WHISPERS
IN THE
ALDERS

H. A. CALLUM

an imprint of Sunbury Press, Inc.
Mechanicsburg, PA USA

an imprint of Sunbury Press, Inc.
Mechanicsburg, PA USA

ISBN: 978-1-62006-911-0 (Trade paperback)

Library of Congress Control Number: 2018958308

FIRST BROWN POSEY PRESS EDITION: September 2018

Product of the United States of America
0 1 1 2 3 5 8 13 21 34 55

Set in Bookman Old Style
Designed by Crystal Devine
Cover by Lawrence Knorr
Edited by Lawrence Knorr

Continue the Enlightenment!

ACKNOWLEDGMENTS

MY THANKS GO TO Lawrence Knorr and the staff at Sunbury Press for publishing this edition of *Whispers in the Alders*. From the beginning, Lawrence and everyone at Sunbury understood what this book was about. Their vision was the perfect complement to my own thoughts and hopes on the direction that the publication would take. The spirit and essence of the book were always the guiding forces throughout the process. As an author, I couldn't ask for anything more.

I owe much gratitude to my fellow members of the Bucks County Writers Workshop. Your guidance and support keeps this writer going. A very special thank you goes to Bev, Bill, Bob, and Don for offering their advice and critiques on my rewrites to this edition.

I've been very fortunate to have come to know many talented authors. Jaylene Jacobus, you were there from the beginning and I am always indebted to you for your support and friendship. Likewise, C. M. Turner, your friendship has been unwavering and you have always known the right words to keep me on track. Finally, K. Alice Compeau, you too are a great friend who has always believed in my work. Your work ethic and dedication have and continue to be a source of inspiration to me. That you all count me as a peer and friend is an honor.

To all my friends and followers on social media, I cannot begin to thank you enough for all your company during the many late nights spent writing. You have all taken much of the loneliness out of this pursuit. You have my deepest thanks for all the friendly banter and for promoting my work. I look forward to more great conversations with each of you.

I couldn't expect this moment without all the readers and reviewers who have invested their time in not only reading this book, but writing about it, too. Without you, there would be no story. A book lives and dies by its readership and you have breathed life into my words.

But none of this would be possible without the unconditional love, support, and friendship of my wife. Lucy, no one understands more the sacrifices made to write than do you. You were the first to recognize my potential, and are always there to remind me that limits are only self-imposed barriers. No other person has shown such faith in my abilities. For that, I am forever yours.

PART I

THE SUBURBAN
GOTHIC

CHAPTER 1

LAST STOP

LITTLE DID I KNOW, but my family's relocation to Alder Ferry would be the last of many moves I endured as a child. It was the quintessential last stop and whether or not I liked it, this would be the place where I would come to define myself. As precocious a child as I was, I could not have imagined that this place would have had the impact on my life as it did. I remember traveling to the mundane town, saying to myself, "God, why can't it be here?" as the quaint towns of the central and upper stretches of the county receded into the fading horizon. Instead, we landed in Alder Ferry—a no-man's land between the gritty, blue-collar city to the south and the captivating, wealthy towns to the north. I egged my father on to go the full monty, and just move us into one of the teeming neighborhoods that sidled up to the border of Alder Ferry. As usual, my opinion was dismissed by my indifferent parents.

I was thirteen years old when we arrived, a mere two weeks before the new school year started. My father, Stuart, was the vice president of operations for a mid-sized manufacturing conglomerate that was increasing its presence along the East Coast. Every year it seemed that another aging manufacturing facility would be swallowed whole by his company. Like a vulture, my father would swoop in and watch over the kill, laying off workers and streamlining processes to squeeze whatever profits he could out of his victim. Once his host was drained, my father would drag us along to the next stop of his tour and the process would neatly repeat itself.

The Caldwell Tool and Die Company became the next victim. The shop employed a fairly good portion of the men of Alder Ferry and was one of the few shops that survived the economic downturn of the nineteen seventies. Founded during the World War II years, it had remained strong and competitive with the small but lucrative defense contracts it secured. The workers and facilities meant nothing to my father's company; it was the contracts they sought. Insignificant shops holding even less significant government contracts were eaten in savory fashion by his company. The contracts would eventually be turned over to the company's main plant for handling. The victim would be mothballed and their workers doled over to the unemployment rolls with haste.

It came as no surprise that my father's company had earned quite a reputation for its tactics. My father was hated before people met him. He was the grim reaper. His appearance most always guaranteed the death of his host. While my callous father couldn't give a fleeting thought about the lives he was trampling, it was always me who faced the consequences of his actions. My father didn't have to assimilate—I did. From the first day at school, I was known by my classmates and teachers (many whose husbands would be laid off by my father) as "the Worthington kid." Try making friends when your father is the most despised man in town; when you will move in another year; when the other kids in your neighborhood refuse to even look at you because "you" forced their daddies out of a job. Being transient was difficult enough, but having your baggage arrive before you made it all the more difficult.

I spent my childhood as an outcast in every town we resided. Home was always contentious—whether from the union picketers pacing the sidewalks to local reporters knocking at the front door, or the drunken men that cursed my father from careening cars as they flung their empty bottles at us. From an early age, I was forced to acknowledge adult problems and deal with them on my own. My parents were too engulfed in their own drama to even appreciate what I was experiencing. Arriving at Alder Ferry I expected more of the same.

Our car continued its course into the town as I tried to melt into the confines of my seat and avoid any conversation with my parents. Strip malls, fast-food restaurants, and elementary schools that mirrored juvenile detention centers, they all gazed back at me through the steely, box frame of the passenger window. I knew they were mocking me, saying, "Ha! Look at you! We have you and will not let you go!" It was my biggest fear that I would someday come to one of the nondescript towns bled dry by my father's company and never leave. I would dissolve into the crowd of locals, my face conforming to those around me, made devoid of emotion by my surrendered dreams.

"Chin up, it could be far worse than you always make of it," chimed my father from behind the wheel. I felt his eyes examining me through the rearview mirror, looking for any recognition from me. His gaze burned and I avoided eye contact at all costs. I pushed myself deeper into the seat, but I was trapped. There were a few times when I allowed my parents to come at me as a unified force. The car was the one place where they took full tactical advantage of situations such as this. Short of throwing myself from the car, which at times I considered, I was all theirs for teasing, ridiculing, and prodding, so they could enjoy the feeling of power exerted over me. I knew it was their sore spot, knowing they had little control over me. As I aged I became more and more indifferent to them. They viewed it as rebellion, an insolent child who had little appreciation for the life they provided her.

"Aubrey, your father is speaking to you," chirped my mother. She always echoed in on his behalf. I sunk further into the seat cushion, my nails nearly slashing through the cloth.

"Aubrey!" My mother exclaimed loudly, always escalating any discussion.

"Yes, mother?" Fortunately, I couldn't see her face through the rearview mirror. I knew it wouldn't be pretty.

"Why don't you . . ." I cut her off before she could get in another word.

"Yeah, I know it could be *far* worse than I make of it. I could start school in a few weeks with *no* reputation." My anger built as I continued my sarcastic retort to the dream world they imagined having created for me. "I could be home like you, alone with my thoughts. Or in a secluded corner office like father!"

"You arrogant little . . ." My mother cupped my father's mouth before he completed his sentence. I took the thrill of it away from him, instead, finishing his thought with my own:

"Yeah, me, your arrogant little bitch of a daughter! I'm the only one in this family who has to face the people in these towns from day one who are filled with nothing but *hate* for you! Two weeks from now I will be in some new school, all alone. Where will the two of you be? All happy in your perfect world! So, yeah, it could be far worse, right?"

Silence. They always went silent after these exchanges. I always wondered if, deep inside, they agreed with me. Their actions through the years would prove otherwise. Every day of my childhood seemed a struggle to maintain my identity and to avoid falling into the life they planned for me. It could have been an easy life, but at what cost, and to end up like them? I learned to show my gratitude in the only way I knew, which was to follow my own path. My success, or more precisely, *my lack of failing*, was the greatest blow I could deal to their pride.

The silence didn't last long, as the argument nearly carried us to the next place that would conveniently be labeled home. I still recall with vivid clarity how we turned off King Street, skirted a few side streets that resembled alleyways, and placed some distance between us and the harried town center. Here we were, no more than a mile from the suburban blight behind us, turning down a well-maintained gravel road that took us back decades. A dreaded feeling of deeper isolation overcame me as we turned our backs to the town that I dreaded only moments earlier.

The land began to slope down and away from us with the gentle undulation of a sheer curtain rippled by a calm breeze. Then they appeared, almost out of nowhere. It was my first view of the alder stand. It was their impressive expanse that made for their memorable first impression, along with being the only undeveloped tract of land for miles. Beyond was the Lowanachen River, its scaly green waters dancing in the rays of the August sun. To the southern side of the stand were the remnants of Alder Ferry's industrial past, waiting to consume my father.

An old stone wall rose up from the turf and paralleled the road as we drew in nearer to the stand. It bordered and held the progression of the trees in check. To our right was a turn-off towards the stand with a large gravel parking area littered by a handful of cars. A path made its way from the parking lot to the site of the old ferry, now a fishing access for the locals. Beside the parking area were four pavilions, a public restroom, and a field about one acre in size. It was the only public park in Alder Ferry, and here it stood without herald. Even when the townspeople filled this space it still had a feeling of detachment from the town. The park was a peninsula of manicured, open space in an otherwise wild environ.

We hadn't strayed far from the center of town, but all spatial relationships ceased after we turned onto the gravel road. My headphones dropped from my ears and for the first time during our adventure I was drawn out of my seat. It was the trees. I couldn't take my eyes from the trees. They drew my eyes in, then

up, and around their border; there were no other ways to go, for I
certainly couldn't see into them. From the shallow rise, the alders
were a sea of green, their expansive canopy commingling on the
haze-laden horizon with the Lowanachen. As removed from the
town as we felt, something eerily calm about this area was causing me to hope that our home would be nearby. I never asked my
parents for details about any of our relocations. After all the years
of moving, I had given up on the minutiae of our existence: the
packing of our lives into neat cardboard boxes and driving, sometimes for days, to our next stopover. The only change that would
render itself out would be geographic. Socially nothing changed
from town to town: I was always the despised outsider.

The park vanished in the dust plume rising up from behind
us, and the gravel road began to fade into the earth, gradually
becoming a two-track dirt road that brought us to the edge of
the alder stand. Our only companion now was the old stone wall,
about two to three feet high, made of local bluestone meticulously
placed one atop the other during some forgotten time. Between
the trees and the wall, the area had a timeless feel to it. Even
civilization had become a memory, as all sounds from town to the
west and the local industrial sites just to the south were drowned
out by the perpetual cacophony of crickets and katydids. The
sound was at times deafening; to this day I am still amazed that I
became acclimated to it.

The dirt two-track was brought to a halt by an old, arched iron
gate, hinged on one side to a cornice in the stone wall. The gate
was the only noticeable break in the stone wall, which continued
until bifurcating into a ninety-degree elbow in two directions: the
length bordering the property, and the other which continued for
a few hundred yards before it disappeared into a small grove of
twisted cedars dominated by a single, towering oak. It was there
that this section of the old wall retreated like a dying cat, disinte-
grating into both time and earth. The wall's endpoint gave off the
semblance of a family burial plot, the lone rise of trees setting an
unmistakable landmark. The solitary oak drew the eyes to it, pulling them up and up, training the viewer's glance to the heavens.
It stood in stark contrast to the alder stand in that its strength
wasn't connected to anything else. Individually it had managed to
survive everything that had occurred in its company over the past
four hundred years. There was a loneliness about that tree, kept
apart from the others, an isolation I knew all too well.

The car squeaked to a stop, my dad breaking the silence only to say, "I'll be right back," as he exited the vehicle to pry open the rusted gate. The dirt two-track transitioned to crushed shells, their pearl essence shimmering and dancing in the waves of heat radiating from the ground. Stolid oak trees guarded the driveway, forming a canopy that dimmed the strong August sun. To our right, the property was bordered by another stone wall being reclaimed by the alder stand.

The oaks all but blocked any view of the structure that would be home in name only until leaving for college four years after making its acquaintance. Our car crawled through the oak canopy toward a point of light. Finally, the trees parted and before us stood a grand old reminder of the colonial past. She was a magnificent example of Federal architecture, its symmetrical design grounding it firmly into the landscape. Its whitewashed stucco exterior pulled in the rays of the sun, giving the old home a gleam that must have been truly captivating in its early grandeur. The signs of neglect were all there: vines had taken hold of the building, peeling back pieces of the delicate stucco exterior in many locations and exposing the weathered brick beneath.

"Ladies, welcome home," boomed my father. "I'm sure we can make this old lady shine again," he boasted. "The price was right too—cheaper than rent!" I noticed my mother's jaw drop at these words. Never before had we owned a home.

"Stu, you didn't . . . I wasn't expecting this," the words seemed to be choked out of my mother's mouth.

"Edith, she's all yours. Do as you please with her," replied my father, passing on control of the property with such a nonchalant manner that any joy in the situation was whisked into oblivion. He did give her carte blanche authority over the property. He just didn't want to be bothered with any of the details. He could care less where we lived as he was never really a fixture in our home with his work schedule.

The house was grand, and I knew my mother was impressed with its size and potential. Not to mention the location of the property, with its feeling of seclusion while being just minutes from town, this could be ideal. For once she would be able to avoid the ire of the women whose husbands were unemployed by my father. She could hole up here, make it her own, and romance her wine collection while my father and I were gone during the day. The property ideally suited our dysfunctional family unit.

We stepped inside, greeted by a wide staircase sweeping up to a second-floor balcony. The interior was impressive, but even more impressive was the amount of work needed before the building could be comfortable, let alone livable. Passing through the home we reached the back door, which spilled out onto a colonnaded portico with an unobstructed view of the Lowanachen. The once manicured lawn had become overgrown with wild rose to the point of becoming impassable, save for a narrow path mown to the boathouse. I looked back at my parents and could tell that this would be their respite, the final stop of the whirlwind tour that was my father's career.

I did my best to keep my distance, not wanting to hint that there was something to this place. Maybe if they weren't in it, I could have made do with the old estate. I peeled myself away from them and climbed into a rusted iron chair on the portico. Even in August, the wind off the river had a slight chill to it. I pulled my arms and knees in close together and gazed across the expansive property down to the river. My eyes traced the boundaries up and down, following the contours of the land that rolled with lazy ease down to the river. The alder stand hugged the property as the house was situated off to the side that bordered the alders. The air seemed twenty degrees cooler than it had at the gate, where the crickets and katydids sang and baked in the tall, dry grass. Here it was cool and quiet. Removed from the world was how it felt, this small piece of turf just as indifferent to its surroundings as I was to my parents. Maybe the chill was just the fact that this was it. This was the place for them, and if I weren't careful, I'd get caught up in life and never get the chance to leave.

Just then I caught movement out of my eye inside the alder stand. Startled, I stood up and hurled myself to the edge of the portico. I leaned over the edge of the rail to catch a glimpse of what caused the movement, but I was too late. Whatever, or whoever for that fact, it was, had vanished. All that was left were a few branches sweeping in to envelop the hole in the brush made by the fleeing intruder that was scrutinizing me. I had become oblivious to everything as I inspected my new surroundings, and this mysterious being took full advantage of my guard being down. A chill ran down my spine as I backed up towards the house and gazed into the darkness of the alders, not knowing what else would come from within their hidden recesses.

CHAPTER 2

STRUNG ALONG

THE FIRST NIGHT at our new residence was passed in peaceful solitude in my new bedroom. It had views into the alders and down the expansive remnants of the lawn to the river. I found myself gazing out the window that night, the moon's silver glow accentuating the skeletal alder branches as they swayed to and fro in the gentle summer breeze. I watched the alders intensely that night after my experience earlier on the portico, and in the end, I surrendered to the idea that it was just a deer spooked by my presence. After all, the property was abandoned for years. Suddenly we appeared and took back this place that had been their home.

The next morning, I pulled myself from bed long before my parents began to stir. I put on the coffee as I always did, the cadence of the drip coffee-maker nearly lulling me back to sleep as I waited. For some time now this had been my morning ritual. My parents didn't seem to mind; the convenience of it suited them just fine. On occasion, I would steal a cigarette from my father's jacket to pair with my morning coffee. The sweet aroma of the coffee mellowed the smoke as it passed over my lips and to my lungs, where it lingered for the briefest of moments before being expelled with the crudded cough that welcomed mornings. I'd been exposed to enough second-hand smoke from my parents that lighting up actually cleared my lungs in the morning.

But that first morning at the new house—the Grand Old Lady as she came to be known—was different. I leaned over the kitchen counter, head in my hands as I waited for the percolation to stop, only to have a fluttering in the morning breeze dancing about my peripheral vision. Opposite the counter was the screen door to the portico, an old hook and eye being the only thing that secured it from welcoming in the outside world. I felt the same chill as I had the previous afternoon. I rose from the counter and moved to the door, my feet falling in silence overcome by the sound of my pounding heart. I staggered my steps and swung out wide from the door to make certain there was no one on the other side. The windows from the kitchen dropped down to ground level, giving me the all clear as I made my final approach. Affixed to the door was a strand of maize-colored rope, fashioned into a dreamcatcher. Alder catkins were woven into the rope with a delicate weave, giving the totem its circular shape. Strands of catkins hung from its core, appearing to have sprouted from it. They dangled with such a natural quality that the slightest breeze caused them to flutter with a lightness that gave them the impression of floating in the air unattached to the physical world. Was this a gift? Or was it a warning? I swore that I would find out before the school year began. I figured it was no more than a prank from one of the townspeople.

But the dreamcatcher was spliced with such a meticulous hand that it couldn't be ignored. I slid my pinky finger beneath this handiwork, and with ginger persuasion lifted it from the door and took it back to my room. It was beautiful in its design and represented the harmony that could exist between the human and natural worlds. I hung it inside my closet door, where it would remain until I left for college. After high school, it was the only piece of décor I would bother to hang. It just couldn't be ignored for reasons all its own.

In the distraction of that morning, I had forgotten the one thing that I craved: my coffee. I went back downstairs and poured a cup. I heard my parents and hurried to the portico, taking my place again in the rusted iron chair. My eyes scanned the alders, my stare etching each and every leaf, studying them all for any sign of the stranger who visited us in the night. I shuddered thinking that this person may still be watching. Maybe if I stared long enough they would flinch and expose their position. I told myself to just stop. For all I knew I could be making myself see things, projecting images of imaginary people moving inside the trees. Perhaps I was drawing on the hope that the person in there would be different—a friend at last in a lonely and evaporating childhood.

I couldn't tell my parents about the events of the previous day or that morning. I knew if I did that I would be accused of acting out and rebelling against another move. Instead, I kept my distance as usual that morning and claimed the portico as my own. I hesitated to discuss anything with them, knowing full well that anything I told them would be dismissed as an active imagination or something worse that would require more fruitless sessions of counseling. It was their way of keeping me down, to simply wave off my concerns and embellish my behaviors so that they could continue with building a life where I was just an afterthought. We never spent enough time anywhere for anyone to see how our family dynamic played itself out.

"Aubrey, I'm heading into town to pick up some things. Why don't you come along?" My mother's invite disturbed my morning peace, but I saw it as an opportunity to feign assimilation.

"Sure," I responded with the drab undertone of a tortured teen. I wouldn't want her to think I was looking forward to the experience.

She reentered the house, and again I was left alone. I looked down into the cold swill of coffee remaining in my cup, gave it a few turns, and splashed it over the rail of the portico. I left the cup there and prepared myself for what Alder Ferry had to offer.

Being alone with either of my parents was awkward. Actually, it was intolerable. Over the years, the course of our conversations had dwindled to the mundane, daily intercourse required just to get along. This day was no different. My mother didn't even try to make conversation. Mechanically, we exited the vehicle, entered the store, and returned to our vehicle. We made six stops in all that morning in near perfect silence. There are some parents who would give anything for the quietness in the relationship between me and my parents. But this was an endured quiet, not one that was enjoyed, a silence as strained as our relationship, nothing more than a cease-fire in the war between us. In time these unspoken words would fuel our battles, gathering momentum with the sidled tension that simmered beneath the surface, only to explode in torrents of rage indiscriminate in choosing their target.

The anguish of being confined with my mother was only met by the lackluster shopping experience in Alder Ferry. Every store was the same, just a different name. Each had back to school specials which, unlike today, actually started at the end of summer. We made our way through the sanitized shopping experience of the American suburb, wandering down endless aisles of useless merchandise to pick out the few things we needed. I had agreed to go on this journey, knowing what it would entail, as I had seen the blasé shopping centers that stretched along the nearby interstate, each being different in style but identical in experience. I chose to go on this boring jaunt for my own selfish reasons, to show my parents that I was at least feigning an attempt to coexist in some peaceful fashion.

We ended our mother-daughter shopping experience near noon and returned to the Grand Old Lady. Leaving the town behind us, I felt again like I was fading into the past as the car pulled away from the paved road and trolled the gravel trail leading to the property. As we skirted along the stone wall towards the gate I caught movement out of the corner of my right eye. This time my eyes didn't lie, but the disbelief remained. In the distance, a figure appeared from within the alders. This figure was small but otherwise any other details of its identity were indiscernible. Seeing our car approach, the figure, with one step, vanished into the alders with all the fluidity of the morning fog. The trees cloaked the figure, making any closer examination futile.

Strange as the situation was, I felt no fear. I was intrigued and was clamoring to escape the car as it clawed at the gravel road. As we pulled into the driveway I began scanning the alders for any movement, unconcerned with my mother. She called my name once or twice, I can't remember for sure, and I dismissed her with a teenage "Uh-huh" as I looked out the window. There was nothing. Not a single sign of life except for the chickadees darting back and forth across the path of the car.

I made my way back to the portico to survey the alders and immediately I saw it. My coffee cup from the morning remained where I left it on the rail, but affixed to its handle was a pair of catkins, hanging from the mug like a pair of tassels. I spilled out of the iron chair, dragging it across the floor as I reached out and pulled them from the mug. I snugged them deep into the palm of my hand. "Who are you?" I whispered under my breath.

"Aubrey, is everything okay?" My Mother called from the screen door, her head straining to see what was going on through the screen that had become stained opaque with time.

"Yeah, just forgot to bring in my cup from the morning," I called over my shoulder to her.

I looked into the trees then at the catkins bisecting my palm. I knew what I had to do. The trees were calling. Soon they would make my acquaintance.

CHAPTER 3

SEEING THE FOREST FOR THE TREES

I COULD SEE THE look of astonishment wash across my mother's face when I announced I was leaving the house for a walk. We had barely spent twenty-four hours at our new residence, and already I had taken a trip into town. Now I was setting out to walk the property. This wasn't my typical behavior and I'm sure that it raised many a red flag in her scheming mind. While I was willfully making an effort in her eyes to get along, it was the mysterious happenings from within the stand of trees that had my attention. I could have cared less about their new home, but before I let them know it, I had to find out what secrets that old stand of trees held.

The trees did have a daunting look to them. I imagined they were watching over the house, contriving a plan to extend their range onto the property and overtake the grand old lady. My parents had come between the trees and their plan and would come to halt the natural succession that had been going on at the property. I surveyed the property one final time from the portico. Instead of embarking from here, I chose instead to follow the driveway out to the gate and make my way to the old elm. From the elm, I could have a wider view of the trees and better plot my entry point through their mysterious veil. And perhaps whoever was playing suitor to me would not be aware of my approach from the elm.

It was a steamy August afternoon, and the old elm offered shade from the sun, but still the air was like soup, thick and heavy, going into the lungs in solid gulps with each breath. I looked down the old stone wall towards the iron gate, where the alders met our property. The air was so full of moisture that the haze was at ground level, giving the whole scene an ethereal feel that only further mystified the alders. I watched the trees from under the umbrella of the elm, taking them in for what seemed like hours, noticing no movement at all either inside or at their border. As excited as I was to make my way inside, the level of apprehension I felt was undeniable. Who or what I would face in there, I didn't know.

I was a stranger here, still uncertain of the land that I was venturing into. Every step would be an act of discovery. Once inside the trees, it would become even more daunting, with no visible landmarks to take a bearing on my location. It would just be me and the trees, an endless monotony of trunks that could lead me in circles for hours. My apprehension was justified: a young girl, alone, with no one to come to her aid. A father who was engrossed in his work and a mother buzzing on wine who wouldn't notice if I disappeared until hours later. Even if by chance someone noticed I was gone, it would probably be too late to have changed my situation anyway.

I brushed those thoughts aside, choosing not to consider the potential outcomes of my actions. The excitement and mystery of it all blinded me from seriously considering the true dangers that I could have been inviting into my world. Apprehension began to fade and contort itself into a wild curiosity that just couldn't be satisfied from a distance. I had to get inside those trees and see for myself how the world looked from their perspective. I peeled myself from the trunk of the elm, my sweat having suctioned my shirt to its craggy bark. I brought myself to my feet and found the remnants of the old stone wall and dawdled along it towards the trees, delaying the inevitable, until I arrived at the iron gate. Crossing the driveway, I stood face to face with the trees that captivated me since I first set eyes upon them a day earlier.

Passing to the interior of the trees proved trickier than I thought. The scrubby cedars that sprouted up in the loamy soil formed a natural barrier that almost prevented my entrance. Almost. I persuaded the branches of the cedars to move aside with a gentle sweeping motion of my forearms. The scrubby and supple branches gave way but were quick to spring back to attention—this I learned all too soon as several of the branches lashed out at me, and struck me in the face, seeming to know where to land their blows, with each one attempting to rake out my eyes. Beneath the cedars a tangle of vines and thorns formed an escarpment that found its way into the eyelets of my shoes, halting my progress every foot or so. Each step proved to be part of a dance, a tango with the periphery that tested my determination.

I looked back and realized that, even though I had only gained about three to four feet into this netherworld, I was swallowed up and hidden from the known world behind me. Even so, I only made it halfway through the bramble that guarded the alders. I was exasperated by the effort I had put forth just to make it this far, and here I was, encapsulated by a thicket that seemed to be gaining a tighter grip on me with each bit of forward momentum I exerted. I lost any patience I had when I entered this thicket, and by now the gentle sweeping motions of my arms had evolved into wide plowing motions, like a diver entering the water. I pyramided my arms and drove them into the thicket, thrusting them apart, pulling myself in deeper. With each thrust, I gained ground, but at the cost of mobility. I wanted to scream but feared drawing attention to myself. I could see the interior edge of the thicket, and knew I was but one more push from making my way into the stand.

By now my feet were so sufficiently tangled in vines that I looked to have sprouted from the earth. A few thicker cedar branches blocked my entrance. With one last hurrah, I threw them to the side, falling forward. My left foot broke loose of the tendrils that had held it prisoner only a second earlier, the momentum bringing my body forward only to be swept out of the bramble by the cedar branches I had just driven out of my way. The branches sprung back, throwing me to the forest floor, my hands being driven deep into the soft, loamy soil and my face planting itself into the ground. My right foot was hung up in the bramble, wondering where the rest of my body had rushed off to.

Quiet.

That's what I remembered about that moment. After all the thrashing there was nothing but quiet. My splayed body hit the soft ground, its impact absorbed by the soil and the sound of my fall was deadened to silence. The ground was so soft, like an earthen quilt that hugged every contour of my body. It was quiet all around. Not an eerie silence, but a peaceful silence that made sound stand still, with the loamy earth swallowing up sound in its soft and airy till. What sounds did escape the earth were captured by the bramble.

My face had plowed into the soil, and the silence was countered by its smell. The soil smelled quiet. It was dark, with a light texture. Running my fingers through it, I imagined that the soil was the cool night air: dark, moist, and ever-shifting, it embodied the night air. If the night air had texture, it would be this soil. It blanketed the earth loosely, grounding the trees firmly but not holding them down, giving the trees support and room to grow.

But there was something about the smell. The earth's smell inside the alder stand was organic—it had life. There was the earthiness of a mushroom to it, countered by a slight tinge of iron that stuck to the roof of my mouth. I'll never forget the smell of the soil in the alder stand. I have never before or since encountered a soil that exuded the essence of life to the senses like that soil did. This soil was the life-blood that nourished the trees calling this piece of turf home.

I raised myself from the ground, finding that I was in touch with all my senses in no way that I had experienced before. For as far as I could see, there were trees. The scent of the soil still perfumed my body, and the sunlight filtered in through the canopy in an array of singular rays that illuminated the forest floor and shimmered with the shifting of the overhead leaves. The air was noticeably cooler than it was outside the stand, and was damp, but not musty. I stood in awe, struck down by the beauty of the stand in all its simplicity. Man had scarred Alder Ferry for years, but here in the stand was a reminder of the good that some individual long ago had done for this piece of bottom ground. These trees preserved the land from the suburban fissure surrounding it. Like me, the alders weren't native to this land but had better than survived in an environment that would have relished in their failure.

Inside I felt small, but not vulnerable. I looked up towards the canopy of the trees, rotating through the kaleidoscope of sunlight filtering down from above, and wondered if it was I that was moving or the ground beneath me. Either way, the trees held their ground and anchored me to this place. My feet felt connected to the earth, rooted in that moment. The mystical awe of the place had me enchanted from the moment that my body impacted the soft earth. There was a peacefulness inside the trees that before only could be found in my imagination. At last I had found a place where I actually felt, well, welcomed. "This must be what it feels like to finally come home," I remember thinking to myself.

I wandered through the stand in amazement. It was tranquil. I was removed from the anxiety of my home life and the worries of another school year. In this place, I was relaxed. There was comfort in knowing that I was finally alone and free to let down my guard. I wanted to become vulnerable to my emotions, and in the stand, I sensed I could do that without fear of showing any outward sign of weakness that could invite an attack. The trees stood guard against the outside world.

Moving through the stand I could feel life again. Through my arms a new energy flowed, as they swayed back and forth, catching the corrugated folds of the trees' bark. I pulled myself from one trunk to the next, swaying through the forest on a horizontal plane that knew no beginning and no end. My arms flung themselves out and in through curves of perfect symmetry; it was the most fluidic movement I had ever performed. This dance through the trees was the first act of extricating myself from the fetters of life that held me in check. I gracefully came to rest against one of the many trunks that had spun me through the stand, its weathered and cool exterior pressed into my skin, and I slid my hands up and around it. I pulled myself closer to the tree, just wanting to melt into it and never have to go back.

In my exuberance I lost all comprehension of time and space—it was both the glory and failure of the moment. Not knowing how far I had wandered into the stand, I stopped myself and pondered my situation as a light peal of thunder rolled in from the distance. Everywhere I looked, there were trees. Then more trees behind them. There were no gaps. The spaces between trees were filled in by others. There was no parallax, and distances seemed to be only a mirage no matter which direction I turned and looked. The trees played an optical illusion, making it appear that I was only walking deeper into the stand, no matter which path my feet chose to follow.

The apprehension that melted away prior to coming into the stand was starting to set back in as the joy of the moment chilled. My exuberance was replaced with worry, not knowing which direction to turn. Sure, the stand wasn't that big, and I could walk long enough in any direction to make my exit. But the last thing I remembered wanting was the inconvenience of adding unnecessary distance to my trek, especially with the coming rain.

At a loss for what to do, I decided to let chance dictate the direction I would follow. I wound myself up into a corkscrew and tensed every muscle in my body. Turning my head upwards into the canopy, I spun clockwise. When my feet finally planted and halted my rotation, I stepped forward. Hopefully, the direction I had chosen would bring me out of the alders within a respectable distance from our property. Another peal of thunder rolled across the sky, closing in on my location.

I began to make my way when I heard the snapping of a twig behind me. I stopped and looked back. The trees made it all but impossible to capture any movement behind me. I chalked it up to a squirrel or a deer trying to outmaneuver the coming storm. I began to move forward, but then it happened again. I froze, and with all my senses on high alert, felt for the sounds with my ears to locate its source. I melted into one of the alder trunks to camouflage my outline. All my senses were made acute by the apprehension of being followed. I looked back to survey the scene, scanning for any type of movement or shape that was out of place.

Another twig snapped. I knew there was something or some-one about to move across my line of sight, bisecting the area I had departed from just minutes earlier. I brought my body down low and absorbed my skin into the bark of the tree, my ears training my eyes in the direction where I thought this being would make its appearance. It was a lesson to trust in the senses, *all of them*, and it paid off. Like radar, my ears followed the sound and guided my line of sight until finally, it happened: visual confirmation of the source of the sounds.

It was an unassuming character, much to my shock. And then I realized that it was the same person I had seen earlier who evaporated into the alders. It was a boy, probably my age, but much smaller than the other boys our age. He was moving through the stand at ease, with no apparent worry on his mind. As I had done only moments earlier, he seemed to be moving along with a sense of calm as he floated into my line of sight with care-free grace, like no one was watching. I was now the voyeur, watching him, perhaps as he had watched me the previous day.

As he passed I assumed it was he who left the catkins behind. I could have been wrong in this assumption but doubted it. There would only be one way to know for sure.

CHAPTER 4

THE PAIRING

THE BOY PASSED through the alders, eclipsed by, and then eclipsing the trunks. His movement weaved an imaginary thread through the trees. Sight was deceptive in the stand, and his passage was proof of that fact. There was nothing in his body language that alarmed me about his presence. He was so unassuming and aloof that I felt some guilt for intruding upon what he probably perceived to be a private moment free of scrutiny.

Much like the privacy I thought was my own on the portico a day earlier. He had probably scrutinized every minute of that afternoon, from the moment we pulled into the driveway until we shut the house up for the night. Now it was my turn.

I stood up, hands on my hips, feet splayed to shoulder width. I must have had an easy six inches on him, and my stance was not inviting.

"Hey!" I yelled out towards him with a tone of authority.

The boy halted and turned towards me. I saw the fear in his eyes, knowing he had been caught.

"Hey, you!" I yelled out again. With that, he took off. His legs sprang into action, fueled by adrenaline. I don't know why, but I gave chase. I was already lost, and now I was following some odd local boy deeper into territory that he knew all too well.

We weaved and twisted through the alders, our feet sinking into the wet earth as we drove closer to the river bank. Here, the land was saturated, the loamy soil acting as a sponge that sprayed a fine silt-laden mist with the impact of our feet. Neither of us showed signs of growing weary. I was fueled by determination, the boy by fear. Our circuitous route now pulled us up and away from the river, the ground growing drier and firmer, allowing me to push off and gain ground on the boy.

I could hear his quickened breaths as I pulled nearer. He turned again, and I followed. But his knowledge of the land proved superior to my speed. Instantly, I felt the ground go out from beneath my feet as one of the many gnarled roots caught my right toe. My momentum sent my soaring, my useless arms flailing at the air, a pointless feat in attempting to break my fall. I came face to face with the loamy soil for a second time. Again, it slighted the effects of gravity as my body kissed the earth.

Every cubic inch of air was expelled from my lungs on impact. Winded, I gasped to regain my breath. For a moment I had forgotten the pursuit. I winced from the pain, holding back the tears that wanted so hard to show themselves. Reality set back in and on cue I turned onto my back, hoping I would catch a glimpse of the boy fleeing in victory. Instead, I found myself facing his outstretched hand reaching down to help me out of my predicament.

I grabbed his hand with a mighty grip to advertise my strength and met him eye to eye. I could see he had his doubts about me, as I did about him. I grabbed both his shoulders and drove him into the nearest tree, pinning him to the subtle pleats in the bark. My left hand on his shoulder, I drew my right hand into my pocket and fumbled for the pair of catkins left earlier to adorn my coffee cup.

Not knowing my intentions, the boy covered up by habit, as if he was expecting to be struck. At that moment, I realized that my fury shattered the sanctity of the alders. As I towered over him, birds flew from the treetops, their calls heckling me. The cool breeze off the river had ceased, and the air became charged with an electricity that sent a current of unease from the ground up through my spine. I was disarmed by this feeling; filled with a sadness that was unexplainable but made perfect sense. When I first entered the stand, I was overcome with peace and felt at ease with my own self for once in my young but experienced memory. I witnessed this boy moving through the stand having the same sense of ease that welcomed me, and I shattered it. I felt abysmal, having destroyed a feeling I had been chasing throughout my childhood.

The boy was the first person that had shown kindness to me in any of the towns I entered, and now he cowered below me, not knowing what to expect. I pulled my hand from my pocket, his rising anxiety noticeable as my hand came closer and closer to revealing itself. I turned my hand over and opened my palm, revealing the pair of catkins.

I closed my eyes and gulped out loud, choking back a string of emotions that only knew suppression.

"Are these yours?" I asked him in the calmest voice I knew. The words rolled out of my mouth in a plaintive tone, seeking forgiveness.

I knelt, realizing that towering above him would do nothing to ease his fear.

"It's all right," I said, as my left hand slid from his shoulder, down his arm, and took his hand with a touch so tender that it surprised me.

"I just want to know if these are yours," I stated coolly. "I'm Aubrey, by the way."

The boy relaxed his body, looked down at the catkins, and then back at me. In a kind voice, he replied, "No, they're yours."

I caught a small grin forming out of the corner of his mouth. No one else smiled like that. It was the smile I would always associate with him, a guarded smile that wouldn't surrender too much to the world around him.

He looked up at me, and from behind his coy smile said, "My name's Tommy."

And that was where we started.

CHAPTER 5

CALLED OUT

I DON'T REMEMBER HOW I got home that afternoon. It was a blur: the chase through the alders, my guilt for cornering Tommy as I did, and the culmination of that afternoon—my first positive human interaction of significance. How I got home that afternoon didn't matter. In fact, that day was far from about returning; it became the departure point. It marked a moment in my history where I would begin to assert my independence and choose the relationships satisfying to me. It came to be a time where my journey through life could be better understood by struggling along with another.

What truly struck me that night as I lay in bed was the realization that I possibly made a friend. Never had I taken the initiative to attempt socializing with the locals. Even if I wanted to, my father's reputation always closed that door before it could open. But here was Tommy, who sought me out. Surely he heard the gossip about my father and his company, and I found it odd that someone like Tommy would want to be friends with me. No one ever wanted to be friends with me. I was always the enemy, and fraternizing with me was treason in the towns my father's company juggernauted. That night I pondered my next trip into the alders, hoping to meet up again with Tommy.

—-—

Maybe it was just too good to be true.

The next morning, I floated down the grand staircase only to be greeted by my parents.

"Coffee's ready, help yourself." With a wave of her arm, I was directed to the coffeemaker by my mother, her head not even rising to acknowledge me. It was typical of the greetings I received in the morning from her.

"Okay," I replied while wading through the fog of second-hand smoke as I found my way to the coffee pot. I poured a cup and caught movement on the portico as I brought the cup to my lips.

"Who are they?" I asked.

"We'll have company for the next few days," replied my father, "Until the threat from the union passes."

"Until then, you're under house arrest until school starts."

I motioned to argue but was cut-off almost immediately by my father who engaged me without even taking his eyes from the newspaper.

"And stay out of those trees," were his parting words as he left to speak to the men who converted the portico into their make-shift command post.

"Someone was seen walking through the trees last night, Aubrey." I looked at my mother as she continued, "And with the union making threats against your father's company, we just can't afford to be too careful."

My heart sank to a new low. I knew who it was out there last night. If they only knew what little threat he posed. Instead, there was this rush to judgment, to prove to my father's ego he was so important that his own security detail was necessary. The unions always made threats when the local shops were bought up and dismantled and I didn't see where this situation was any different from the others. The previous day in town passed without any event. Where was the concern then? My mother and I were free to venture into the gut of enemy territory. Now, we were relegated to this place, prisoners to our circumstance.

My fingers furrowed open the paper left on the counter by my father. Maybe it was different this time. The headline read: *"Union Vows to Fight Worthington at Every Step."* Typically, it was my father's company called out by the papers. But this time my father made the headline. If the union couldn't beat the machine, they would go for its operator. Below the headline was a picture showing a group of men blocking my father from entering Caldwell Tool and Die. Behind my father were a group of reluctant police officers, placed in the awkward position of ushering in the angel of death for their neighbors. One of the men stood front and center, his meaty forefinger firmly planted in my father's chest, giving off the impression of drilling a hole clean through his suit and straight to his core. This man had a look about him. His appearance was menacing, with years of hard work and hard drinking worn thick into every crease in his furrowed brow. The seething pool of anger in this man was displayed prominently in his eyes, those eyes black as coal with a red aura fanned by contempt and blistering with hate. Those eyes brought the monochromatic newspaper print to life. They stared back at the reader, daring you to step into his world. Those eyes became emblazoned into my memory.

I creased the newspaper to hide away those glaring eyes and slid it away from me across the counter. I collapsed into myself, crumbling onto the counter like a wet rag. Wanting to be alone, I peeled myself off the counter and skulked back to my room. Never before had I wanted to engage my surrounding environment, and now that I finally wanted to, it was taken away from me. My reality was cruel in that it always found a way to strike me down.

Taking the catkin dreamcatcher Tommy left the previous morning, I sat by my window and gazed into the alders. With my hands on the catkins, I wished myself back into the stand. The catkins were rough but yielding. As my fingers traced their surfaces, the individual buds of each gently parted, rolling with my passing finger like the waves in the river just beyond the alders. A tear came to my eye, gradually building in mass until it rolled down my cheek and splashed onto my hand. Another followed, then another. In short time I had all but broken down, muffling my cries to avoid drawing the attention of my mother. I pulled the catkins up close to my face as I wiped the tears on my sleeve, and caught the essence of the catkins, gingerly spicing the air about my nose. The smell was soft and earthy. It bore the sweet earthiness of the soil that I remembered.

I lay down on my bed, propped up by a pillow, the catkin dreamcatcher strewed across my chest. Looking out the window, I caressed each individual catkin as I viewed their ancestral home. Holding them was now the closest thing to being there. I was transcended from my room to the stand by their slight scent, my imagination giving me a brief reprieve from my confinement. The thought of the trees coupled with the rhythmic strumming of the catkins was soothing, and the tears that had been set free stopped their flow. My muffled sobs broke into deep cleansing breaths as I came to terms with my situation. Eventually, I would be granted my leave from this prison, but in my mind was one concern: Tommy. I finally made a friend, I thought. The relationship was so fleeting that I hadn't even been given the chance to take it for granted.

Over the course of the next two weeks, I surveyed the trees from every possible angle. No one stepped forward from the alders to make themselves known to either myself or the entourage gathered on the portico. I surrendered to the fact that my new friend sensed my abandonment of him or gave in to the talk about me and my family. It was useless to try and imagine having a friend at all. The one moment I had with Tommy was probably the closest thing to friendship I would ever know. I was convinced we would never cross paths again.

As monotonous as the time I spent locked away at home was, it was still not enough time to delay the inevitable first day of school. It was always the most difficult day of the year, walking the gauntlet of inhospitable faces from the car to the front door. As my mother's car pulled away, I was left to fend for myself. Every year it played out the same, and by day's end, I would be twice as lonely than I was before I entered the classroom. With time the process became more bearable, the cycle repeating itself with a seasonal regularity every September.

I was enrolled at the school for St. Germaine Parish. Religion was an afterthought to my parents; a Roman Catholic school was the only homage they paid to their faith. As I made my way from the car I passed beneath the black iron gates and entered the institutionally inspired architecture of the nineteen sixties embraced by every Catholic school in my experience. The look was dated when it was built, and twenty-five years later it was all but obsolete in both style and function. If anything, it offered a bit of familiarity, each new school year beginning with a feeling of déjà vu from the previous.

I was shown to my homeroom by one of the mothers assigned to monitor the halls. I could always hear the chuckles and gossip as I made my way down the hall. I never understood these women: why would anyone spend their time here, for no pay? Needless to say, the women in these places never impressed me. Even as a young girl I felt patronized by the male hierarchy that seemed to subjugate the nuns and lay teachers. I only assumed that St. Germaine would be no different than the other parish schools I had attended.

I was among the last of the students to arrive and took my seat at the back of the classroom. At the head of the room stood a tall, thin, middle-aged woman of no particular status. Her clothes were plain, and her wide-rimmed glasses seemed to make her eyes look like fish bowls, with her irises darting back and forth like minnows evading capture. I took her in along with the other students. The cinderblock walls painted beige with three walls of chalkboard were anything but stimulating. But stimulation wasn't necessary; after all, we were only there to learn.

"Good morning everyone," her voice boomed, filling the room. Although powerful, it was actually pleasing to the ear. "My name is Ms. Kaliczenkoff, for those of you who don't know me, and I hope you all had a pleasant summer."

She seemed well enough, and I thought to myself, "I could actually listen to this one," with the way her words seemed to roll off her tongue and travel across the room in rhythmic waves that lost neither volume nor inflection in the rear of the classroom where I sat. She had a gift for speech, a rare quality in a teacher.

Ms. Kaliczenkoff began with calling out roll, each student standing when called. One by one I watched as each of my peers stood then sat, the staccato cadence of their cresting and falling almost a lullaby, like the waves upon the shore. Each student in this room had the potential to be my nemesis. I examined each as best I could to try and measure their potential as an adversary. The room was anything but a classroom to me; it was instead a jury pool, and I was conducting voir dire to best assess my chances at survival for the coming year.

"Alton Mackay," called Kaliczenkoff, amidst hushed giggles of the classroom.

"It's pronounced Ma-Kay, Ms. Kaliczenkoff," and instantly I recognized the voice as he rose from his seat. It was Tommy. Another place, another name, but it was him. I wasn't sure whether I should be mad or happy. As if the boy weren't odd enough, I came to find out his real name in such an unusual way. I sat and wondered why he told me his name was Tommy.

"Aubrey Worthington," called Ms. Kaliczenkoff. I was still pondering what to think of Tommy, oblivious to the fact that my name had been called. "Aubrey Worthington, are you present?" I rose, embarrassed by the giggles and stares that accompanied my name and aloof welcome to the class. "Ah yes, Ms. Worthington. I've heard about you. Take your seat, please." All eyes found their way to my direction, and the giggles and under-breath comments previously directed to Tommy, a/k/a Alton, were turned to me.

With that, my introduction to the sphere of St. Germaine was complete.

CHAPTER 6

FRIENDS

WAS LAST TO retrieve my lunch that day, more so to avoid interacting with the other kids. I entered the coatroom to find my lunch ransacked, spilled onto the floor, and flattened into the aging linoleum. I picked up what remained of it and headed to the cafeteria. Fortunately, the cafeteria was large enough so I could escape the scrutiny of my classmates.

The scene was about what I expected. Cliques of kids gathered at their own tables. Each table assumed a stratum in the social atmosphere of the school, reminiscent of the feudal hierarchies we discussed in history class. In some ways, it matched the power structure of the church: it was clearly defined who answered to who, and you best not dare speak out. I gathered up the courage to enter, boys eyeing me cautiously and girls whispering to one another as I passed. The occasional bread crust found its mark, but I managed to part the crowd unscathed. I spotted a table in the back with one lone occupant, the wavy blonde hair tipping me off to who it was. The other boys slapped the back of his head as they passed on their way out to the playground, each blow causing his hair to spray outward and circle the crown of his head before falling back into place. He just sat there and took it repeatedly, barely flinching.

I came up behind him and cleared my throat.

"Is this seat taken, *Alton?*" I placed a strong accent on his name, mainly out of curiosity, not seeking to add further insult to his predicament.

"No, please do." Tommy looked up as he answered, just in time to catch a passing smack from another boy heading out to the schoolyard.

I instinctively stood up and yelled, "Hey, you quit that!" Shocked by both my forthrightness and volume, I immediately backed away.

The boy was quick to turn and grab hold of my arm, "Quit what?" He paused, and with an introspective glance drawing a bead that pierced my eyes retorted, "Oh yeah, that's right. Better straighten up before daddy fires me, too. You should watch it. You're in a tighter spot than this idiot is all I'm saying."

I pulled my arm loose, breaking eye contact with the boy in a conciliatory acknowledgment of defeat. The boy gave another quick blow to the back of Tommy's head before taking his eyes off the two of us and making his exit.

"Never mind him," Tommy said with exasperation, "he's harmless, all wind and no gusto." I sensed that he was more embarrassed to be played like that in front of me than for being hassled by the other boys.

I took the seat beside him, avoiding the awkwardness of his having to face me if I sat across from him. I took out my sandwich from the plastic wrap, flattened to the point that the bread and fillings morphed into one singular object, with no taste or textural difference left to give it any aspect of being a sandwich. I took a small bite, chewed, and started: "So," pausing for another small bite, "what should we call you?" My question trailed off with a bit of farce in my tone to temper the situation.

"It's not easy being *Alton*," Tommy commented. "Especially in a place like this."

"I can only imagine," was my reply. "Why Tommy?"

"Well it's common enough not to draw attention," was his answer. "Plus I always liked Tom Sawyer, you know, so I guess I borrowed it from him."

"Fair enough." I nodded in agreement. I turned towards him, still maintaining a bit of the personal space between us. I knew all too well how rough it was being the outcast. It felt good in an awkward kind of way to know that I wasn't the only target at school.

"I guess you may be wondering where I've been the past couple of weeks," I asked it both as a question and as a matter of seeking forgiveness. "I'm going to go really far out on a limb and assume you know who my dad is." It was painful doing this, letting on who I was, even though I was certain he knew. There was still fear that my family could put a halt to any friendship between us.

"Yeah Aubrey, I do know, and trust me, I have no issue with that." Tommy's answer was disarming and heartening as he leaned into the words to give them greater emphasis.

I went on, "It's just that . . . with the unions and everything . . ."

Tommy cut me off, "I totally get it. Trust me. If anyone understands, it's me."

A huge weight lifted, knowing he understood. I could only assume that he knew someone at Caldwell affected by the takeover.

I extended my hand to Tommy, and leaned in, asking him, "Friends?"

Tommy took my hand, letting his guard down ever so slightly, and with that coy smile from the corner of his mouth that would always stay with me, he answered, "Friends."

CHAPTER 7

DOWN UNDER

"WHATCHA DOING LATER?" Tommy's question surprised me at the lunch table and had me on the ropes. "Nothing, I guess. Why?"

"I was thinking maybe we could meet up after school, hang out a little while, you know?"

Tommy didn't need to ask. Anything to get me out of the house was a score. Throw in another lonely soul to commiserate with, now that was a bonus.

I hedged my answer, just to toy with him: "You know, I don't think . . . Oh, okay. Sure." He hung onto every word, and I took more than a little pleasure in seeing the thrill of his doubts rollercoaster into sheer joy.

"Great! How about we meet in the alders again?"

I looked at Tommy and nodded my agreement with slight hesitation. It was a bit peculiar I remember thinking to myself. "Tommy, I nearly got lost stumbling into that place the last time. I don't even remember where we were before let alone how to get there."

Tommy looked up. One thing I would admire about him is that he always seemed to have a solution, especially when it involved helping me along. He was a rarity in that regard. Since then, I've known no other who would go out of their way to make me, well, happy.

"Here's what we'll do," Tommy continued, "Stand by the elm at the corner of your property, look down the stone wall towards the alders, and I'll wave you over to where I am. From there I'll show you around the alder stand, just to get your bearings."

"Sounds like a plan, see you around three-thirty." With lunch ending, we both gathered up and prepared to weather the final three hours until freed from our prison.

One could hardly imagine the two of us would end up being friends. We came from totally different worlds, and the social predicament of "*Caldwell Tool and Die v. Worthington*" almost made it impossible. We didn't see the bounds that society built around us. Lonely and depressed, we were an odd couple that made perfect sense, the ignorant eye completely unaware of how alike we truly were. Our rejection by everyone else drew us together. No matter what the people around us did to make us feel different towards one another, our compassion for each other's predicament prevented that split from occurring.

Our beginnings were anything but similar. In time, I would come to learn from Tommy all about his past, and the pernicious events that would shape and drive the torment deep within that always left him unsettled.

When I first met Tommy, he seemed to appear from and disappear into the alders with a supernatural energy. There was magic in those trees, and he played the part of their sprite. The level of comfort he displayed there imparted on me a sense of peace. In the alders, Tommy was always carefree. There were no eggshells underfoot, no need to look over his shoulder. The alders allowed Tommy to be Tommy.

The alders were to Tommy, unlike any other place, home.

— —

It was a warm April evening in 1974, and spring fever was in full swing as the last of the winter snows finally melted from the memory of Alder Ferry. There was something about the first warm day of the year that invited a party after a long winter—especially after a winter that seemed like it would have no end. That night the beer flowed freely, with the local kids gathered in the parking lot at the alder stand. Headlights illuminated the gravel lot while the engines of Detroit's finest machines revved and purred to the mood of the crowd.

Everyone was loose that night: loosely clothed, loosely wound, and uninhibited from the alcohol splashing about and the reefer wafting through the night air. As the night wore on, the crowd slowly drew down, and one by lonely one, the cars departed. Until only one vehicle remained, isolated in the back of the lot, and free from scrutiny. The 1974 Dodge Challenger swayed from back to front, mirroring the motions of its occupants, its hefty springs bowing to the thrusts and heaves of the couple inside. In the shadow of the alders, Tommy came to be and his life's predicament formed. Mothering him, the alders were the one place where he would always receive shelter from the predicaments presented to him by life.

—–

I managed to make my way to the elm and waited patiently for Tommy's signal. Nothing. I had all but given up on him making an appearance when I caught a glimmer of white cloth moving just inside the curtain of cedars that hailed to the alder stand. I skimmed along the old stone wall, bounded across the driveway, and peered inside.

"Psst—over here," Tommy's hushed voice guided me to the best point of ingress through the cedars and into the stand.

"Thought you'd forgotten about me," I remarked as Tommy parted the branches and I passed through with little difficulty.

"Ehh. Took a bit of doing to get away from home. Anyway, we're here so let me show you around." Tommy reached out his hand and I stepped fully clear from the cedars and into the alders. The portal behind me closed up giving the impression that I had been swallowed whole. What opening was there just a moment ago sealed itself up against the outside world. There I was, for the second time, inside the alder stand. It was just as I remembered it being, the light filtering through the canopy in shimmering iridescent patches that were lucky to find the forest floor. The light filtered into magnificent rays that softened the mood. The feeling I remember most was how disarming it felt to be inside the stand. It was a good type of disarming, a peeling away of fear and apprehension that left me in a state of serenity that defied explanation.

"This way," Tommy shook me out of my moment of clarity with nature. He moved with ease through the stand, the terrain seeming to be part of his subconscious mind. We seemed to move in a circular pattern through the trees; then again, moving through the stand usually seemed to be a circular movement. The interior of the stand seemed to be the center of the universe, with everything unraveling from it. For us, it would become the center of our world. We moved through the alders like deer, browsing and prancing, nimbly navigating the gnarled root bases and skirting around the swampy depressions in the earth. Tommy had a knack for seeing these depressions. To my untrained eye, they just looked like the rest of the ground. My feet followed Tommy's, but still, I occasionally bottomed out in more than a few of the many depressions, my new sneakers tattooed by the earth's tannic ink.

We made our way through the entire stand that afternoon, and by trek's end, I was comfortable with making my way in and out. At least I knew which way was home. This was a feat all its own for my directionally challenged mind that was rare to veer from the archetypal path.

"Think you can make it back?" Tommy mixed his question with doubt.

"I'll manage, Tommy," was my response, slightly under my breath. I was part exasperated from the excursion and part put-off by his comment. Still, he was right to ask.

"Let me show you something," Tommy announced and began pulling away again.

"Wait!" I remember being pissed to the point of wanting to slam him into the ground for the past hour, and now he wanted to take off again.

"I just want to show you something, it's not far. Promise."

"All right . . ." My words trailed off, the disgust of ever coming along beginning to make itself apparent.

Tommy kept his promise. We walked less than ten minutes and moved deeper into the alders. There, abutting from a depression in the earth, were several boulders the size of large sedans. Over time, soil deposited atop them, and to my astonishment, a few of the alders grew in that shallow soil. Their gnarled roots gripped at the stones and held them tight inside of their earthen palms. From a distance, the boulders were barely discernible as the forest floor all but hid them from view. Tommy put his arm out as we approached.

"Careful," he whispered, looking around to make sure we had not been followed. His sudden concern was surprising.

"I don't ask much," Tommy spoke with an intonation of hesitation in his voice, "But I need to know if I can trust you with something."

I looked at Tommy, bewildered. Here we were, alone in the middle of the alders, and I was wondering what bomb he was about to drop.

"It's just that I'm very private, and . . . I can't risk losing something that's been a part of me for a long time now."

"Tommy, I didn't come out here to take anything from you," my patience tested as we stood in the middle of the alders. "I came as your friend."

"All right," Tommy let out a huge sigh and looked me in the eye. His eyes bordered on trust and faith as I remember them scanning my face for any sign of reticence in maintaining his confidences. "It's just that this has become a very special place for me . . ." I looked at Tommy with quizzical eyes. After all, he had just shared his entire knowledge of the alder stand with me.

That is, with the exception of one final detail.

Tommy swept away some debris from the forest floor to reveal a square of plywood, weathered to a pale shade of gray. He slid it over and revealed an opening to a small cavern hidden beneath the forest floor. The reveal of the cavern's entrance astonished me. I didn't see this coming; from any angle, the opening was perfectly camouflaged. Here was an opening to another realm, more precisely a realm within a realm. The alders were a mystical place that already defied any explanation. Now a whole other world, with a mystique all its own, was opening before me.

A makeshift ladder led us down into a cavern that was about six feet square. The air was damp and cool and had the musty smell of the earth that grounded the alder trees. Inside my eyes grew wide at what I saw. Tommy had built himself a makeshift home here, just a few feet beneath the forest floor.

"I've been coming to the alders for as long as I can remember," Tommy started, "it was my backyard. Still is, I guess. I have the stand all to myself. No one ever bothers to come inside. You know how much of a hassle it is to get in, then there's the mud and such." I could sense the pride he took in his forest abode.

"One day I happened across the opening. I checked it out and covered it up as best I could." I gazed at Tommy and then at the small room in disbelief. He continued, "After I'd been certain no one else knew it was here, I claimed it for my own."

I looked around the small cavern. There were a couple old wooden chairs, a hammock, and straight ahead of me, a small collection of books.

"What do you think?"

Honestly, I didn't know how to answer the question. I was more in awe of the space and what he had done to it to make it his own.

"Well, I'm more than surprised. It's not at all what I was expecting," Tommy's face drooped but picked up when he responded.

"I know it may seem weird, but being in town we had no real yard. Sometimes I just needed to have my own space, you know. After all, I usually had nowhere else to go."

I totally understood the need for space. After all, I was nearly suffocated by my parents, even though if they could, I'm sure they would have loved to lock me away in a cave somewhere.

"It's not weird Tommy, just not what I was expecting," I sensed a little bit of ease returning to him.

I scanned the small collection of books. As I would get to know Tommy better, one thing was certain: I could always find him with a book. He never went anywhere without something to read. The shelf before me held an eclectic mix of classic and contemporary works. For a boy his age, it was a small but impressive collection. A few stood out, like *The Adventures of Huckleberry Finn*, which is where Tommy found his namesake. In some ways, he reminded me of a modern-day Huck Finn, the lonely youth taking on the world around him and trying to recreate it to suit him as best he could.

There were a few others, *The Lord of the Flies*, *To Kill a Mockingbird*, an anthology of Shakespearean dramas, and Whitman's *Leaves of Grass*, to name just a few. I reached into the stack and pulled out Hardy's *Far From the Madding Crowd*. Holding the book, I looked back at Tommy and remarked, "How appropriate." We both shared a laugh. It was great to be with someone who understood my dry wit.

"Here," Tommy reached out his hand to mine and placed several catkins inside my palm. "These will be our signal. Whenever you want to hang out, just leave one inside my locker at school." It was the sweetest gesture I ever received.

I took the catkins from Tommy and said to him, "And you do the same."

CHAPTER 8

BUSINESS PARTNERS

I NEVER HAD ANYTHING good to say about my father's business dealings. When he went into a new town, the layoffs always targeted the older employees. With rare exception were the older employees nearing retirement age allowed to finish out their careers and leave with their pensions. Hardly ever did my father show any semblance of respect or dignity to his workers.

Not long into the new school year, I remember my father coming home and laying into my mother about how his day had gone. It went beyond the typical talk of overhead, profit-margins and whatever else drove the man to do what he did. Instead, he was talking about the union. More precisely, their attacks on him.

"Edith, I just don't know how to take this crew," said my father, "typically people are happy to stay employed. But this union, their steward, seems out to break *me*."

"Stuart, it's nothing personal I'm sure," was my mother's comment. Even with the lifestyle that my father's position created for her, she took very little interest in his dealings.

"Edith, this man, Mike Genardo, is about to throw away the last thirty years of his working life. For what? To save a company that in all honesty would fade into nothing if left to its own devices?" My father was inquisitive towards himself, as my mother had stopped listening before he'd started. "I'd rather not let him go, but I sometimes worry about what he's capable of."

Now, this caught my mother's attention.

"Really, Stuart? Some uneducated, broken down old man has got you worried?"

She knew how to catch him at his weakest. She had a knack for that, instead of nurturing, she went for the kill. She could be ruthless, and at times I understood why my father chose to risk being fragged by his employees instead of being exploited by his wife.

He turned his head towards my mother, and I caught the gleam in his eye that let me know when his trigger was set. She backed off and let him continue, knowing the minefield had been laid and everyone should now tread this territory with the lightest of steps.

"The man is a loose cannon, he doesn't care what he loses, or how he gets to me." My father paused, looked my mother in the eye, and warned, "*How he gets to me.*"

"You can call back the security detail if it gets any worse, right?"

"I suppose I can. It's just the man's playing the game very well."

It was peculiar for my father to dwell on any single employee like he was with this Genardo character. As I aged I came to disagree with my father's business model to even greater degrees, but even still, I could see some truth to his point: whether or not my father's company had taken over Caldwell, the plant would have eventually shut down anyway. Genardo would still have his pension, and the other workers too young to retire would be added to the unemployment rolls. The friction between these two men was almost personal, a battle of the wills.

I kept my silence throughout the conversation, but as usual, I couldn't be ignored.

"You're awful quiet tonight," was my father's greeting to me.

"I guess I don't have much to add to the conversation," was my quiet response.

"No, nothing at all. I'd expect as much from you," he spoke to me like one of the many men he had laid off over the past two decades. My mother's indifference was the only thing that iced the conversation from escalating. I caught her glancing at both of us, each eye seeming to independently seek one of us out and lock us down. I could never tell whose side she was on but knew that it probably wasn't mine. If anything, my mother was always playing to protect her stake.

My parents were as odd a pairing as were Tommy and me. The striking difference was that they conformed to social norms. My father was the "Type A" personality driven to succeed at any expense: his marriage, family, and health meant nothing to him if they interfered with this career. The only time I mattered was when we played the part of the "all-American" family, me tugging at his pant leg as he spoke to the media or his employees. My mother would always be in the picture, but quietly observing from behind my father, conservatively dressed to play the part of loving wife and doting mother.

Which couldn't have been any further from the truth. My mother was just as calculating, just as domineering, and just as ruthless on the home front as my father was in the business world. On the outside she was the proper housewife, holding together the perfect modern family to give the ideal photo opportunity that hid the truth from the public. The fact was that my mother rarely left the house. Instead, she locked herself away day in and day out, a functioning alcoholic at peace only when left alone, drink in hand.

My mother was born into a world of privilege. Her father was an executive for a large multi-national oil company that came into its own following the Second World War. My grandmother never worked a day in her life, and my mother had been raised with the most elegant lifestyle and received the finest private education that was meant to prepare her for a carefree life, meant to carry on conversations at the cocktail parties she would eventually host for her husband's co-workers and clientele. Instead, she met Sgt. Stuart Worthington, who was on leave after returning home from Vietnam. The rest, as they say, is history. But history has an odd way of making its way to the memory.

Like any inquisitive child, in my free time, I pillaged through my parents' personal effects, if anything just because these things were there. Nightstands, dressers, footlockers: they were all there to be explored, like treasure chests. Mostly what I found was of no interest to me: my dad's dog tags; loose change; an assortment of old medications; really, nothing of interest. On the surface, my parents were the most blasé couple. Not even a box of condoms, or a guide on sex that most couples kept in their nightstands. They were as white-bread as they came.

Except for the letters. Why they survived I couldn't imagine, except for maybe they were simply hidden away, just to be forgotten. It was at that time the most damning thing a child could have laid eyes upon. It became the evidence that nurtured my need to be liberated from my parents.

At the base of my parents' bed was an antique footlocker. It would speak to the imagination of any child, with its worn brass hardware, dark mahogany exterior, and the dings and gouges that evidenced its many voyages. It was a mysterious piece, and I was drawn to it. Inside was nothing of seeming importance. Nothing but clothes. Old, forgotten clothes that had faded from fashion resided within the ancient footlocker, waiting for a fleeting trend to breathe life back into them. It was like an archaeological dig, each stratum of clothing being older than the one above. I still remember pulling out a pair of bell bottoms and being fascinated with a pair of pants whose flared legs could serve as a skirt on my childish frame.

I pulled the clothes out carefully, laughing at some and admiring others. I stacked each layer meticulously so that I could reset them into the footlocker to appear as though never disturbed. I noticed the bottom had a bit of give when I pushed on it and bowed under the pressure. It was a false bottom. I worked the thin veneer of wood loose from the frame and laid claim to the letters exchanged between my parents. They were the evidence of an affair disapproved of by my mother's parents, my father being an ill-suited social match for their daughter.

The letters were far from romantic and bore a business tone to them. They captured one night, a night that would forever haunt them. They were initiated by my mother for one reason: she became pregnant on the night they met. I was a mistake. Without telling me that directly, their treatment of me for as long as my memory would allow supported that fact.

The exchange went back and forth for over a month. Abortion? Not an option. Adoption? Maybe. The letters addressed every situation in how to rid themselves of this problem they created: me. I found nothing in the letters where they discussed my birth or raising me as their child. Everything centered on one thing: how best to sweep this under the rug so that the both of them could move on in their separate ways. It was evident that neither one had intended to select the other for a life partner.

In the end, religion won out. My grandparents became aware of the pregnancy and demanded that the two marry and raise the consequences of their actions. At nineteen, my mother was pregnant and married. She was shunned by her parents, the only allowance being that my grandfather connected my father to an associate who took a chance on the young army veteran. My father would never have had such an opportunity fall into his lap if he hadn't knocked up my mother. The life he enjoyed wasn't his, it was mine. All mine and he never thanked me once for giving him the opportunity to succeed in the business world.

In all this, my mother seemed the victim. But I didn't feel sorry for her. Her charmed life was gone, and instead of showing me love, she dug in her heels to protect what was rightfully hers from this arrangement. She was a willing accomplice, seeking to regain what she would have established through a more traditional marriage if she had never met my father.

I was ten years old when I found those letters. There was nothing in them that hinted of joy or love. I was simply an impediment. I was the glue that bound their relationship, a piece of baggage reminding them each day of how they found themselves in a loveless, lifeless marriage that sustained itself only because it was a necessary evil. To a ten-year-old child, this was shattering. I always knew that my parents were different than the other kids' parents at school, but attributed this to their standing in the social order more than anything else. I had become a victim of religion through their marriage. Everyone in America, I would say, is a victim of religion to some extent. But when it's you, it cuts deeper. No child wants to be the mistake that would become progeny to a succession of mistakes.

That evening's transpirations about the union, my father, and my mother's reaction to it all wore on me. My father's comments to me, and my mother's cool reaction to us both reminded me of the letters. I was the wedge between them and at the same time the only thing that kept them together. It was easy to understand why they never divorced. My father had found a life that was comfortable financially and shared it with a woman who could care less about what he did so long as she could maintain a quality of life fitting for someone of her upbringing. This he did and did it well.

I pulled myself away from my parents that evening, knowing I was licked again. There was no winning for me. In a way, I was the Mike Genardo of our family. I could play along and take what they gave me, or I could fight. To fight, I would risk losing everything. Longing to be loved was one issue, but to fight would mean to give up any possibility of leaving on favorable grounds, to attend college far away, out of their sight: a buy-out for my acquiescence to the terms of their arrangement. In my room that night I thought of the alders. It too seemed like the only place I had left to go, the only place where I was welcome. I pulled a pair of the catkins from my nightstand and looked at them. I remembered Tommy saying to me about the stand, "After all, I usually had nowhere else to go." At that moment I knew how he felt. I just wanted to be free of the people on the floor below me who were pulling me along with them as an afterthought.

I looked back at the catkins and thought it was good to finally have someone to talk to, someone who just might understand where I was coming from. It was reassuring to know that maybe, for the first time, I wasn't alone. There was another person out there who may get me, who could relate to my relationship with my parents. If not, at least I knew he would listen and not run away.

CHAPTER 9

BOUNDARIES

"JEAN DE ROCHAMBEAU, Jean de Rochambeau. Say it with me class." Ms. Kaliczenkoff allowed our studies in American history to take a turn that day, becoming instead a lesson in French. The names rolled off her tongue with elegance: Rochambeau and Marquis de Lafayette were not just names when she spoke them. Her pronunciations of them were romantic and captivating. It was my first exposure to the French language, and her command of it was symphonic to my ears. No other teacher before seemed as enlightened and airy as she. She was an enigma and had a manner about her that breathed life into what it meant to be educated and sophisticated. She was in a league far above the other teachers and staff at St. Germaine.

St. Germaine parish defined the term parochial, and not in the religious sense of the word. In many ways, its stifling parochial bent suited it perfectly to Alder Ferry. The parish was strict in adherence to its rules and protecting its interests. Change was never welcome; it challenged the powers that be in both the parish and in the town. Fortunately, religious dogma was typically opposite that of the secular world, and it gave the parish a crutch to prop itself up with and turn its back against the changes ushered in during the late twentieth century.

At the helm of St. Germaine was Father Richard Pekennick. He was a tall and overbearing man who used his stature to make anyone standing in his way uncomfortable. Not used to being challenged, he ruled his parish with a close eye, being very guarded in all aspects of parish operations, and maintaining close confidences with few individuals. For as close as he oversaw his modern fiefdom, he ruled from afar and always maintained a distance from his parishioners. To most, it was proper for their religious leader to separate himself from his flock, and they thought nothing of it. To the few that questioned his way of doing things, they were quick to refrain from challenging him out of respect, and fear.

Alder Ferry's past lent itself to Protestants and Quakers, who settled the town long before the Catholics began immigrating to the area. The Catholics were newcomers, and from its inception, the parish was consistently seeking to protect its interests so that it could eventually focus on attending to the spiritual affairs of its parishioners. Harkening back to the days when a parish was the local governing body, St. Germaine was one of the few parishes that also conformed to the political boundaries of a town. Geographically and politically St. Germaine was an overlay of Alder Ferry. It defended its territory vigorously in its youth against Protestant vandals and a local government that was not the least bit interested in serving justice on behalf of the Catholic newcomers. Many years later it was understandable how the leadership of the parish had come to be secretive in its affairs; any display of its inner workings to the outside world was strictly forbidden to protect its property from vandalism and its members from harm. Even though Catholicism had since gone mainstream, Father Pekennick was keen to maintain this wall of secrecy.

Father Pekennick managed a parish body numbered at close to one thousand parishioners. Assisting him in that operation were the occasional seminarians on temporary assignment and Deacon Robert Hatton. It was a structure that bode well for Pekennick; his inner circle was modest, and outside of the diocese, he reported to no one. For an organization as large as the parish, he maintained the confidences of its operation close in hand, micromanaging its affairs as best he could to avoid intrusion on his affairs. To keep church matters close, he relied upon his deacon, a man that was a social pariah in the community.

The deacon was a widower and retiree from Caldwell. A recovered, raging alcoholic and fists-first man, Hatton was known in Alder Ferry for his drunken exploits and his aptitude for settling matters with violence. When he finally came to, it was his church that brought him back into the community, it being the only place where he could find any sort of welcome given his past. For Hatton, it was the one way to reinsert himself back into the community as he struggled with his faults and to maintain his sobriety. For Pekennick, Hatton was his perfect suitor to serve as his deacon. An outcast from the community, Hatton could carry out his commands while deflecting any scorn from making its mark on the pastor.

Hatton was quick to rise to the position and to subordinate himself to Pekennick. Hatton found it difficult enough to find his place in Alder Ferry after losing his wife to cancer. A lonely man who guarded his privacy to such an extent that it raised suspicions among his neighbors, the church became his opening to the outside world, his chance to show that change was possible for a sinner like him. Pekennick was the only person who gave this sinner a chance, and for that, Hatton showed his gratitude through loyalty and submission.

To be honest, I never enjoyed church. Even when it allowed for a reprieve from home life, I still didn't enjoy it. Its rigidity and stuffiness abhorred me; going to mass was punishment. My parents must have shared my sentiment; they casually dropped me off every Sunday and arrived sixty minutes later to cart me away. I suppose it was too much of a burden to allow me to intrude on their Sunday brunch, or for my parents to assimilate into the communities we used as mere rest stops. Perhaps my stubborn father would have seen the families he destroyed: there they would be, praying their hearts out to escape the financial ruin his company's actions caused them as they took up residence in the pews each Sunday. Maybe he had a conscience but just couldn't bear to hear it.

At St. Germaine Parish I enjoyed going to church for the first time in my life. It wasn't to save my soul, or receive communion, or be seen by the school faculty. St. Germaine had one thing the other parishes never had: an altar boy named Tommy. Sunday mornings became another ritual in our friendship. From the front row, I would watch him, casting an odd face when no one was looking, trying to get a rise from him. On more than one occasion I succeeded, but at Tommy's expense, I was certain. The old ladies were quick to fire a steely glance my way, which I deflected through abject ignorance of their cold response to me. It only seemed to pester them more, which I quite enjoyed. Sit me in those pews against my will, and I will do the best to get what I need from it. My soul was hungry, not for God, but to interact with my kindred spirit kneeling at the base of the altar in humble obedience.

I never caught up with Tommy after mass. It was probably for the best anyway, I remember thinking, only because this was a very public place. We drew enough attention to ourselves as class outcasts from Monday through Friday that we more than likely could spare subjecting ourselves to the same on a Sunday morning. It was after all the Lord's Day, and who were we to subtract from it?

Our Monday through Friday experience at St. Germaine was only softened by one individual who seemed to be on our wavelength, and that was Ms. Kaliczenkoff. If Father Pekennick had an antithesis, she was it. The school was run under the auspices of the parish by guidelines from the local diocese. Ms. Kaliczenkoff knew the politics of operating a Catholic school and played the system as best she could. Where most other teachers flew under the radar, she was quick to rise above it and let her intentions be known, teaching by her own style, while straddling the rules to bend them as best she could. A local woman, her roots had protected her to some extent. Father Pekennick knew this, but all along I was certain he was lining up his facts to eventually remove this black sheep from his flock.

Ms. Kaliczenkoff did not seem to be an ordinary fit for the school. She was just too different, too elegant, and quite beyond what the school could offer its students. But there she was, her talent limited and her potential far from ever being realized as an educator. That was my perspective as a young teenager when I first met her, praying that I would never end up like her. Little did I know it, but I would grow to become a woman whose outlook on the world was forged by someone who at first glance seemed to allow her very own being to be limited by the world that surrounded us. It was a contradiction that only life would allow, as is always the case. These are the contradictions that abound and allow us to escape the mistakes of the past if we open ourselves to recognizing them.

"Jean de Rochambeau, Jean de Rochambeau." Ms. Kaliczenkoff continued to rattle off the names of French officers that aided in the cause for independence. Her staccato tempo earned her the nickname of "Ms. Kalashnikov" in honor of the Soviet weapon of the same name for her rapid-fire style. Without a doubt, most students at St. Germaine couldn't appreciate Ms. Kaliczenkoff for what she was; neither could I at first, I'll admit. But her difference from the rest of the staff drew both Tommy and me closer to her, almost as if she knew exactly what we were experiencing as we came of age in Alder Ferry.

As that day came to a close, I made it a point to sneak a catkin into Tommy's locker. When school let out, I dropped my book bag at home and made my way into the alders. Tommy was already there, waiting. "Got your message," Tommy said with a chuckle in his voice.

"Well, I didn't want you to think that getting together here would always be your idea," was my reply. I reached inside my jacket pocket and pulled out two cigarettes and a lighter I had "borrowed" from my mother before leaving the house. "Wanna smoke?" Tommy hesitated, then acquiesced.

"Next time I'll bring the wine from the sacristy," and we both choked back a cough as we inhaled.

"What's your take on Ms. K?" I asked Tommy.

"Well, she's different. But in a good way, I mean, she seems to get me. Do you know what I mean?" Tommy's response struck a perfect chord with me.

"I do, it's just that she seems so out of place. It's almost like she's doing someone a favor teaching at our school."

Tommy took a short drag off his cigarette and exhaled in puttering breaths to choke back his cough and enjoy whatever buzz he could from the nicotine.

"I know nothing about her," Tommy responded, "except that her family is from here. Maybe she is like everyone else, you know, wants to get out but this is home for her. Beats me."

I looked towards Tommy but sort of through him, "I get that, but you know there's more to it than just being here. No offense, Tommy, I know it's where you grew up . . ."

Tommy cut me off before I could finish: "It's not my home. Never has been and never will be. This alder stand is the closest thing to home I've ever known." There was a touch of bitterness in his tone, and when he spoke he seemed aged beyond his years.

"Hey, I'm sorry, I didn't mean to just assume, you know. I really don't know enough about you to make that assumption I guess."

"It's all right, and I didn't want for it to come out that way. I'm sorry."

"Tommy, no need to apologize, it was my fault." It was the first of many times he would apologize for an action outside of his control. Even when he would speak up to politely assert himself, he would become apologetic. Whatever life had already thrown at him started to wear him down at a very early age.

Tommy looked down and away. I did the same to make an awkward situation seem less awkward; it was all I knew to do.

"Look, I know what it's like to not fit in, trust me on that. So, whatever it is that you've had going on, it won't scare me off. My parents are about as screwed up as they come."

"If you only knew," Tommy's response was a bit lighter, but still I knew that he probably didn't have it easy growing up in this town, being the reclusive bookworm that was misunderstood at school and from what it sounded like, at home, too.

"Back to Mrs. K." I hoped shifting the conversation a bit would help lessen the tension.

"She's the only teacher I've ever liked or trusted in that school," said Tommy as he livened up again. "When I'm around her, I feel, good. Kind of like when we hang out together."

"Yeah, I get that sensation from her too. Deep down I think she understands us. I just hope that, well, someday I can move on from this place. I can't imagine being here forever."

"None of us want that, ˋBree," Tommy took it upon himself to shorten my name into a more familiar form. I let it go because I liked it, no one had ever done it before, and it was endearing. These were the things that always drew me close to him, even when he didn't try he knew how to make me feel essential. After episodes like our earlier exchange where I nearly ripped his heart out, he would always come back at me in this way, usually with no effort, because he always poured his heart out. If either of us ever violated the sanctity of our relationship, it was always me.

Tommy went on, "But it just happens, right? All your life you dream of getting out and exploring the world, but then life just grabs you by the foot and pulls you back in."

He was too young to be that jaded, and I could see the conflict in his eyes: he had witnessed this all too often was my guess, the cycle of broken dreams in Alder Ferry. It was that cycle which was responsible for his creation. Tommy's life story was another notch in the belt of this town's circle of life.

"Maybe it doesn't have to be like that, Tommy. Maybe we give in too easy."

"You're right, Bree. I guess it's just that I don't know where to start, you know?"

"None of us do. I guess that's the hard part," was my answer. Tommy nodded in agreement, and we both looked to the sky which was growing dark fast.

"Same time tomorrow?"

"Sure," I said, and with that, we parted for the day.

I took a few paces towards home and stopped. Tommy was still in sight and I took it upon myself to reverse roles and follow him home this time.

We made our way to the gravel road, and I kept just enough distance between us to avoid being noticed. I wasn't sure if he would care that I was following along, but at times he was so secretive that I knew I had to do a little digging on my own to get inside his head and understand him better. I didn't see it as prying, but as educating myself to become a better friend to this boy who moved through the world almost unnoticed.

It wasn't a far walk from the gravel road to Tommy's neighborhood. We passed through a narrow grove of trees that separated his property from the gravel road. I stayed back and watched as he disappeared into a squat little bungalow, with cedar siding that had been long weathered to an ashen color and was curling up at the edges. The bungalow was one of many that stood in a row along the trees here, just on the outskirts of town, and by convenient design out of its sight. It was the "poor" section of Alder Ferry: old factory housing that had served its purpose to the many trade workers who toiled away their lives in the factories that faded into forgotten memories. The homes were far from well maintained. Most of the properties had a barking dog chained to a tree, with chicken wire strung between them as makeshift fencing. It was a depressing sight, and I felt for Tommy later that night in my well-appointed bedroom. As much as we had in common, there were plenty of differences between us that should have prevented our friendship from taking root.

I was about halfway through a turn to make my way home when I saw a peculiar sight. It was Tommy, and he was running. Running in circles, lapping the boundary of his property repeatedly, like a hamster in its wheel. I was more than mesmerized. I was puzzled. The boy was strange, I thought, but this was weird. I counted twelve laps made by Tommy around the property before he returned inside. He came back out and set a bowl by the back step, called out with a clicking sound and waited, then went back inside. A scrawny, feral-looking cat felt its way out of the shadows, and with wary footing drew itself up along the side of the bungalow to feed. The cat was Tommy's feline alter ego. Both moved with an apprehension that was without explanation. Both were secretive in their movements, always looking behind them, with a fear that they were the subjects of intense scrutiny. I backpedaled from the property and turned for home, more questions than answers now brewing in my head.

CHAPTER 10

COVERING UP

THE NEXT DAY, I met up again with Tommy in the alder stand. I wasn't sure how to approach what I witnessed the previous evening, but if anything, figured it to be just an extension of his eccentric personality. I knew I would come off as intrusive for following him home, but in my mind, I justified it with the fact that I had once been the object of his very same voyeuristic curiosities.

"Tommy, I have a confession to make."

"What do you mean?" Tommy looked at me with an inquisitive glance.

"Last night . . . I . . . I followed you home." My head was down to avoid eye contact as my toe traced figure eights with long, anxious curves in the loamy soil. "I know it wasn't right, but I just went along and did it. I didn't mean to intrude or anything, it's just that, well, I just want to know you a little better."

"You know Bree, it's not that you followed me home. It's just that we have such different backgrounds, and I know my home isn't special, I'm more embarrassed by it than anything."

I caught a look of sadness in his eye and knew he probably felt that he was being judged by me over his living situation. We did come from different worlds, and under most circumstances, we should have hated one another for being on opposite sides of the fence that partitioned our worlds. But we didn't. We had more in common than we could have ever imagined. If we allowed society to dictate our friendships, we would have been at a loss, having never ventured to gain what we became so fortunate to enjoy.

I knew Tommy felt ashamed of his home in comparison to the Grand Old Lady. We both had our heads down now, looking away, each waiting for the other to break the silence. I knew it wouldn't be Tommy, he was too meek to be the first to speak up, so I took it upon myself.

"Tommy, I could care less about where you live. I'm interested in you." I stopped, hoping that he would come to at my words, but I knew he would take a little more goading. "Listen, I go home and look forward to when we'll get to hang out again, and that's it. Following you home, to me it was just an extension of our day. I didn't want to go home and be alone with my parents. I just wanted to stretch out the day a little longer. Sorry if you think it was weird or anything, but that's it, I swear."

Tommy looked up and I saw that he was about to let his guard down.

"What was all the running about? You know, it was a little odd."

Tommy turned to me and sighed. "Bree, I have to run before dinner. My grandfather says I'm too fat and that I need to work up an appetite."

It was the last thing I expected to hear. Tommy hadn't begun to trim out like some of the other boys, but he was far from fat.

"I don't have a great family life, Bree. That's why the alders here are so important to me. It's my only escape from that place. You're the only person I've ever shared this with. It's not easy to talk about."

"I know." My response to him was succinct and resolute. "Just because my parents have money, a nice house, all that, doesn't mean that I enjoy being home either. It's the last place I wanna be, too."

I explained to Tommy the letters I had found hidden away in the footlocker. I knew that if Tommy was going to open up, then the same would be expected of me. It was only fair. And as painful as my conception and birth were, talking about it reminded me of the pain I was probably asking Tommy to relive by sharing his experiences with me.

"I know my mom doesn't really love me. And as sick as it sounds, whenever she really gets to me, I just tell her: 'You wish you had aborted me.' I thought it would really make her hurt. But it didn't. She would just say, 'Maybe you're right,'" and walk away. It doesn't matter what I say to her. No matter how hard I try, my words just don't cut as deep as hers."

Tommy interrupted before I allowed the sadness in my voice to overcome me. "I remember my mom telling me that I don't have a middle name because I didn't earn it," Tommy recalled as he brought his upward gaze down and looked at me with a wry smile. We came from different worlds, but here we were misery enjoying company. Our common suffering at home was the bridge that gapped the social distance between us. In the end, we were both two misbegotten children thrown to parents who could have cared less about us, except for the fact that we had had the audacity to circumvent the plans they imagined for their lives.

"I was a mistake, too," Tommy stated matter-of-factly. "My parents met up before my dad shipped off to Vietnam. He was killed in action days before I was born." I caught Tommy looking up to the heavens as he spoke, almost as if he was calling out for the father he never met to connect with him in any way whatsoever. "A few weeks later the war ended. Maybe he'd still be here if he hadn't enlisted when he did."

I interjected: "Well then maybe you wouldn't be here then, right? They weren't thinking about the future, you know. Your mom probably figured he'd ship out and forget about her anyway."

"Maybe you're right, Bree. It's just that I never seemed to exist or matter at home. I don't even look like my mom or her parents. Look at me. Do I look Italian to you?"

It was true: Tommy's father was born to Irish parents who immigrated to the United States after World War II. His pale complexion and blonde hair would be the last thing to lead anyone to believe that he had any Italian blood running through his veins.

"All I know is what I've been told." Tommy kicked the dirt as he rehashed the first decade of his childhood. "My dad's folks died long ago, leaving him an orphan. Odd how history repeats itself, isn't it?"

I continued to watch Tommy, captivated by his story. He knew he had my attention, and there was something therapeutic about airing out all the wrongs that had taken up space in our lives. Tommy was a natural storyteller, his penchant for words uncanny even at a young age. Without effort, he could draw out any emotion from you as his story unfolded, and at times I would forget he was talking about himself. In the alders, discussing his life with me was the surest way he could distance himself from the pain of his childhood.

"My grandfather always called my dad that 'mick bastard.' And I was his son, a second-class mick citizen living in his house. As long as my dad was Irish, I would never be good enough to be his grandson." Tommy's dissociation with his family made perfect sense to me as he continued in with his story. "My grandparents took me in out of duty. To what, I don't know. Maybe it was God or religion, but for whatever reason, they did it. But it doesn't mean that they had to make life enjoyable at all."

"Tommy, I know the feeling. From the outside, it seems like I have it all, but life is plain miserable living with parents who wish you had never come to be." Tommy looked at me, and I at him. I knew it was a stretch to try and compare our existences. It just couldn't be done. I may have been unwanted and unloved, but Tommy was somewhat of a forgotten reality by his family.

"Bree, I know we both have it hard at home. My Mom is never around, except for when whoever she's dating gives her the boot and she comes back to my grandparents' house until the next guy comes along. At those times I know exactly how you feel: she is there but harsh as anything. I know she hates me."

"It's just hard, I know, seeing all the other kids with their parents. Then I look up at mine and just wonder why they just had to bring me into the world. Why not adopt? No, I have the pleasure of being the worthless Worthington, the anchor that ran their grand dreams aground. I know that hate, Tommy."

"I know you do, Bree. I didn't know it when we first met, but I know it now. And I know that you understand me, as best you can, which is better than anyone else. But let me ask you this: why do you go home?"

The question caught me off guard. Why did I always go back home? Why not run away? The truth of the matter was that I was a coward. Afraid all the way through high school it would turn out, afraid to turn my back on my parents for the simple reason that they provided for me. As bad as it was, I could always go back home. It was all I knew, and maybe I actually enjoyed the torment; it was the only constant in my life. My dysfunctional home life had been the only permanency that I understood. Like an addict, I kept going back for more.

"Tommy, I can't answer that. I just don't know, but where else would I go?"

"Well, what if they made you leave?"

"What do you mean?"

"Every day for as long as I could remember I was told to get out of the house." I watched Tommy, his dramatic pauses drawing me in, for what I anticipated to be a finish that made my home life seem finely knit in comparison to his. "When they would leave for work, I was made to leave the house. When school was in it wasn't really an issue. But during school breaks and summers it wasn't easy."

"Did they really put you out like that every day?" I asked in disbelief at the unfolding story.

"Every day. Not much different than the dogs chained up in the neighbors' yards. If I was thirsty, there was the hose. If I had to go, there were the trees. If I was hungry, I'd have to wait for my grandmother to come home on her lunch break."

"Tommy . . ."

"Don't even ask about number two."

His dry humor gave some airiness to his story. Still, I couldn't believe it. I didn't know his family at all, and when I would finally get to know them, I wouldn't be shocked at how this timid and unassuming boy had been shoved to the wayside. These adults bore the burden of raising Tommy, a duty imposed upon them by religion and familial ties they barely adhered to, and it showed. He had been born into a hatred that his birth aroused in all of them. For his grandfather, it was the impure Irish blood that spoiled his progeny and interfered with his homestead; for his grandmother, it was the imposition of another mouth to feed; and for his mother it was the reminder of a drunken night that stifled her partying ways, at least until he was old enough to somewhat fend for himself.

Tommy had been nearly on his own since he was five years old. Since five years old he was thrown out into the world, basically on his own. And this wasn't the suburban America of the past, where kids could roam free. It was a day and age where predators waited at bus stops and cruised the mall parking lots looking for their next victim. Tommy would have been the perfect victim. No one would have noticed if he went missing, not until it was too late to do anything about it, anyway.

Fortunately, Tommy survived that fate. I would sometimes wonder if he had hoped for some stranger to come in and take him away. His existence at home was just that, an existence. His family would never appreciate him for his intellect, and even if they tried, they lacked the capacity to even come close to appreciating his potential. This small, timid boy had developed an imagination to counter his home life. The vulgarity of his childhood allowed his mind to take him places that would bring an escape, if only temporary, from the horrors of his childhood. His imagination fueled his inner spirit and kept the demons at bay. Tommy's creativity was born from the pain he was forced to live through, a beautiful contrast to the world that had called him its own for all too long.

The alders were part and parcel of his imagination, his escape from the reality that was his captor.

"In some ways, it's good that it worked out the way it did, Bree. That's how I ended up here in the alders. I guess the alders and I, we kind of found each other. It was the first place I could go and have some peace. My family never cared where I went off to, and on those nights at home when the arguing got too bad, I could come here. Your first night in town, it was one of those nights. My Mom came home, both her and my grandfather were drunk, and I just had to get out."

I was speechless at his story. I had never known the troubles he had known. While my father's rage could turn violent, it never turned on me. It would occasionally make its way to my mother, and at times trickle down to me in the form of a cold breakfast or a day spent isolating in my room. But I had never known the struggle to survive like Tommy. I never had to cover up or disappear to protect myself. Tommy always had to anticipate the uncertainty of his near future, keeping one step ahead of a torrent of rage that could swallow him whole.

"What if the weather was bad, Tommy? Rain or snow, or just plain cold?"

"At first it was a little hard, I'd pull myself up alongside the doorway to keep dry. A few doors down, we had a neighbor, that would bring me in sometimes." Tommy's acknowledgment of this act of kindness was so matter-of-fact that it was odd. Given his experiences, it could have been that he was unsure how to accept such an act of generosity.

"That was before I found this place," Tommy motioned with his arms about him in the air, giving off a gesture of thanks to the trees. "By the time I was ten I had this place all to myself. By then I preferred to be here, alone."

I could appreciate his distrust for adults, but he was young— way too young, to be so cynical. He'd never known an adult that he could trust, and here I was, the first person that came to know his entire story. I remember that day, feeling both saddened and honored by the fact that he shared it with me. That day forged our friendship and earned Tommy a loyalty in me that would be tested, but that I would never allow to be broken.

CHAPTER 11

THE TIPPING POINT

T HAT FIRST YEAR in Alder Ferry passed quicker than any
other year I had ever known. It came to mark the beginning
of a seed change allowing me to break free from a family life
that was only a mere formality. It was also a year that saw the
emergence of an incredible friendship with Tommy that would
define my character, and chart a course allowing me to open up
to another with no fear of reprisal. Never before had I been able
to place such trust in another person. My friendship with Tommy
changed that and gave me some hope that there could be light in
other people as well.

That year also marked my transition from grammar school to
the morass of high school. If I had ever felt like an outcast before,
entering high school bore a greater burden on me; it could only
magnify my isolation from my peers. The only saving grace of
entering high school could be its size; perhaps I could melt away
into the crowd and live the next four years in anonymity. Being
that I was Stuart Worthington's daughter, this thought did not
seem to bear much potential.

The school year at St. Germaine closed with a token graduation ceremony in the church, followed by an informal reception in
the school cafeteria. We donned black robes and strode down the
aisle, organized by height like a chain of dominos being strung
through the vestibule and into the front pews. Tommy was several places ahead of me, his worn suit collar pushing its way
through the robe, rising and falling in cadence to his footsteps. I
kept time along with Tommy's fluttering wardrobe as our solemn
procession made its way, running a gauntlet through the crowd
of faces that examined our every step, especially mine it seemed.

Father Pekennick celebrated mass and called out each graduate's name. Each child's name was greeted with surly cheers and

hurrahs typically reserved for the football stadium, a response indicative of the raucous blue-collar crowd forming the backbone of the parish. I could care less for the others in my class and listened for Tommy's name to be called. I brought my hands together, quieted by my program in hand, to celebrate his achievement of surviving eight long years at this institution. Tommy's name didn't get the cheers that the other graduates received. Instead, all I heard was a tepid clapping of hands echoing from the rear of the church. My name, without surprise, was given the silent treatment. If it weren't for the fact that we were in a church, I am certain the response would have been quite vulgar.

We began our procession out of the church following mass, and to my surprise, both my parents were in attendance. They were hidden from view in an out of the way side pew beneath an aged stained-glass window depicting the second station of the cross. I held my head high, pretending not to notice them. They, in turn, did their best not to notice me, a demur to my denial of their presence, and to avoid making eye contact with the locals. Regardless, I was shocked to see the both of them in attendance. It was the first time in my memory where both of my parents attended a school function on my behalf.

Once inside the cafeteria the class was allowed a few moments to themselves and their teachers before the gallery of parents, family, and friends were admitted. Under any other circumstances, it would have been an awkward, lonely moment. But it wasn't. I found Tommy, and together, we headed straight to Ms. Kaliczenkoff. Over the course of the school year, she had become a beacon of hope for both of us. Of all the teachers I had known, she recognized how unique we were and the potential we held. She also sensed the friendship that had taken root and sensed that our relationship could be the one thing that prevented the outside world from bowling us over.

She had given us the permission to refer to her simply as "Mrs. K," an acknowledgment on her part of both the difficulty in pronouncing her name and the strong teacher-student relationship we formed. It was obvious to everyone that Tommy and I were different. To Mrs. K our differences from the rest of the class were what made us unique. Instead of seeing us as rebellious or non-conforming out of spite, she knew the challenges that we faced in the daily rituals of school life. If only she knew what had been happening in our lives outside of school.

But she didn't, and the challenges we faced defined not only who Tommy and I were as individuals, but they also gave us the incentive to better our circumstances. The challenges we faced brought us closer, bringing about solidarity in our purpose: to challenge the status quo manner of living in Alder Ferry and to escape with our futures intact. What she did do was notice the fire in each of us, and she did her best to direct that energy back into our selves. Mrs. K saw how our circumstances matured us far beyond our peers and recognized where we could go if given the chance. It was almost as if she recognized in us some missed opportunity in her own life.

"Tommy, Aubrey, congratulations!" We were greeted by Mrs. K's open arms and a beaming smile. "Here we are, you made it. A chapter in your life closes, and the next is set to open."

Her use of the term chapter to define these periods in our life was appropriate, especially for Tommy, whose escape from life was often shuttered between the chapters of a book.

"Thank you, Mrs. K." It was a worrisome moment for me. My thanks to her were genuine, but in some ways, I just didn't want this school year to end. For eight to nine hours a day, the class-room could be intimidating. Now, the one person who had made the school experience more than tolerable was being removed from the equation.

"Listen," Mrs. K felt out the sadness that accompanied the achievement of graduating. "I know high school seems scary. But just remember this: I am always here. If there is ever anything that either one of you needs . . . I am here for you. Always. There will be plenty of change over the next four years for both of you. But I know you both have what it takes to succeed. In each of you, there is a spark that can set fire to the world around you. Right now, you may not notice it. But I do."

Tommy and I looked at her, tears welling up but being held back with great effort. The conversation almost seemed too adult for us, and looking back, I knew she was offering advice to be carried into the future when life would present its greatest chal-lenges. Ironically it was Tommy who interjected his thoughts into the conversation: "I won't miss St. Germaine, but I'll miss your class, Mrs. K. It was the only place I ever felt . . . normal."

"Don't be silly, Tommy. You are normal. As a matter of fact, you both are normal. You are your own normal, and don't let what other people do or say define who you are. Ever." It was some of the greatest advice we ever received, and to this day I carry those words with me. Anyone who tried to define me, how I should try to conform, my attitude, anything about me—I came to eye with suspicion.

Mrs. K let out a grin to take away from the gravity of her words. "Come on, we're here to celebrate."

Tommy withdrew a weathered camera from inside his suit and motioned for the three of us to come together for a picture. The doors to the cafeteria were about to be opened to family and friends, and Tommy rushed us together to get the picture taken before the ensuing crown could prevent its happening. Mrs. K stood between us, her arms draped over and around each of our shoulders, pulling us in close. Another staff member stood several paces from us, motioning us this way and that, to properly frame the photograph.

As the shutter clicked, a thick, meaty hand swiped at the camera, sending it to the tiled floor. It landed with a crack, the plastic housing splitting open and the canister of film catapulting itself back towards the man. The film came to a rest by his left foot, which crushed its plastic cylinder with no discrimination. The man grabbed Tommy, looked at me with an icy glare, and commanded, "Come on, Alton." The anger seethed in his voice. Tommy's body went limp under the pressure of his grip, while his head tried desperately to pull towards me. I saw the desperation in Tommy's eyes as if he had feared for his very life. It was a look that I had only seen before in wildlife films shot in Africa. It was the same icy, foreboding look that came from the eyes of a gazelle being drug away from its herd by a lioness, her claws buried into its shoulders as her mouth engulfed its throat in a suffocating hold that prevented the escape of any sound.

Tommy embodied this look of utter defeat as the man pulled him from the room. Tommy's eyes followed me for as long as they could until he disappeared into the crowd. It took me a few moments to gather myself, Mrs. K tightening her hold on me, as my body grew rigid with fear. I knew that face. It was the same man who blocked my father's entry into Caldwell the previous summer. It was Mike Genardo.

I looked up at Mrs. K with glassy eyes not knowing if Tommy would be all right. I had never sought solace from an adult before like I did at that moment. If it were my parents by my side, I would have shrunk away from view and hid out of sight until the danger passed. Mrs. K held onto me though, and even in the whirlwind of what had happened, I felt safe. As bad as the moment was, I didn't want that feeling to ever end. The security I felt in her arms was like none other. I questioned why it took such a violent act to make it happen but took comfort in the fact that someone was there to finally keep the world away.

The crowd resumed its activities as nothing had happened and I wondered if this was the norm. Did Tommy really matter that little to all these people? Or was this man such an enigma that people simply stayed out of his way? The crowd didn't seem to think twice about his reaction to the situation. They simply went on with the matter at hand, like this was an everyday occurrence. Maybe for most of them, it was a testament to the hardscrabble lives they knew. Most of the people in the room were cut from a blue-collar mold that they held onto more than anything else. The scene at the reception would probably repeat itself throughout the night as the celebrations moved to backyards filled with smoldering barbecue grills and coolers of beer.

"Aubrey, I got you, everything will be all right." Mrs. K turned towards me, one hand on each shoulder, her eyes gazing into mine with such sadness and sympathy that I broke down into tears. "I think Tommy will be okay, his grandfather is temperamental to say in the least." I buried my face into her blouse. Deep inside I felt fear for Tommy. "Listen to me. Everything will be okay. Tommy will get through this, you will get through this." But it wasn't good enough. I knew why Genardo acted as he did. As much as he may have hated Tommy for who he was, he hated me even more for who I was. My friendship with Tommy caused this scene, and now because of me, Tommy was probably in jeopardy.

"It's all my fault," I sobbed into Mrs. K's blouse. "I didn't realize Tommy was related to him. Now Tommy is going to get hurt because of me, because of my father." She pulled me in closer. Still, the celebrations went on around us, oblivious to our situation.

"Aubrey, you did nothing wrong. Don't blame yourself for what that man just did. You had nothing to do with his actions and whatever happens is not your fault."

Still, I couldn't help but feel responsible for having placed Tommy in this predicament. I pulled myself back from Mrs. K, and she wiped my tears with a tissue. It seemed that teachers always had tissues on hand. As I wiped my eyes, my parents began to make their way toward us. For once I was glad they were late to the party. I could not have imagined the scene that would have unfolded if Genardo and my father happened upon us at the same time.

"Good afternoon Mr. and Mrs. Worthington. Aubrey and I were just looking back on the past year. She will be missed! Honestly, she has been one of the best students I've had the pleasure of teaching. All these tears of joy, oh my! Here Aubrey, take another tissue." Mrs. K deflected from the gravity of the situation. She knew the best course would be to keep my parents unaware of the incident they barely missed, salvaging my friendship with Tommy. I would be fraternizing with the enemy in my father's eyes, and I'm certain that he would have done everything in his power to keep me and Tommy apart.

"Thank you, Mrs. Kaliczenkoff. She's never been known to be . . . let's just say she's been a challenge to teach. But Aubrey has spoken highly of you, and I must say that this has been by far her most successful year of school." My father's praise was odd, but it rang true. The past year at St. Germaine had gone by without incident, in part to Mrs. K and in part to my friendship with Tommy. If not for them, it would have been like years past, with time spent in detention and at conferences with school administrators to discuss my conflicts with teachers and students. My year at St. Germaine became the highlight of my grammar school education.

My parents motioned to leave. I looked up at Mrs. K, who gave me a hug and whispered into my ear: "Remember, anything you ever need, I am here for you." We withdrew and exchanged smiles that spoke volumes. In those smiles were sentiments and intentions too complex to be understood at the time.

The drive home was short, but the silence of the trip drew it out for what seemed to be hours. I dined with my parents in silence, and afterward we all retreated to our own spaces. There was no after-party, no continued celebration into the night. I shuffled the dinner plates into the dishwasher, sneaking a couple of cigarettes from my father's sportcoat draped over the dining room chair as I went through the motions of cleaning up after dinner. I made my way to the portico, melted into one of the old iron chairs, and gazed into the alders. This day had been difficult, and I couldn't keep from worrying about Tommy. The alders always reminded me of him.

I moved my body from the portico and strode to the river's edge to enter the alders unnoticed. Immediately I felt relief, knowing that I was out of the reach of my parents and could finally let my guard down. I took out one of the cigarettes and took in its vapors with deep, luxurious breaths. I was always amazed at how something so impure could at the same time have such a cleansing effect on my psyche. Each exhalation expelled the smoke from my lungs which chased away the stress of that day. It was at that moment that I knew I couldn't just stay there, all alone. I needed to see if Tommy was all right.

— —

As I made my way through the alders I looked for any sign of Tommy, stopping midway on my journey at our secluded hideaway. There was nothing to insinuate that he had been to the alders recently, and all alone there was an eerie silence that cut through to my core. Tommy by and part made the stand come alive for me, his energy seemed to feed the mystic aura surrounding these trees. I snatched a few pairs of catkins left hanging from one of the branches and stuffed them into my pocket, if for anything they were to have something to hold and smudge into oblivion with the nervous energy I began to feel. I made the circuitous route through the alders to the gravel road that divided the stand from the edge of town. It was an imaginary line of demarcation, a place where a young boy traveled to escape the rigors of his life. I was certain that the events earlier that day made the alders all the more welcoming to him.

I crossed the road and moved through the grove of trees that bordered Tommy's property. A flock of ravens lightened from the branches above. The rustling of their wings startled me, the branches erupting violently as they scattered. Their cackles cut through the evening air but only with shallow intrusion. The moist June air all but swallowed up and suffocated their calls. Quiet again. I made my way to the property, side-stepping through the trees with stealth, this time scanning what was ahead and above me to avoid detection.

As I moved, the decrepit structures that passed for housing came into focus through the undergrowth. My mind pulled my feet along in this journey. The trepidation was real. Tommy's grandfather was a pistol and if I were seen—I let that thought escape my mind. I had to check in on Tommy, even if it meant risking my own hide. I heard a rhythmic drumming the closer I approached. Nearing the residence, I ducked down to a near crawl and latched onto the chicken wire fence strung between the trees. My face planted itself into the weave of the fence, meshing with the ramble of vines claiming it for their own.

I fought with the vines for a seat to scan the property. As I finally made room for a clear line of sight that covered the entire backyard, my eyes witnessed a scene that shocked me to the core. I watched as a large wooden plank rose and fell with rehearsed rhythm. In anyone else's hands the plank would have appeared oversized, but in Genardo's meaty grip it found perfect accommodations. A shirtless Tommy was bent over a broken sawhorse, his neck pinned to the dirt carpet by Genardo's left hand. The plank landed on Tommy's rear with repeated precision, every so often missing its mark and scoring a hit to his lower back. Even from the distance of my vantage point, the bruising was apparent, its purple hue advertising the plank's victory.

Genardo was relentless, stopping momentarily only to take a long swig from his beer. Beside him were the remnants of his afternoon: spent beer cans littered the area surrounding his feet, and would occasionally rattle when his blows struck Tommy. With each strike, all breath was expelled from Tommy's body. He was past the point of crying, his body in shock from the beating it was withstanding. His body lay limp, and he appeared to be all but lifeless, failing to even tense before each blow struck him. The only sign of life I witnessed was his head turning ever so slightly from the bare-ground where it had been planted to anchor him into place. Between blows, Tommy managed short, pained breaths that gurgled from the froth that bled from his mouth. My eyes welled up as I watched.

It was during one of these breaths when Tommy's head turned and he somehow noticed me. I don't know how he was able to manage it, but he did, and with the last amount of strength he could muster, his mouth lipped the words *"Go away."* The tears by this point were streaming down my face and I had begun to sob through spasmodic, hyperventilated breaths that became more difficult to muffle. Tommy's glassy eyes contacted mine once more, and I grabbed onto the chicken wire fence so hard that it sliced into my palm. My eyes were locked into Tommy's. Another blow found its mark, causing Tommy's head to turn away from me, his mouth sputtering in the small mud puddle created by his expectorated saliva.

I pulled back from the fence with the slowest motion my quivering body would allow, not wanting to be noticed. I must have backed through the small stand of trees on my hands and knees, keeping a low profile and doing my best to keep an eye in the direction of Tommy's house. I was certain I wasn't seen, but every instinct in my body was on heightened alert as I found my way back to the gravel road that bordered the alders. My feet reacquainted themselves with the ground, and fueled by adrenaline, I pushed into the alders like a deer bounding away from a hunter. My legs moved on their own, taking me back to our retreat in the alders.

The entire drama of that past hour exhausted me physically and emotionally. I lowered myself down into the cavern and lit the second cigarette on impulse. An eternity had passed since I left the house. The magnitude of the situation had in effect lengthened that encounter, causing it to take up permanent residence in my mind. As the moments passed my guard came to relax. Every muscle was spoiled from the release of adrenaline moments earlier, leaving me to collapse into the hammock strung across the space as I finished my cigarette. I wept for Tommy. I wept for myself. I wept until I couldn't cry anymore until every ounce of sorrow had turned into a stolid disposition. A disposition that would drive my determination to escape this life at any cost. This was the nexus that ended the paltry youth I had known.

The tears receded in no due haste and my sobs grew shorter. My breath became my own again as I took in my surroundings. As often as I had been here, I had rarely taken an interest in the books that Tommy had acquired for this escape from reality, but at that moment, they were the only connection I had with Tommy. My weakened legs wobbled as I rose, floating towards the makeshift bookcase hewed into the rock. The whole moment was ethereal; the trees above had begun to sway in the evening breeze coming off the river; it was enchanting. I moved towards the books in the fading sliver of sunlight that managed to peek through the canopy and find its way to the floor. It kept perfect time with my steps, its line pulling me toward the books.

I ran my fingers over their spines. No certain title called to me. I only wanted to hold these books because of Tommy, because I knew how important they were to him; for years they were his only friends. These books were the distraction from the prison of his life. Never before could I have imagined why he needed this place, this retreat. Now my imagination need not apply. It was all perfectly clear, the sanctity of this place for him. No other place offered the refuge and calm of the alders.

As I drew my fingers across the titles they found a composition book that had become sandwiched between two larger volumes. Their spines had worn from age, creasing over the composition book and hiding it from view. I pulled it from the shelf and opened the cover, to be greeted by a blank page yellowed to the color of an autumn sunrise and stiffened by the elements. Twenty blank pages later I contemplated putting the book back, thinking there was nothing more to it. My thumb scanned the edge of the book and halfway through found a few scribbled lines. I stopped, not knowing if I should pry, but looked anyway. I began to read what I noticed to be Tommy's handwriting:

> *Escape to the trees*
> *Nothing is left to be*
> *Here I am, no one knows*
> *Do they care?*
> *Doesn't seem so to me.*

Immediately I felt regret for prying. I thumbed ahead quickly, and page after page followed. Tommy's experiences were captured here in this book. I wanted to read, but at the same time wanted to hear it from him. I knew enough already; could it get any worse? I shelved my curiosity along with the notebook. It was far too personal and far too emotional at that moment. To take it in would have been nothing more than gawking at an accident scene. I couldn't allow myself to do that to Tommy's feelings and his emotions. Far too many others had already done that. I refused to allow my selfish curiosity to betray him.

The daylight had all but vanished into the western sky. Darkness was calling. I closed my eyes and took in a deep breath, allowing the earthiness of the stand to overwhelm my senses. The calming effect filled me, renewing my strength for the walk to my parents' home—not my home. It could never be that. I knew I would have to leave for the night, and felt like I was abandoning Tommy as I prepared to make my way out. I found it hard to release the composition book. It was like holding Tommy, his essence emblazoned onto its pages. With reticence, I pulled away in what felt to be slow motion, my eyes trained on it, remembering how Tommy had looked into my eyes as I watched him languish at the hands of his grandfather. I released my grip on the composition book with reluctance, much like I had done to the chicken wire fence earlier, the scar it left becoming the stigmata of that evening. The fading light cast a pallor glow over the space that caught movement out of the corner of my eye. From the composition book, a small, black and white swath had found its freedom and took to the ground in an innocent spiral. The Polaroid photograph landed squarely at my feet. Ignorance would not be an option.

PART II

THE DYSTOPIAN
PLOT

CHAPTER 12

IN THE NAME OF
THE FATHER

T HE BOY HELD the scene all his own. Without knowing it,
he had a demanding stage presence that any professional
actor spent years attaining. He was a striking model with
his ivory skin gleaming under his golden crown, and the bowl-
style haircut perfectly framing his rounded cheeks yet to be chis-
eled into distinction by age. The lighting passed on an angelic
aura about him. It was soft, the light, much like his skin, and it
complemented his tone to perfection. It was pure innocence: a
cherub, framed for a moment in time, exposed to the world with
no care to what people thought of him. His appearance was still
intact, still unspoiled in some way; it hadn't been exposed to the
scrutiny of the world. His body's language was still fluid, gracing
the frame effortlessly, unwilling to succumb to the pressures of
the outside world, if not out of principle, then out of pure ignorance to the cold realities of life.

He held his head high and cocked with a slight tilt to the
right, eyes toward God. Was he watching God? Only he would
have known what his gaze was set upon at that moment. It was
a gaze that leaped off the canvas of the photograph and stared
through the viewer, into some greater unknown. One couldn't
help but notice the brightness of his eyes, accentuated by the
pleating rays of light that shone down upon him, emanating eerily enough from the rosewood-colored crucifix that hung in the
background. At that moment, he appeared to be seeking grace,
his pensive mood almost dismissing the cherubic innocence that
accompanied his figure.

The boy's right hand was neatly folded under his chin. It
wasn't holding his head up but was more contemplative, and

almost a forced gesture. His eyes avoided direct contact with the photographer. While his right arm arced away from his body and nested under his chin with a graceful arch, his left arm fell in the opposite direction, guiding the eyes downward, following the contours of his naked body. His left hand terminated at his groin and was cupping his prepubescent genitals to bring them into focus for the lens of the camera. No, it wasn't for the camera. The camera didn't do this. It was the person behind the camera.

I placed the photograph down. The boy, of course, was a much younger Tommy. I couldn't quite process what I was looking at, so I turned the picture over. The innocence still shone in his eyes, but his mood hinted that he knew something wasn't right. Still, there he was, all for the taking. I didn't want to know what happened next, I only hoped that this encounter ended with the picture. That was the only favorable outcome to this situation that I knew possible. There before me was Tommy, exposed to the world, and taken advantage of by some unknown person that he probably trusted. Tommy was the child at risk you always heard about, and never did I fathom that I would come to be acquainted with such a situation.

Tommy was sweet enough when I met him. My mind knew that a much younger Tommy, free from years of abuse, could have only been sweeter and more innocent. And an easy target. A young boy, forced out of his home when the adults were working. A young boy still innocent and trusting. A young boy looking for that warm and compassionate adult to take him in and give him the attention he wanted and deserved. The person behind the camera became that adult.

— —

Tommy vanished the summer before high school. I made my way to the alders as often as I could, leaving notes that I had been there waiting for him. Each time I returned, I was met with the loneliness of lost friendship, a friendship that I couldn't help but blame myself for destroying. A friendship that was now wrapped in the sorrow I felt for Tommy after finding the picture. The abuse I witnessed him suffer was now only an afterthought. This picture changed things: this sweet boy who sought out my friendship had won my heart months before, and I now wanted to protect him, to hold him close. But I couldn't. I was left with my last memory of him, telling me, "*Go away*," out of fear for my own safety, while he was beaten nearly lifeless. Now I was alone with this picture, his innocence snuffed out.

I had nowhere to turn. My parents were out of the question if anything they would have loved to see Tommy destroyed. I struggled all summer long with what to do. I ruled out the police, not wanting to draw unnecessary attention to Tommy. After the beating he just took, the last thing he needed was this ire and the controversy that would surround him and his family. I needed someone that could help without raising red flags, without causing a circus. Someone that would keep Tommy's interests as a forethought before reacting. I considered reaching out to Mrs. K, but she too was away. As the days wore on I struggled with the picture, and that I had done nothing about it. A summer with no distractions only put more pressure on me to do something.

I took the picture out of the alders to preserve it. I hid it away in my room to keep it safe, this evidence of a crime against a young boy that shouldn't go unpunished. My heart ached for Tommy, and it ached more because I had been so indecisive on his behalf. I sat at my desk and pulled the picture from within my St. Germaine yearbook, where I tucked it away. Holding it in my hands, I knew that I couldn't wait any longer. Maybe that was the answer to the dilemma, I thought. In the end, I settled for the one institution that was supposed to look over its flock: the church. I still knew no one in Alder Ferry, with the exception of Father Pekennick and his staff, and even then, this was little more than a casual acquaintance. It wasn't the best option, but it seemed the only option at the time. At a young age, my mind was already wary of organized religion. Still, I chose to conduct an informal visit to the rectory and challenge my instincts, hoping to prove them wrong and to see Tommy's lost innocence avenged.

I had never seen the inside of the rectory at St. Germaine. Nothing about it was inviting. If anything, the exterior of the building was as drab as the town, a monolith to the bland architecture of the nineteen-sixties that epitomized the institutions that had come to dominate American life. Schools, churches, government buildings; they all looked the same. None of them were inviting to the people they were intended to serve. These institutional monoliths were designed to push people away, to avoid becoming overextended in providing the services that they were tasked to provide.

The rectory at St. Germaine was no different. It and the school were beige brick that disappeared into the landscape, offering nothing that appealed to even the casual observer. The buildings were neutral, much like their inhabitants. Neutral to the needs of their parishioners and to the community. The only neutrality Father Pekennick and his staff didn't hold was in their allegiance to the church, and to the inner workings at St. Germaine. Those two priorities always came first. Nothing and no one ever caused a deviation from that attitude.

I made my way to the rectory on a warm, muggy August morning. The air was thick, smog blanketed the town, hazing away any object that reached into the gray morning sky. It was a morning where electricity filled the air, the moisture generating an electric charge by the friction it made against my face as I reluctantly pushed on, hoping for the best outcome possible. I stood before the white storm door, stained by time, and holding tight to its hinges but pulling away from the jamb. It clung loosely to the building like a muslin cloth. Behind it was the main door, which prevented any preview of the goings-on inside the building.

I paused on the concrete steps leading up to the door. They were rounded by the thousands of footfalls before mine, edges softened and adding a welcome feel to the entrance way. I traced the steps with my eyes to delay the inevitable. In each I caught its flaws; more precisely, its individuality. The bottom of the three steps was the most rounded and softened. It wasn't gouged or pocked in any fashion but rounded into a smooth finish that made it gleam and appear slick to the touch. The middle step was less rounded in its edges, with a few pockmarks dotting its surface. This step was a bit rougher in character, but nevertheless a bit more intact than the bottom step. The uppermost step was truest to its original form. The squared off edges were still visible, defining its angular shape. The steps reminded me of God, and of grace: the closer to God, perfection was more apparent. Obviously many didn't make it this far; the worn nature of the bottom step in relation to the upper two made it clear that very few were granted entry to the rectory.

I couldn't be concerned with these details, these distractions from the matter at hand. That is all they were: distractions. I struggled with the picture since I found it, and it became my nemesis that summer. And so, I made it here, to the entrance of the very place that I never thought I would find myself. All in the name of friendship, and of something else I had slowly come to understand: love. I loved Tommy. I cared for him deeply. No other person had ever stirred these emotions in me before. And because of that, I found myself staring up at the rectory door at St. Germaine. Since meeting Tommy, I found myself wandering outside of my comfort zone with increasing regularity. And I did it each time with less and less inhibition.

I gulped down a long swallow of the thick, muggy air and choked back any regret for being there. The beaten storm door pulled away with such ease that my grip almost pulled it along with myself over the side of the stairs. I wasn't prepared for the ease with which the storm door opened. Its presence seemed a mere formality; its function lost and its necessity in question. I wedged my body between the storm door and the more foreboding wooden door that sealed off the rectory from the outside world. The wood of the door was stained dark and it was perfumed by the incense used in the church, the lingering afterthought of countless rituals.

My fist was greeted with the door's hefty mass. The wood almost absorbed the sound of my half-hearted knock. I struck a second time, this time rapping my knuckles against its hardened exterior, rather than pounding on it with the fleshy underside of my palm. I waited; it seemed like forever passed, but I waited. I didn't dare turn my back and walk, not just from this situation, but from Tommy. I wouldn't walk like everyone else had done. I knocked a third time so they knew I wasn't leaving. I would wait them out if that was what it took.

The elderly housekeeper came to the door. Father Pekennick was far too busy running his parish to keep his own home.

"May I help you, dear?"

"Aubrey Worthington. I'm here to see Father Pekennick."

"Well, I don't think he has any visitors scheduled for today, dear."

To say that the woman was condescending was an understatement. But I knew to get in I would have to bite my tongue and play along.

"It's not a scheduled visit, ma'am. It's kind of urgent. You see—there's this boy."

The woman put her hand up to stop me from saying any more. She was probably too much of a prude to listen further anyway. As wholesome as most religious people hold themselves out to be, the first thing to always come to their mind is sex. I learned that from the very classrooms they built. From third grade on, sex was bad. That's what I was taught. All they cared about was who we slept with, and that we were married—to each other. But here, a fourteen-year-old girl mentions a boy and all bets are off with this old woman. I struck the right nerve.

"Right this way, just sit here and wait."

She looked at me with a mixture of disgust and curiosity. I took in my surroundings as I waited. The room was no different than a waiting room at a doctor's office. Except there were no windows, no magazines, no television. Only a handful of worn chairs, a smattering of pro-life pamphlets, and some forgotten Operation Rice Bowl collection envelopes. And the smell. There was the smell. The odor from the front door inhabited every breath. It was the same nauseating smell that accompanied each Christmas, Easter, funeral, and wedding mass. Incense. The rectory was stained by its odor. It had seeped into the carpets, the woodwork, and the heavy curtains that covered the windows in the narrow hall between the waiting room and the entrance. The smell was a sort of psychological warfare to weaken the senses. Meant to ward off evil spirits, it was having that effect on me.

"Father Pekennick will be with you shortly, dear."

"Thank you, ma'am." My response heavily accented the ma'am. She squinted and turned her back to me, stomping off to resume her matronly duties on behalf of the pastor.

"Aubrey?"

Father Pekennick's voice boomed and his figure filled the doorway of the waiting room. He was a tall, fit man, built to intimidate. His imposing stance brought me down from the cocky position I had taken with the housekeeper. I shuddered on the inside as a chill ran up my spine and down to my fingers. Business was now at hand.

"Yes, Father." They were the only words that I could muster.

"Come with me."

Without hesitation, I rose from my seat and followed him to his office. Inside, a door to my right led to the breezeway connecting the rectory to the church proper. This room was different from the waiting room. Floor to ceiling windows washed the room in golden sunlight. The curtains were wide open, our meeting in the office an open affair to the outside world. It was almost too bright after being in the dank waiting room that held the aura and odor of a funeral parlor.

Father Pekennick motioned me to a chair in front of his desk. I took my seat as instructed, and he took his behind the desk. My eyes were down, avoiding contact with his. I feared to look into his eyes, his presence was so overbearing that I didn't want to give him any edge in reading me or taking the conversation in a direction that would prevent me from broaching the topic of Tommy.

"How can I help you today?"

Silence.

Father Pekennick cleared his throat. "Aubrey."

With the little courage I could manage, I brought my head up and there it was. I was blindsided by what I saw. It was the antithesis of my reasoning to come here.

I locked my eyes onto Pekennick's jaw to avoid direct eye contact and remarked in a matter-of-fact tone, "Wow that is some crucifix." It was some crucifix. A dark, rosewood-colored crucifix exactly styled like the one that watched over Tommy in the picture.

"I had it commissioned for the parish by an artist from seminary. You won't find one anywhere else. I'm glad you appreciate it," Father Pekennick's comment cemented what I had feared as my eyes locked onto the crucifix.

"Now how is it today that I can help you?"

"I'm sorry to have bothered you, Father. I don't think I'm ready to talk about it just yet, and I hope you can forgive me." All I wanted was out of there—it was a crime scene. I wanted to escape as fast as I could. I only hoped that the rush of nervous energy I began to display was mistaken for just another awkward teenage moment.

"Well, whenever you're ready, the door is open." I was sure it would be. Or maybe I was too old for him. He stuck his hand out, and I slid my clammy palm into his, sickened to be making any contact at all with him. Him—the man that took advantage of Tommy.

"Here, let me show you out."

"I can manage, Father, thank you." I withdrew from him without reservation. He had a look of slight astonishment and I caught him shaking his head lightly from side to side as I made my way out. I pulled the door shut and clicked the storm door into place with a tender touch to avoid commotion. There was enough commotion competing for my attention inside me at that time. I made my escape a haphazard affair, alternating between running and walking, my clothes saturated by the humid morning air. My breaths were shallow and rampant. Like my thoughts, I couldn't control them.

Nothing was sacred, and nothing was holy. Everything was a mirage. There was no one to help. No one to understand, and no one who wanted to understand. Maybe Mrs. K, but I couldn't wait for her. But I also couldn't tackle Father Pekennick on my own. Tommy was taken advantage of and abused by every authority figure he had known. Innocent, sweet Tommy. He never hurt anyone. I didn't even know if he had it in him to hurt anyone. There was just nothing left to do except tear it all down—tear down every structure that had run roughshod over this little boy's fragile existence.

CHAPTER 13

TRUTH AND
CONSEQUENCE

I COULDN'T WAIT FOR school to start. I needed the distraction from this life that, without any warning, had finally happened. It happened without me asking for it to happen, and it was remorseless. I found myself morose, feeling sorry for myself, for the situation that was delivered to me. My existence was in a world all alone. All alone, that was, until I met Tommy.

Which is when I realized that it could be worse. I was a victim of both cold circumstance and religion; that was all. My body had not been violated. My innocence was still mine for the losing. My psyche had not been penetrated by pervasive outside forces looking to exploit my body and soul. I was no victim. Tommy, he was a victim. Tommy reminded me that, no matter how trying my life could be, that it could always be worse.

I spent the remainder of that summer preparing for the inevitable: high school, and becoming an even smaller fish in a pond far larger than I had ever known. I passed the waning summer days sitting on the portico, gazing into the alders, wondering just where everything was going. It was a lonely existence, like the years before, but now it was plain lonesome. I had finally come to know friendship. And having lost it, as I perceived the situation to be, I finally knew loneliness; real, sad loneliness. Before Tommy, I was simply alone. Without Tommy, our escapes from the world, and our conversations in the alders, I was truly lonely. Alone I could accept; lonely was a painful state of mind against which I struggled in desperation to find the means to cope.

There were few breaks to the monotony of that summer's waning days. I became more open to doing anything that would break up those long days, anything to take my mind off the events of the previous three months, anything to make me forget all I had seen. My eyes aged far in advance of their natural years that summer. Time was the enemy, and in my loneliness, its numbers overwhelmed me.

Maybe that was why I went: boredom and withdrawal from life. The portico was a lonely place. The alders called me constantly, but I stopped going. Without Tommy, being there reminded me of sleeping in an empty house. There was no sound, and little if any movement. Every sound I made was swallowed whole by the emptiness of the alders. It had at one time felt like a home of sorts, a home founded on our friendship. It was always reassuring and safe in there if anything for the memories of the place that were created with Tommy. Without us though it was empty. It was still there but somehow failed to fill the void within me. It was a reminder of the few beautiful memories I had of Tommy; a painful reminder as I allowed summer to slip away.

And so I agreed to go, to Caldwell, and visit my father's office for the mundane task of making photocopies of school transcripts. I had never been to Caldwell before that day, as it offered nothing of interest to me. It was a gray building almost relinquished back into the landscape, kept alive only to fuel a sputtering local economy. Its exterior was nondescript, the rows of windows along the production area blackened by years of metal dust and oil spray that also served to lubricate the lungs of its denizens. I still remember my father coming home in the evenings from Caldwell after our first week in Alder Ferry. From his nose spewed a gray sludge, unseen particles of the industrial process captured by his nasal cavity, the remnants of the metal parts ground into a usable form for industry that invaded every square inch of living and inanimate space they encountered.

I wanted no part of that. The dirt, the grime, and the persistent cough that workers there developed. It was a reminder of the need to escape Alder Ferry altogether. Working there was a sure method to eliminate years from one's life. I would not partake in the ritual circle of life here, neither as an employee nor as a survivor of some future loved one left to succumb to Caldwell's disease. On no level at all would I become a part of that cycle.

But I went that day out of boredom and curiosity. Maybe I would see what drove my father to seek out these places. Maybe I would see what drove men like Mike Genardo to wade through life knee deep in misery, drowning anyone that fell into their wake. As much as I said I would try, I knew I couldn't approach Caldwell with an open mind. It was the reason I had arrived in Alder Ferry, and to an extent, it brought me to Tommy. For that role played by Caldwell, I was more than grateful. But the gratitude ended there.

I knew going to Caldwell could be dangerous. Genardo was there. If he had approached my father about me and Tommy, I'm sure I would have been held accountable to that fact at home. But I hadn't been. Still, Genardo was a wild card that couldn't be read. In the back of my mind, I always thought that he was waiting, for the right moment, to reveal the unlikely friendship between Tommy and me. We were two kids that should have been enemies from the start but were wise enough to see beyond the black and white existence everyone else had come accustomed to living. If Genardo saw me there at the plant, I was certain he would cause some level of disruption, anything to take a stab at my father, at me, and at Tommy. Anything to destroy the nemesis that was my father, and to destroy any chance of Tommy ever searching me out again.

I was filled with apprehension as my mother directed our car towards the plant. The lot was a pale reminder of what a parking lot should be, its asphalt burrowing back into the earth, crumbled into pea-sized bits of gravel that still oozed oil that slicked over the puddles after each rainfall. The lot appeared glaciated, scoured through the years by the abuse it suffered at the hands of the elements. All that remained was an outline of the lot that once consumed this space, a shell of what it had once been. Its worn surface was indecipherable to the eye; numerous springs constantly kept the potholes filled to the brim with water that bore the oily sheen of the asphalt, its membranous glue released back to the elements. We slalomed through the lot, circumventing the craters, avoiding the chasms that could certainly swallow the front end of our vehicle.

The car creaked to a halt by my father's sedan. The workers' vehicles were relegated to the rear, their aged and decrepit cocoons of Detroit's past kept from the sight of visitors. I was thankful for this bit of segregation, not wanting to make contact with Genardo or any of the other employees that may have borne his same demeanor. I sat still, at that moment feeling a twinge of regret for making the journey; a twinge that was also spiced with excitement, complementary to the fear I had felt.

"Let's go, Aubrey," was my welcome to Caldwell as my mother pulled my door open, allowing my slumped figure nearly to spill out onto the pavement. I found my feet and followed along, stopping at the front entrance. It was a glass vestibule, flanked by arborvitae dwarfed by the lack of sunshine and the inhospitable soil where they made their home. The glass was hazed from years of exposure to the elements; no amount of scrubbing could ever restore even a vague amount if lucidity to it. Above the entrance, in stainless steel block letters, was the title "CALDWELL TOOL AND DIE CO." The letters were the only semblance of character to a building that otherwise had no personality.

I fell in line behind my mother as we passed through the vestibule, which opened into a small waiting room. To the left, the wall was adorned with the various awards and industrial certifications bestowed upon Caldwell throughout the years. To the right were employee photographs, most notably the annual group pictures of the entire workforce dating from the plant's inception. On this wall were the lives that provided the human lubrication to the gears that kept the plant in operation. It was these lives that somehow made the plant immortal, their blood and sweat fueling its production lines, and giving credence to its presence. Like a parasite, the plant lived off the men who were now only memories, allotted only a small space on a faded, whitewashed wall. This wall was their memorial, their final resting place. Atop the wall was a picture of my father, watchful eyes gazing down on his charges. Below his picture was the inscription, "S. Worthington – President."

It must have been a cruel blow for an outsider to come in and assume total control of what amounted to be Alder Ferry's economy, outside of the boom in retail outlets reshaping the suburban landscape of the town at an apocalyptic pace. Caldwell was all that remained of industry in Alder Ferry. It was the only place where tangible things were produced. Now an outsider had come to roost over Caldwell.

Straight ahead was the receptionist desk. Commanding the desk was a tall, lean, green-eyed blonde whose purpose was to capture the attention of visitors. She was probably twenty long years younger than my mother. She greeted her with a bubbly, "Welcome, Mrs. Worthington." I could feel the hatred for her seethe from my mother. It was envy and fear, all wrapped into a neat and solitary package. I saw what I gathered to be the reason for my father's late nights and early arrivals at the plant since this is what would be greeting him. But he couldn't be totally to blame. Their relationship had been so icy and devoid of love, that any outside attention would have attracted him. But this, this specimen, this Athena-like figure of a woman, was too much. Far too much for my mother's fragile ego.

I gawked at the receptionist and caught my mother looking at me. It was an awkward moment frozen in time. My mother coldly cut through the moment, grabbing my hand and tearing me away from the scene.

"Good morning, Denise. We'll show ourselves in. Aubrey, now."

My mother's eyes left me and found their mark on Denise. Like tendrils, they grabbed her and dropped her immediately back into her seat behind the reception desk, her near perfect figure now slouched out of view. Denise's warm smile was erased from her face by the gaze my mother shot at her, setting her in her place, filling her with the fear of what would happen, if – the unspoken "if" that was hanging over the two like an ominous storm cloud set to release its fury. It was a wordless, gestured warning, communicated by body language only spoken and understood by women. My mother had projected her will across the room towards her younger rival. Denise had been duly warned. It was a poor lesson in femininity from my mother, one that I refused to carry on into my own adulthood.

She didn't knock when we approached the door to my father's office, graced with his title, President Worthington. I remember thinking I would rather die than address him by this title. His office made his position known, its spaciousness and finely appointed furniture fitting for any executive. His workers on the floor below would have been fortunate if their living rooms came close to the size of his office. It was a stark contrast to the two worlds that stood juxtaposed to one another at Caldwell: that of an auspicious executive peering down on the struggling working class, a body of men that fueled the fortuitous lifestyle we knew.

My father appointed his office with fine modern furnishings and finished the space with details that set it apart from the rest of the building. Inside, it was a fresh, modern, and finely detailed space, disregarding the filth of the remainder of the building. It contrasted with the aged workspaces and break rooms allotted to the employees. The employees were rarely even allowed inside; he saw to it that they did not soil his office with their presence and the filth of industry that followed them, although they were the same soils that lined his pockets.

Floor to ceiling windows formed my father's aperture to the plant floor below. Tall drapes framed the glass, drawing the eye up towards the crown molding he had installed to add to the room's grandiosity. I looked around the room and at its appointments. I couldn't help but smirk, likening my father to be referred to as "El Presidente," his perch above the workers below was more a mark of dictatorial power than corporate authority. I almost let the title flow from my mouth, but stopped myself short. I didn't have it in me that day. That summer had all but sapped the will to fight out of me.

"Good morning, ladies," was my father's greeting to us upon our entrance. His eyes remained fixed on the documents before him, our presence but a minor distraction. "Let me know if you need help with the copier, Denise can . . ."

"I'll get by," interjected my mother, cutting him short. My father's eyes rocketed upward from the documents on his desk that only a moment earlier held him captive. With a wave of his left hand, he motioned my mother towards the copier. His right hand fiercely gripped his fountain pen, mimicking his hold on the bayoneted rifle in his picture from Vietnam that was prominently displayed in the shadow box hallowing his awards and commendations. My mother made her way to the copier, her eyes talking him down without him even knowing it, relaxing his guard. He was a matter-of-fact man, and could not bear the insinuation in her voice that there was any attraction between him and Denise.

I maintained my neutrality during this exchange and made my way to the windows to survey the action below as the throng of workers moved among their machines in what appeared to be a choreographed procession of the functions being performed. I moved the curtain nearest the end of the wall aside for a better view, while propping my body up against the wall to hide the silhouette of my figure from the men below. I was shocked how close they were, for it was a totally different world from the office that sheltered me from the harsh reality of their hassled work day. I could see their faces, watch them strain as they toiled, read the profanities escaping their lips out of frustration and anger.

I almost felt too close to the plant floor. Looking down, I couldn't help but imagine myself up on a pedestal, overseeing each and every action below me, scrutinizing the men as they processed through the motions of their tasks. Beneath me; they were beneath me and on many levels. My vantage point was the seat of power, the very locale from where the destiny of each worker would be determined. Who would stay; who would go. The decisions from this room were far-reaching, extending well outside of Caldwell, influencing which mortgages would be paid and which cars would be repossessed. All those details were determined from this seat of power.

By relation, I was part of that mechanism, like it or not. I would never be welcome here because of my father. It didn't matter that I despised the man as much as the men below. There could be no Shakespearean plot, no romantic interlude; nothing could ever bring our two worlds together or into focus. I would be forever opposed to Alder Ferry by birth, not by my sympathies. My sympathies could never be appreciated by the men below me. If they would only open up to know how I truly felt, then perhaps I could find a way to fit in. However, this was not meant to be.

I continued to watch with amazement at the processes unfolding below. The plant floor was filled with danger, given the amount of movement and the machinery being used. One lapse of judgment was all that stood between the men and escaping the workday unscathed. I went unnoticed to the men; any distraction could be deadly, and in the least, would earn a reprisal from their foreman.

One person did stand out from the crowd. I watched as an ashen work glove made its way to the sky with ambiguity, attempting to make its presence known in discrete movements. Beneath it a blonde head bobbed, swaying to the rhythm of the broom he leaned into as it glided across the concrete floor. Behind the broom was the boy I had been so desperately missing all summer. There was Tommy, moving about to keep the workspaces clear of debris. He was a boy, moving among men, his grandfather in all irony shielding him from the men on the floor. It was a grim reminder of what life had to offer Tommy if he failed to escape this town.

I pressed my face into the glass, my palms pushing on it, trying in vain to break through. Tommy tried to pass between the machines so that I could see him, glancing up on occasion and casting his wry smile towards me. My heart melted knowing he was safe. He was still here, only hidden away at Caldwell to keep him away from trouble. Me—I was trouble. Genardo wanted nothing of our friendship, the near-death experience he bestowed upon Tommy was proof of that. Short of locking him in their home, this was the best place for Tommy, where Genardo could watch over him, and see to it that we were kept as far apart as possible.

A smile splashed across my face for the first time that summer. I was now in a world all my own, watching the only true friend I had ever known coast about the floor below me. I was oblivious to the moaning of my mother at the copier, and to my father who was hunched over his desk, eyes straining to read the documents prepared for his review. Nothing else mattered at that moment except that boy on the production floor. My form filled the window in my delight, and my eyes darted back and forth like minnows as they followed Tommy's every move across the floor. Tommy looked up, and for the first time in months, our eyes met. This time it was out of relief and happiness that they locked onto each other. It was a reunion, and I almost felt alone with him at that moment.

Until life on the floor came to an abrupt halt and jeers broke out, breaking the monotony of the workflow. Over the crowd one voice boomed, "Hey Alton," in a teasing, whining tone, "Hey Alton, there's your girlfriend!" The girl was drawn out nice and long to make sure Tommy could enjoy every bit of embarrassment being created. Tommy became bright red, the color of a fully-ripened watermelon's flesh. The jeers came to a halt, silenced out of respect it seemed, as the form of a large man stepped out from behind one of the machines. Genardo took notice. He cast an angry glare at my figure in the window. I was made infinitely small by the look he gave me, the same look I avoided when I spied him inflicting his brand of brutality on Tommy. His stare was cold and caused a chill to ice my core. He stepped up behind Tommy, hovering over him. Tommy dropped his head low and leaned into his broom for support. He had now come front and center, and there was nowhere for him to hide, no protection from the dozens of eyes that watched him out of morbid curiosity, wondering just what action Genardo would take.

Genardo swiped the broom from Tommy's hands. Its handle appeared to be nothing more than a matchstick inside of his fist. Without any trouble, he snapped the handle in two and threw it to the floor. The hollow sound of the wood crashing to the concrete echoed throughout the silent building, tolling the impending doom Tommy and I were sentenced to face. Genardo grabbed Tommy's collar and growled, a growl that was audible even through the thick glass that was the only barrier between us. He murmured something to Tommy as he lifted him from the floor. His thick, calloused lips prevented me from deciphering what message was delivered, but I knew it was vulgar and violent by the creases in his forehead that began to swell as he looked back and forth between me and Tommy. Tommy's legs dangled, with no traction to gain for even a feigned attempt at escape. Genardo turned Tommy towards me, looked up, and grinned through his stained, broken teeth.

Caught in the moment I hadn't noticed that my father had been standing over me like Genardo was to Tommy to view the drama unfolding below. The silenced machines must have awoken him from the trance cast over him by the documents which moments sooner absorbed his entire being. I gulped as I peered backward at him, also keeping an eye on Genardo. I feared what was next; whatever was bound to happen would not be good, and would undoubtedly change the course of my future. My father slipped ahead of me and to my left with a great sidestep, and drew the curtains fully open and gazed in wild wonder at the spectacle below. My mother was by his left side and slightly behind him, also amazed and perplexed by what was transpiring. I shied away from the glass, trying my best to melt away from the reality of it all.

Then there was abject silence. Not a sound was made in a moment that seemed to have no beginning and no end. It was now a contest between Genardo and my father, the two staring at each other with intense hatred, waiting for the other to blink. Neither gave up any ground nor motioned at all, and the no man's land that was buffered by the wall of glass remained empty, with the exception of the broken broomstick, the first casualty of this encounter. There was real fear in the air which was now charged between them, the current insulated only by the glass curtain. Every man on that floor had come up behind Genardo, ready to back him, their eyes set upon him and waiting for the order to advance. Genardo sensed the stage he had and took full advantage of it.

Genardo stepped forward, glancing back with an evil grin to his co-workers and waving them off. He dropped Tommy into a crumpled heap at his feet. My legs were turning to jelly. Still, I stayed, waiting to see what was next. My breakfast had begun to work its way back up from my stomach, coagulating into small, white, acidic curds that lodged themselves into every crevasse offered by my teeth. The taste lingered there, like a festering wound.

Luckily, it was the only physical reminder of this encounter I would be left with.

"Worthington," Genardo hollered out to my father. He shot a snarky grin back towards the other workers, enjoying his moment. My father fumbled through his pockets, looking for something to do with his hands other than breaking out the glass window that separated the two men.

"Keep that daughter of yours away from my grandson, you hear?" Genardo nudged Tommy's gut with his foot and let out a cocky laugh from his aged mouth as he tipped his head up and away from us, trying to call us out. He turned away from the window, while Tommy remained motionless, frozen from fear. Without hesitation, life on the floor returned to normal at Genardo's cue. Tommy pulled himself to his feet after his grandfather returned to his workstation and picked up the remnants of his broom. He looked up at us; we could only watch as he stood there alone, not knowing where to turn. Above him was the man who had no interest in him whatsoever. Behind him were his grandfather and the other workers, a daunting gauntlet for the young boy to run through if he wanted to leave. I watched as Tommy crept back to the loading dock and hopped down, disappearing from my sight, again.

My father turned to me with rage burning in his eyes. His own blood had betrayed him; I knew that is what he thought. On top of that, he had just been humiliated by Genardo in front of the entire plant. It was my fault alone for the scene that just played itself out.

"That?" My mother ended the silence and grabbed my collar with both hands. Her stare burned through my eyes. "That is what you spend your time with? Pathetic." She ended on a note of disgust and pushed me away and into my father. Her eyes stared me down, backing me into the corner of my father's chest. I pulled myself away and retreated to the reception area as their incendiary gazes escorted me from the office.

I knew that I would pay for this debacle, even though in reality I had done nothing wrong. The only wrong that day was the blow to my father's ego. The pain that Tommy and I endured during that tenuous moment mattered to nobody. There was nothing else to be, in the awkward silence, the three of us staring at each other. Everything had already been said. Consequences were all that remained.

CHAPTER 14

INTO THE GREAT UNKNOWN

TWO EVENINGS LATER it was raining steadily by the time
I managed to fall asleep. The rain kept perfect time, its syncopation lulling me off to sleep. Its drops pattered against
the window panes and the roof of the house, drumming a cadence
ushering me into the realm of dreams. There are few sounds in
the world as comforting as the rain. It has always been my lullaby.

I was woken in the middle of the night by a change in tone.
A new rhythm had begun to accompany the rain's song. Half
asleep, my ears followed along, tracing the source of the sound
to my window. I stared in the dark, allowing time for my eyes to
widen and adjust to the low light. I noticed the rain slowed to a
pace that made it nearly inaudible. But there, at the glass, the
rapping continued.

Tap, tap, tap. It was solid, the tapping sound. In the pale light
cast by my clock radio, I caught a glimpse of something rebound-
ing off the glass. Then again, and again. I finally made out what
was causing the noise: pebbles. One after another, in rapid-fire
fashion, they made their way to my window, begging my attention, succeeding in their plight to be noticed.

I peered through the window with caution. It was an eerie
occurrence. The rain and movement of the trees outside added
to the mysterious happenings just on the other side of the glass.
Down below, partially hidden by the forgotten and overgrown rose
garden, was Tommy. I should have known it was him; no one else
would dare an entrance under such odd circumstances. I waved,
gesturing him to wait as I attempted to open the aged wood sash,
now swollen shut by the humid air. With every effort to move it I
was greeted with a hollow bugling made by the sash as it pushed

against the wood frame. The frame was obnoxious in its resistance, trying with all its might to hold back the sash and prevent it from allowing any exchange between me and Tommy to occur.

"Hey!" I uttered in a hushed but commanding tone through the window which surrendered to open itself halfway. Pebbles being thrown at my window? If anything, I expected something a bit more original from Tommy. Already, my expectations were beginning to exceed reality when it came to the opposite sex.

"Are you crazy?"

"Maybe, but lonely, too," was Tommy's response.

"Yeah, me too," I replied.

Just like him, I had been lonely that summer, for sure. The only difference was that I didn't have to face alone the fearsome troubles he was made to endure.

"Meet me in the alders tomorrow. Three o'clock, straight after my shift at Caldwell." Tommy's words were brief, and foreboding in tone.

"I'll be there. Now get, before we get into it any deeper."

"Just be there. It's important we talk." Tommy's parting words were worrisome. I feared that life had been too much for him by now—so much from his family and co-workers that, perhaps, all was through for our short-lived friendship.

It was always hard to dismiss Tommy. He was so genuine, so kind, that I felt bad whenever I had to send him off. Especially under these circumstances, where we had been separated for close to three months. I smiled down to him, shooing him away with both hands, catching his smile in return, a smile that eased any anxiety tomorrow would bring. I waited until he vanished into the alders, and watched as he melted into their solitude. He had a way of making an exit that made his presence seem non-existent. He was a ghost, almost forgotten to the outside world. Except by me, which made our friendship all the more special, knowing that it would always be just the two of us: the only two in the world that held the key to understanding one another. That was our bond. With a heavy heart, I closed the window, shutting out the humid air that birthed the memory of that evening's encounter.

Sleep escaped into what remained of the night. By the time morning had broken I was exhausted. Yet I was also filled with the anticipation of knowing that I would finally be able to spend time with Tommy later that day. Time to catch up on the events of that summer, time to maybe heal the wound that our separation caused.

Suddenly the alders spoke to me again. They were once again relevant to my life, and to our relationship. They weren't the empty house to which I would return with a hollowness in my heart. Their sanctity remained, and we would be sheltered there again later that afternoon. There we would be free from scrutiny, free to talk and laugh as we pleased, with no fear of retribution. We could be ourselves.

— —

Tommy made it there first and was reclined upon the rock that formed the roof of the hidden enclosure. The few rays of sunlight that made their way through the canopy caught his blonde hair, giving it an effervescence among the grays and greens that were the summer canvas of the alders. He jumped down and ran to me, both of us holding our arms wide open and falling into a tight hug that had no beginning or end. Tears of joy were liberated, my eyes finally seeing this boy that had been hurt so much and defined by the brutality of his life experience. I had never hugged anyone else like this before. As a small child, I never experienced this longing to be with another, and to feel the need to be close to them for the sheer comfort of it. Tommy was fast becoming more than a friend. We both experienced from each other what had always been missing from our lives: honest affection.

I held onto Tommy's hands as I lowered myself down into the chamber. I was amazed how his hands had changed in appearance and texture. They were rough and calloused, transformed into the hands of a working man. In the space of one summer, his tender skin had been pulverized into a leathery hide that lost the ability to feel anything that touched its surface. I was saddened by this; another piece of him had been taken away too soon, and without any protest.

We sat face to face, his hands in mine. I felt their toughened exterior which offered a sharp contrast to his boyish face that had yet to begin the transformation into manhood. As I traced the scars and callouses, I couldn't help but feel overwhelmed. I came to the edge of a near total breakdown, feeling I had failed him.

"Tommy, I am so sorry," tears streamed down my face. "I am so sorry . . ."

"You have nothing to be sorry about. All he needed was an excuse. If it wasn't the graduation it would've been something else. It wasn't the first time, you know . . ." Tommy's voice trailed off with that last sentence, and he gazed skyward while searching inside himself at the same time.

I did know. I knew too much. I knew that this boy had taken beatings like that for as long as he could remember. Better yet, he had taken beatings for as long as his mind wouldn't allow him to forget. These were his memories, the mile markers of his childhood. No trip to a magical kingdom, no family vacations, no photo albums filled with smiling faces. This was his reality. Only in here, protected by these trees, did he ever manage to escape.

"But it was all my fault . . ."

Tommy wiped my tears away with his right hand and put my head on his shoulder.

"Bree it was my fault for not telling you he was my grandfather. I knew better, I knew how he would react. But I didn't care."

Like anyone that had been abused into submission, Tommy took full blame for the events of that summer. He placed the weight of the situation upon himself, another burden he was willing to carry. This is what he had become through the fault of his family. He was the reason for his mother's depressing self-pity, a party girl turned junkie, her social life terminated by his pregnancy. He was the one that sapped his grandparents' resources dry, forcing them to clothe, educate, and feed him in his mother's absence. It was all his fault. He deserved every bit of agony he had been dealt. I refused to allow him to take full responsibility for my actions and to allow me to do him like everyone else before me. I was certain he didn't even know he was doing it. Still, it wasn't right, and that emotional tailspin needed to stop.

I knew the feeling all too well. My mother's social standing was exuded through her pregnancy. What it once was had become me, born into the world unwelcomed. My father may have gained a career, but he was nevertheless shackled into a marriage in exchange. Divorce was out of the question for him. His father-in-law made it clear that divorce from his daughter would equate to a divorcing of his career. But unlike Tommy, I wasn't physically abused and neglected. I was merely set aside to cause the least amount of disturbance to the coerced state of their marriage.

Tommy looked back at me. He would engage me with the strongest, kindest words to lay their kiss upon my ears.

"Bree, I'll never tell anyone I'm sorry for being your friend. Never."

I was moved. Only true friendship could stand the divide that others put up. Only a true friend would rather suffer than lose the one relationship that mattered most. Ours was that strong, and that special. We had sensed it, but it had never been tested as it had been over the course of that summer. I knew it wouldn't be easy maintaining this friendship in a place where everything and everyone always seemed aligned against us. All this made the significance of leaving Alder Ferry a determined truth of our existence.

And then he dropped the bomb I didn't but should have, see coming.

"But, there's one thing. I'm moving, well, kind of."

"Kind of moving?" I knew there would be some kind of catch. In my growing cynicism, I always waited for the catch. I never accepted anything, no matter how significant, without expecting another shoe to fall.

"I'll still be here on weekends. During the week, I'm gonna be living with my aunt in the city, to go to school."

This was Genardo's way of not only keeping us apart but also perpetuating the misery he could bring to Tommy. He was being sent into a neighborhood that several decades ago sent most of its inhabitants fleeing to the outer ring of poor suburbs, like Alder Ferry. He would be out of his environment; not in that poverty was shameful, but simply for the fact that he had been a product of our sheltered suburban America. He lacked any instincts to survive four years at an inner city high school.

"We'll get to hang out here on the weekends still, right?" Faith in this statement was lacking in my voice, fearing that the distance and time apart would eventually prove too much. We would also be inhabiting different worlds, moving among different circles, our lives drifting further apart instead of closer together.

"I'll be here every weekend, working at Caldwell. Another gift courtesy of the magnanimous Michael Genardo," Tommy spoke with a matter-of-fact tone, very embittered with his situation. I had my fears of not being able to see him on the weekends he returned, with the dread of working at the plant sapping what life remained from him after surviving a week alone at a new school and neighborhood. I was relieved in part that he had Caldwell, a reason to return to Alder Ferry.

"Promise me, Tommy . . . promise me that we won't let this come between us."

"I promise, Bree. This place is home, here—the alders—you and me. It's my escape from out there." He craned his head over his shoulder, motioning to the universe that seemed light years away, but was just beyond the confines of the alder stand, waiting in perfect patience for us to stumble. The alders had become my only escape from the outside world as well. I could always slip away from the house unnoticed and steal away a few hours there to myself.

"Then it's a deal," I stuck my hand out to Tommy. He took it in his and gave it a firm shake, consummating our agreement, working around the schedule imposed on us. We both laughed with a bit of practical caution. In the end, it was a compromise that represented our true goal: preserving our friendship and securing our freedom from the rest of the world that we enjoyed in the alders.

We both felt the unease that the impending school year would bring. And now, instead of having a familiar face to see each of us through this transition, we were to go it alone. The awkwardness of the teenage years, magnified by our peculiar personalities, would cast a huge chasm between us and our peers. Even in an environment as large as high school, I couldn't help but acknowledge the fact that we would still stick out in glaring fashion.

"Good luck with the move," my dry sarcasm gained me a wincing smile from Tommy.

"I'll need it," was his response, as I sensed fear and sadness in his voice. As trying as life in this town was for him, he never knew anything else. At an incredible juncture in his formative years, he was now being thrown to a social mix that he was ill-equipped to confront. He was the despised outsider making a backward move to the city. His awkwardness may have preceded him, but it was his suburban roots that would make him a desirable target among his new peerage.

"Remember our signal," Tommy held out a pair of catkins. Like the catkins, our friendship was organic and alien to Alder Ferry. They had come to represent the perfect symbolic embodiment of our friendship.

"Always will," I plucked the pair of catkins from Tommy's hand and buried them deep in my pocket.

"I gotta go before they start wondering where I've been," Tommy stood, obvious that he was not wanting to leave, but knowing he had no choice. A late arrival home would only give his grandfather another reason, another opportunity, to beat him into submission.

I spoke up, "I won't be far behind you. Tommy . . ."

I couldn't bring myself to say good-bye. Neither could he. Instead, we held each other one last time. Tommy melted from my arms and vanished into the alders. He was their pixie; this place having given birth to his being and his essence. As he evaporated from sight I couldn't help but ignore how long it could be until we would see each other again.

I found myself alone again in the cavern that had come to be our shelter, a rest stop on our journey through life. Time always seemed to stand still in the alders, allowing us to catch our breath. I pulled out a cigarette and pulled on it long as the match touched off its cherry, flaring its flame brightly in the lackluster evening light. It did soften the edge of that moment, a distraction of what had just transpired and the reality of it all. At the same time, I caught my fingers tracing the spines of the books that lined the makeshift shelf. Time and weather had aged each volume to distinction.

I was distracted for a moment by the beer cans tucked away behind the ladder. I eyed them, then shunned them from holding any significance. Tommy had brought back wine from the church many times before, which we drank down in mischievous delight. If anything, the beer cans were an upgrade over the flash-fermented and sugar-laden wine used by the church. The thought of him sitting here alone and drinking never occurred to me. I was more troubled by the fact that there were none left for me. A beer would have been the perfect chaser to that evening.

All the while my fingers drew a lazy trace along the row of books. Like a fingerprint, each volume was distinct to the touch. Some had been worn far less than the others while some had barely any spine remaining. There were those that remained steady and true to their original form, impervious to time and the elements. In a way, they were like people, each with its own story to tell, if someone would let it be told. Their place on this shelf in part invoked the magnitude of their existence to their owner, a young boy who turned to them for companionship and escape. To me, this was their story, their singular reason for gracing the shelf.

My fingers continued along the row of books, gently appreciating the imperfections that made each unique. I didn't hover; my fingers skirted across each of them, my time equally devoted to each as I had no favorites. None of them grabbed hold of my fingers as they draped across them, not until I reached the composition book. There my fingers stalled. The aura of the composition book held them in place. Its black comb was rigid and steadfast. The rough-hewn edges were innocuous on their own, but every single sheet held the edge of a razor. These attributes spoke to my fingers, tempting them to turn its pages while being warned to enter at their own risk. I retracted, not wanting to violate this space, but only wanting to peek inside and hear Tommy through the words he scrawled across its pages.

My fingers withdrew, remembering the last time they violated the sanctity of this personal totem. This book, more than anything else, ruined that summer. But in some ways, it did open me up to appreciating what scraps of good had entered my life, no matter how minimal they seemed at times. The composition book filled me with sorrow. Inside were brilliant examples of Tommy's potential. In contrast, however, these examples of his potential also chronicled the harrowing moments of his childhood. Moments that made the rest of his life seem mundane, uneventful, and even acceptable.

And then there were the memories that paled all others. Like those witnessed by the rosewood colored crucifix in the Polaroid. The very Polaroid that I failed to act upon. It would become the catalyst bringing definition to both our futures.

CHAPTER 15

RHYTHM

I N THE BEGINNING, we made good on our promise to meet as often as our conflicting school schedules allowed. Tommy continued to come home for the weekends to work at Caldwell; I would anxiously await the end of his shift to be brought up to speed on all that had been happening in his world and his foray into high school.

Those meetings were special. We were never certain when, or even if, they would occur. When they did it was like a holiday. When they didn't it was pure disappointment. It was like watching a heavy snowfall, dreaming of a day away from school, only to have those dreams funneled away by the passing snow plow. The gratitude for our meetings was always apparent in the flurried exchange of ideas, recounting the new experiences we encountered as we moved headstrong into the final phase of our primary education.

I must have outgrown religion by the time I entered high school. For the first time, my parents enrolled me in the public-school system. I didn't mind, and I welcomed the gesture. I was through with the parochial school system, sickened by it for obvious reasons.

From the outside, the Alder Ferry public high school was just another non-descript building thrown at the landscape. It landed where space allowed, where it would fit, the needs of its inhabitants secondary to its purpose. With its chain link fencing, beige block construction, and lack of windows, it bore more of a semblance to a minimum-security prison than a school. It was beyond my comprehension how anyone could foresee that this blasé structure could foster the minds of the youth entrusted to its care.

As drab as the Alder Ferry high school was, Tommy still wasn't quite as fortunate as me. His indoctrination into the Catholic faith would be drawn out another four years at Monsignor Devon High School. There was one positive for Tommy there: it was safer than the public high schools of his Monday through Friday neighborhood. It was a minor relief that he could attend Monsignor Devon, a small favor paid to him by his grandparents. This suburban child, who sought refuge at the last natural place in his hometown, needed every bit of reinforcement to aid his survival in the transition to urban life.

While life had done its part aging us to this point, high school seemed to mature us further. We seemed older now than we were just weeks before. We were becoming more experienced, even worldly in our views. It was a description that never applied to us before, two kids stifled by their tiresome suburban reality. But we were different. We desperately wanted more than what was offered to us. Our conversations developed a cosmopolitan flair. For his age, Tommy was very well read, having grabbed whatever book, newspaper, or magazine within his grasp from a very young age. I wasn't far behind, having followed his lead. I learned from Tommy that in literature I could not just escape life, but sometimes could find the answers to the problems that dogged me.

It was the third Friday in September. I remember the warmth of the early fall sun, the dryness of the air, and the breeze sweeping off the river. It was, like any Friday had been, routine: return from school, complete what assignments were due the following week, and ponder how to pass away another weekend alone.

The Grand Old Lady was empty, as was usual. I don't know why, but I never entered through the front door; it was always through the kitchen door that emptied onto the portico. That day was no different; there was no abeyance from my routine. The Lowanachen sparkled, tossing diamonds of daylight about its gentle waves in the bright sun at the end of the expansive lawn which was now reclaimed after being let to the hands of nature for many years. The alders, they swayed gently in the breeze, murmuring to themselves. They were whispering a jested hint towards a secret they were trying to keep from me.

I climbed the trinity of stairs to the portico and was greeted, to my delight, by a pair of catkins undulating from the storm door handle. "A little risqué, Tommy, a little risqué," I spoke to myself. I clutched them dearly and gazed with serenity into the alders as a gentle smile imparted itself across my face. The next twelve hours couldn't expire soon enough. But they did pass, and our first meeting in weeks was finally going to happen.

— —

"You shouldn't keep a girl waiting," was my greeting to Tommy, arriving several minutes late. Typically, it was he who would arrive early in an unfashionable manner.

"Sorry," he smiled through his apology and all was perfect again. "So, I have some news. I joined the football team."

"What?" I was shocked. The boy had no athletic moves about him whatsoever.

"It's the only way to keep safe at school, Bree. The football players take care of their own."

Private or not, Monsignor Devon High School was still an inner-city school with inner city demons. Rival neighborhood gangs patrolled the halls, and each neighborhood kept the other in check. Drugs, guns, knives: all were mainstays at the school, though rarely displayed on the campus. Tommy had no neighborhood affiliation. He was a lone wolf. The pack mentality there would have torn him to shreds in no time at all.

Instead, the football team became his pack. On the field he would be the team's tackling dummy, absorbing hit after hit, satisfying their needs to let out their aggression in an appropriate and accepted fashion. He lifted his shirt at that meeting in the alders, revealing a torso tattooed with bruises that glowered back at me in an angry purple color. I could see him wince and adjust his body to avoid extraneous discomfort as he moved.

I was shocked he was mobile at all, especially after completing a grueling shift at Caldwell following his first game of the season. He learned to breathe through the pain. Most important was the pride he showed of himself. He took pride in figuring out how to survive in that new environment, of how to find allegiances to keep him safe during the school day. Survival! It was what he had learned from the experiences of his earliest years.

In exchange for his service to the team, he was hands-off elsewhere on campus. It was an unspoken rule, a code, that athletes were not to be targeted by the neighborhood factions. Tommy was smart. He took his beating wearing a full complement of protective gear, rather than being punished in the bottom of a stairwell or riding the El after school.

"It's brutal in there," Tommy's eyes lit up as he continued, "There was this kid, he was new, and they threw him down the stairs. Like he was nothing."

I was a bit shocked by the story, and the senseless trauma inflicted upon the boy's body. Tommy recounted how his head had landed squarely against the radiator at the bottom of the stairwell. His skull fissured, leaving the body to twitch in a semi-comatose state.

"Everyone just stared," Tommy looked into infinity as he continued, "Even the teachers stayed away, and the ambulance just kind of showed up it seemed." I looked at Tommy, and he appeared to be in shock himself as he recounted the story.

"All because he was different because he was new. It could have been me." He gulped; I gulped. He was right: it could have been him.

"Just promise me you'll watch your back," I cautioned. The last thing he could do was to let his guard down. I had my doubts that a group of jocks would come running to his aid if he found himself at the center of a neighborhood turf war.

Tommy continued with his story, "And I tell you what, if there really is a war on drugs, we're losing. The stuff is everywhere, anything you can imagine." This was a world for us that, up until a few months ago, only appeared on the evening news. Now we were living it; actually, only Tommy was living it, but I lived it vicariously in his telling of the story, my concerns for his safety being real. Every Sunday evening, I feared for him when he returned to his urban nightmare.

"Glad you're getting by, Tommy." My remark was morose and drab, to hide the fear I felt for him. I also had nothing to counter it with. My school days had none of that drama. Every day passed with no celerity, each one melting into the next, the repetition becoming déjà vu. The days were like my shampoo bottle instructed: lather, rinse, repeat. No beginning or end, just a monotonous cycle. In reality, I was a bit jealous of Tommy. I needed some excitement; the dulling effect of town was draining. I wasn't sure if I could handle the excitement of an inner-city school, but at that point in time, I would have tried anything. I was jealous, too, because Tommy had joined the football team. He had friends, of sorts, while I remained shunned, the curse of being daughter to President Worthington.

"Don't be jealous," Tommy came back at me. He must have been reading my mind, my body language, or both. "The guys on the team, they aren't friends," he paused to find the right word to describe his relationship with them, "... they're just an extension of school. Right here is always where I want to be."

"Lucky I like you, just a little bit," I tried but couldn't contain the smile that exploded across my face. We both laughed and knew this was true friendship. We ran the risk of causing trouble we couldn't comprehend if we were ever discovered meeting this way; any meeting between us would exact someone's wrath. Only something as real and profound as a friendship like ours was worth even fathoming that risk. We took it in stride, accepting the dangers. It was more dangerous being alone and vulnerable than it was being under fire together.

"Read me something," It was out of the blue. I was tired of the talk of school, especially since I had nothing to add to the conversation.

I cleared my throat, "Read to me, Tommy."

Tommy hesitated, then rose and approached his eclectic book collection. He looked at me with his head cocked; never had I asked him this, and never had literature been a topic of any great substance between us. Sure, I would read the books he recommended, but it stopped there. I never had anything to add. Tommy was always so eager to talk about what I read that I would let him ramble on, expressing how those works moved him.

The tables were turned. Now I wanted to be part of that conversation. I wanted to make sure I remained a part of his world, and give him something, anything, to look forward to so that our meetings would continue without stagnating.

He ran his hand along the volumes, stopping at one tucked away in the middle. "Here, this is my favorite," he spoke while removing a poetry collection from the shelf. I watched as his eyes swam across the page, rising and falling with the verse. His eyes were the lungs to his soul; they breathed in each word and brought life to them as they danced across his lips. Tommy had no great stature. He was short when it came to the male gender. But his voice, that voice of his, it was prepossessing when he recited poetry.

I watched and was entranced by the magic of his invocation. His eyes mirrored the pages, reflecting the words straight off them. I could almost read the words myself by following his eyes like a deaf man could read lips. His annunciation and cadence were perfect. It was beautiful. His voice had a lyrical flow that made the words almost appear and linger in the air about us. My mind was swimming; Tommy's introduction of poetry to me in this way gave me a real appreciation for the genre. He articulated the words in a manner that would lead the listener to believe they were his own. It was Tommy's recitation of Seamus Heaney's "North" that captured my soul. It almost brought out the brogue spoken by Tommy's grandparents, the same brogue that was intrinsically linked to his DNA, and a perfect accompaniment to the suffering of his life. Tommy's articulation of the words softened him but made his experience beyond his years even more apparent.

"Heaney's one of my favorites. It's real, isn't it?"

I nodded in agreement, still floored by his performance—describing his reading of the poem was nothing short of a performance.

"Yeah, it is. Real," I responded, again having nothing I could add, even if I tried. I was blown away by Tommy's reading of Heaney, and struggled to bring myself to my feet.

"Hmmmm . . ." I coasted over to the row of books, brushing against Tommy, wanting to make a selection of my own. He watched as I examined each and every one, my fingers stopping here and there, pausing. I furled my lips, acting dissatisfied in my search.

"Wait," I broke the silence, "what's this?"

The composition book. To Tommy's chagrin, I "found" the composition book.

"That's really nothing," Tommy moved to grab the book but I turned, thumbing through the pages with fury as I looked over my shoulder at him.

"Oh really? Nothing? Then I guess you wouldn't mind . . ."

Tommy swiped the book from me. I saw the look on his face, a look that he had just been violated, and knew that I had gone too far.

"Hey, sorry. I didn't mean to pry."

"It's no big deal. Forget about it."

"Well, what about it then?" I just wouldn't let it go, and I could see that I had worn him down just enough to yield his indulging me.

"Just a second, I'll find something a little more polished."

While Tommy sifted through the book, I could tell he was looking for something more than which poem he should share with me. It was the picture. He rifled through the book, an anemic shade washing out his face when he realized it was missing.

"What's wrong?" I tried my best not to let on that I knew, that it was somewhere safe, ready to be the first shot fired in a war nobody would win. For the moment, my ruse was working. He was too concerned with the picture itself to consider, for a moment, that it wasn't he who misplaced it.

"It's nothing—I think I just misplaced a few of my notes, that's all."

No, Tommy, you didn't lose anything. I stole it. I stole it to make certain that whoever did that to you would be made to pay for what they poached from you: your childhood.

"All right, you ready? It's still a work in progress so go easy on me."

"Don't worry, just get on with it," I smiled and spun around, sitting on the opposite end of the space so I could take in every word and every movement he made. This was going to be a performance. I was filled with anxiousness to finally have a sampling of what he wrote in the composition book, without having pilfered it first with my eyes. His reading of "North" had mesmerized me, and I wanted more. If he hadn't read that poem, I wouldn't have ventured that day to ask him to read from the composition book. But the moment was powerful, and I was caught up in it.

I sat on the edge of the old, worn, office chair. It creaked with my every move, sounding off like timbers in a ship that had spent one too many years at sea. The chair groaned, its swivels grinding into the dirt floor as I leaned forward, intently staring at Tommy's eyes as they made their way down the page:

> Slivers and streams
> Of light;
>
> I could find no more
> To see;
>
> It's always the dark
> That seems;
>
> To find me alone, vulnerable;
>
> Washing through the wood
> It's dark;

Over my shoulder I see
Nothing;

For once alone, secure;

They wrap me in their
Breath;

Harken to the past
Forget;

The future is out
Of sight;

But the now,
It is here;

Ready for the taking, acceptance;

A gift, golden

Not to be opened

But merely

Enjoyed.

"That needs absolutely no polishing." I was enchanted by the words he crafted, the rhythm that gave them life, the sound of their escape as they rolled off his tongue. On paper, they were just words—words I would have read without any second thought. They rang out from Tommy, caught somewhere between the rasp of a boy and the baritone of a man. His eloquence of speech gave these simple words a profoundness that they would never know on their own. I could never craft something as moving, or read it as inspired as he did. I lacked the pain and the inner strife to become a poet. Tommy, on the other hand, was the perfect suitor for the medium.

"Just don't share it with anyone else. It's very personal."

"You have my word, Tommy. It stays right here." I pulled his hand to my heart as I reinforced his security in knowing that his writings would retain their sanctity. It was a gift being the first audience to be moved by what he wrote, and I wasn't sure that I was quite ready to share them with anyone anyway. That moment was ours. I would do nothing to spoil it.

The remainder of the school year came and went in much the same fashion: meeting when we could, as often as we could. Tommy would read to me. I would listen with ears closed off to the rest of the world. I became his muse. During the times we were apart, he would write with a pace so voracious that the worn composition book could no longer contain his imaginative wanderings. Soon it overflowed with his creativity, filling numerous journals. Each time we met there was more to be read, and more to be heard. Inspiration was always just around the corner, waiting to strike.

CHAPTER 16

SEPARATION ANXIETY

W E MANAGED TO survive freshman year unscathed. Tommy's acceptance into the football locker room (although a very unlikely scenario at the outset) ensured he was hands-off in the halls of school. As for me, I kept to myself, finding it easier than I thought to disappear into the crowd.

Unfortunately, the summer between freshman and sophomore years was not meant for us. By now Tommy was expected to work full time at Caldwell, Genardo seeing to it that he earned his keep and contributed to the costs of maintaining the household. Fifteen years old, and he was supporting himself. His grandparents and vagabond mother, when she appeared, squelched away his meager earnings.

While Tommy toiled his summer away, I was sent to an all-girls camp several hours from town. My father saw to it that I was out of sight and out of mind, which in his restricted point of view was the perfect cure for his problem: two teenagers set to interfere with the power scheme of the world he constructed. All the while he watched Tommy for eight hours on the production floor, ensuring his confidence that we would be separated long enough to lose interest in one another. It was a perfect situation for my father. As for me, I was miserable.

One hundred teenage girls, all from established families and spoiled, sweating away in rustic cabins while cursing their parents for this banishment. I had nothing in common with them, except for one binding tie: our parents all had earned or inherited a measurable amount of wealth. There was one other common thread weaving through these girls: teenage angst. Their summer loves were interrupted, and the topic of conversation always turned to how they missed their boyfriends, each one struggling to outdo the other with their tales of romance.

I could play this game and beat them at it all day long. Tommy and I were the furthest thing from boyfriend and girlfriend, but they didn't need to know that. Our relationship had grown far too intimate to even liken it to a mere friendship. We were and always would be far more than just friends. Our relationship was one of love that defied explanation; it surpassed the boundaries of the contemporary definition of love. It could never be explained. It needed to be experienced to be comprehended.

There I was at camp, and eventually I wanted, but in truth actually needed, to talk to someone. To fit in with that crowd, I assigned the role of boyfriend to Tommy. Talking about our time together was the only thing that palliated the pain of being separated from him and our taboo rendezvous in the alders. To the other girls, he was the consummation of the perfect boyfriend, a prototype for their beaus to follow. They hung on every word as I divulged the secret meetings between us, all of them appreciating the fact that I let them in on this secret. We were born romantics, stealing away time together whenever we could, cementing a love forbidden by our families. We were Romeo and Juliet to them; but I ascertained that none of these girls had ever taken the time to read the real *Romeo and Juliet*, failing to see the tragedy that befell the two lovers, and to understand how dangerous our relationship was to the both of us.

I recounted the poetry Tommy would read aloud, and how the words poured out from his heart onto the page with incantations of our love. Few of the poems were about me. But they were romantic in the sense that they revealed his innermost thoughts, fears, and pain; romantic in that he made himself vulnerable to reveal his most private thoughts to me alone. I laughed deep inside, watching them become starry-eyed over this boyfriend of mine, the working-class hero reciting poetry to me, the girl who was the progeny born from the nemesis to his social order. Inside I felt superior as I pulled one over on them. But that feeling retreated each time I spoke of Tommy. I knew, to the outside world, that this was how we appeared: lovers who were fortunate in everything but circumstance.

The time away that summer was refreshing in that it gave me a renewed gratitude for our friendship. It was also amusing, to some degree, to see how the other girls reacted to my stories. Envious at times though they could be, their envy was not misplaced. Tommy was one of a kind, gentle, and loving. His affects towards me would melt the heart of any girl. I was even more fortunate in that he wasn't wooing me. His affections were genuine, meant to bring me closer, and not to disrobe me mentally or physically. He was all mine, but the other girls didn't know and were still too naïve to comprehend just how that came to be—boy and girl, wrapped up together, for the sake of companionship and comfort.

My time at the camp did turn out to be a welcome distraction from the mundane world of Alder Ferry. For a brief time, my guard was down. I was separated from my cold, forced unit of a family, and separated from the innate world that failed to welcome any dissent from the existence it insisted we follow. Both circumstances were oppressive in their haunting of me, ominous clouds that loomed on the horizon threatening to disturb the serene escape I enjoyed.

It was the first time I remember understanding how good it felt to leave Alder Ferry and the trauma that would accompany returning.

PART III

REVENGE AND TRAGEDY

CHAPTER 17

HEAD GAMES

W E BOTH ARRIVED in Alder Ferry within hours of one another as that late summer's day began its recession into the memory. A memory only to be darkened by the changing seasons of human conduct and repressed by the winter of the mind to prevent the arrival of the spring. The timing of that day was impeccable, almost prescient of things to come, of things that had to happen.

Somehow the postal service, in its artless function, was the mechanism that came to sow the seeds sprouting the events to rule the coming year.

The letter spent its summer in hiding, cramped down between the seat and the floorboards of the old jeep conscripted into duty for the postal service. There it spent nearly eight lonely weeks, a witness to the mud of the summer rains, the dust of the summer heat, and the tailings of a public servant's life littering the floor about it. With patience, it waited to be discovered and ultimately delivered to its intended recipient. In concurrent fashion, we were both delivered to the hands of fate.

It didn't matter if it were consequence or coincidence. It was hard to decipher which it was anyhow. Regardless, a bluff had been made; a bluff that would be called. A bluff that couldn't be dismissed by the players brought to the table.

———

Father Pekennick sat at his desk sorting papers and scratching out his homily for the coming weekend. He always started too late, he knew that; throughout his career, he was told that he always waited far too long to prepare his message. More interested in the business of running a parish, he knew his detractors at the diocese were right. But they couldn't argue. He kept the shrinking parish solvent and delivered his message each Sunday without remiss.

Until that Friday.

"Father, here's today's mail," the elderly housekeeper was matter-of-fact, all business. Each day was the same routine: announce the mail's arrival, place it on the desk, slide it halfway toward Father Pekennick, and exit the room via an abrupt about-face to the door. This day was no different in effect. The only difference was the message being delivered.

Father Pekennick dismissed her with a wave of the hand and a nod of the head. She was all but nameless to him, the familiarity between the two nothing short of the interaction of a tired couple that spent decades together. The routine misplaced the conversation, removing it from the equation. His face remained fixed on the homily, the words dying before they could make it onto the page. Rather than pain over those lost words, he took up the mail for distraction.

"Bill, bill, bill . . ." Pekennick stopped when he came across the envelope, eyeing it with curiosity. It had been weathered into a dull, yellow color over the course of its summer vacation atop the floorboards of the old jeep. It was odd, he thought, to receive correspondence from a parishioner this time of year. The envelope certainly wasn't official correspondence based on its outward appearance. Outside of the Christmas holiday season, he rarely received correspondence from anyone, save for the token invitations to the wedding ceremonies he was paid to perform.

He slid his silver letter opener between the flap and body of the worn envelope. It penetrated easily, creating a clean wound and exposing its contents to the world for the first time in two months. Not expecting much, he withdrew the single piece of paper from the envelope. With a flick of his thumb, the letter recoiled open from its tri-folded condition with all the enthusiasm of a spring released from its latch. Like a jack in the box, it sprung its surprise on the cleric without holding back.

"Lord, help me!" was his response, eyes full as the harvest moon with the shock of the image before him. His pupils were just as startled, retreating to the back of his head, not believing what they had seen. His head shrunk back from the paper, his arms looking to have doubled in length as he tried to distance himself from what he saw. Finally, he pushed the letter away, and it shrunk back into itself, forming a triangle covering up its obscenity. The reverse side of the paper offered up a minute clue, an inkling as to the source of this devious endeavor.

— —

My father and I ended our long, quiet drive and pulled up to the house. Upon our approach, we noticed another sedan in the driveway, and as we neared, another vehicle next to it. It was a police cruiser from the Alder Ferry Police Department. Driven by instinct my father accelerated and closed the gap to the house, skidding through the gravel to a halt by the old hitching post that now served as a parking stop before the cascading front steps. My father rushed from the car and burst into the house. I took my time, not knowing what I was about to encounter.

My father waved me in, signaling all was clear. I slipped in through the half-opened door. It was worse than I could have imagined. All color left my face, allowing it to grow pale as a corpse. Immediately inside the front doors, in the sitting room, were my mother, Detective Fennimore, and Father Pekennick. I shrunk from the ensemble and made my way to the kitchen, attempting to overhear their conversation without becoming a part of it.

"Edith, Father . . . what's going on?" My father looked about the room quizzically, taking on the look of having walked squarely into an ambush.

"Stuart, we need to talk. Privately." Detective Fennimore's years of experience showed, his command rolling off his tongue with the air of a pleasantry.

"Right this way," my father motioned the men into his study that was a bit farther down the hall, at the opposite end of the home from the kitchen. Any possibility of eavesdropping was severed from the equation for me. As soon as I saw Father Pekennick, I knew why they were here. But how could they know? My mother wandered back to the kitchen, returning the coffee service. I shot her a look, which she returned my way. Both of us women were removed from the conversation, a conversation left solely to the men. It was one of those rare occasions when we understood one another on a level that required no words to be spoken. I acknowledged her with a slight nod of my head and retreated to my room to await the reckoning that was to come. I knew the understanding between my mother and me at that moment would be soon forgotten.

——

Back in the study, the conversation began to take on a more stolid tone.

"Stuart, I need you to identify this for me if you can." Fennimore slid what appeared to be a blank piece of paper encased in an evidence bag across his desk.

"Look here." Fennimore's left index finger drew Worthington's eyes to the bottom of the page, which bore the embossed block letters that read, "CALDWELL TOOL & DIE, ALDER FERRY, U.S.A."

"Do you recognize this?"

"Certainly, it's the old letterhead, we use it in the copy machine for in-house printing. We have plenty of that old stock around."

"Where is that copier?"

"It's in my office . . ." Worthington regretted that answer. He was forced into it, and now he was feeling the pressure of being set up by Fennimore.

Fennimore didn't flinch, and continued, "Who has access to it?"

"Me, my secretary, that's it." Worthington looked up, and went on further, "Unless someone was in there without my permission, we do have a cleaning service come in."

"Is the office typically locked?"

"Yes, only my secretary has a key, it's always locked."

"And that stock you were talking about?"

"It's in a couple boxes, in my credenza." Worthington's face grew red, wondering where the line of questioning was going.

"Listen, I don't know where you're going with this, or why he's even here," stated Worthington as he motioned to Father Pekennick, who had been seated, quietly observing Fennimore in action.

"Stuart, we're not here to blame you. Before you go and get defensive, let me just say this: I'm pretty certain this isn't about you. It's about one of your employees."

The air calmed for a moment. They were now at the eye of the storm. Worthington was disarmed by Fennimore's comments, placed at ease in his chair, his grip on its arms beginning to relax. The beads of sweat that formed on his forehead began to evaporate in the cool, air-conditioned comfort of the room.

"I still don't know why he's here," remarked Worthington, directing his comment towards Father Pekennick.

"Father, please do the honors." Fennimore stepped aside as Father Pekennick approached the front of the desk. His hand planted itself on the evidence bag, causing it to submit to the pressure he exerted, the sweat on his hands causing the plastic to attempt escape before coming to be pinned under his palm.

The priest was fraught with obvious nervousness, caught between an executive known for his short temper and a law officer pushing him to this point. He prefaced his next move by saying, "Stuart, I received this in today's mail."

With a flick of the wrist, his sweaty palm pulled the evidence bag from the table. He reversed it with an imprecise movement that gave the entire action a feel of occurring in slow motion. The reveal was delayed to a degree, but the view of the image was not obfuscated in any way. Father Pekennick did his best to avoid looking at the image again, his retinas still scarred by the shock of its first revelation to him.

Worthington's chair rocketed backward, gouging the chair rail that encircled the wall of his den. He rose with a fury reserved for the tensest of moments. This moment qualified in that regard.

"Jesus H. Christ! What the fuck is that?"

The picture, of course. It was the picture of Tommy, bathing in the view of the crucifix that peered down on him. Across the top of the page, in neat cursive, the sender had written: "Pekennick the Pervert." Worthington's reaction confirmed what Fennimore said earlier, that he was certain this case didn't involve him. By some misfortune, he was associated with the incident by the piece of evidence, the letterhead that somehow contracted the image and made its way out of his office.

Fennimore placed his hand on Worthington's shoulder, guiding him back to his seat. He turned the evidence bag over, hiding the vulgar scene from view.

"Sit down, Stuart. We're just trying to find out who sent this. The picture obviously predates your arrival here."

"Do you know who the boy is?" Worthington asked of Fennimore.

"We certainly do. And that's the second part of the problem," Fennimore glanced at Father Pekennick who chimed in to respond, as if on cue.

"It's Genardo's grandkid."

"Great," this was the only response Worthington could summon. He shriveled back into his chair. Not only was there a pedophile somewhere, maybe even in his plant, but Genardo's grandson was the victim. Worthington realized that Tommy was a victim on many levels; he just didn't care. What he was facing now was a crisis that could topple his leadership at Caldwell. Genardo's grandson was victimized by a molester, and the evidence was sent from his office. It was almost too good to be true. This could be a perfect score for the union if it became known to them. The previous summer Tommy made his entrance at Caldwell, for the entire plant to see, and embarrassed Worthington. Now he was back, in dire circumstances caught on film, the boy whose sordid past threatened to topple Worthington's kingdom.

"Look, Stu," Father Pekennick interrupted the conversation, and was probably the only man who could get away with calling him Stu in the heat of that moment. He was trying to deflect from the situation, and continued, "for all we know, the boy could have done this, he is working there, right?"

"Come on, Father. You really believe that?"

But Worthington did like where he was going with that idea.

"But, let's say, someone, someone from the labor side found this picture, and wanted to make management look, well, bad?"

It was true. Anything that could discredit management, discredit the corporate powers now behind Caldwell, was a turn of the screw that favored labor.

"I wouldn't put anything past Genardo, I don't care if that's his grandson in the picture. He'll do whatever it takes to get at me."

"Listen to the two of you. Before we go about protecting your reputations, I'm going to find who took this picture in the first place." Fennimore set both men, worrying over their small kingdoms, into their places.

"Now, looking at that picture, I am going to say that it was a religious individual. The crucifix, Father. I'm going to need to interview all members of your staff: teachers, janitors, housekeepers, religious personnel. Everyone."

"And for you Worthington, same thing goes. That includes Genardo and your secretary."

Father Pekennick and Worthington looked at each other in disbelief; the rug had just been pulled out from under their feet.

"Listen, we need to complete our due diligence here. In case you forgot—we have evidence of a crime, a very serious fucking crime. Now get over yourselves."

Pekennick jumped in, "Detective, what about Tommy? Did you think about his welfare at all? You go out there and investigate. I guarantee the next thing that happens—that kid ends up beat to hell. You know what his grandfather and cohorts are like, isn't that right Stuart?"

"He's right, as much as I hate to admit it. You go showing this picture around and it's over for the kid."

"Stuart," Fennimore was edging his way in, to see where he stood, "aren't your daughter and the boy—"

"No." Worthington was emphatic in the statement. "She's been away all summer, and the two go to different schools. They have nothing to do with each another."

"Well enough." Fennimore had tested those waters; he had to. In the least, it was to push Worthington a bit further and give him something else to grind his teeth on after he left.

"I'll give you both two days to sort it out with your people. Keep it on the down low. After that I'm opening a full investigation, no holds barred. Understood?"

Both men nodded in agreement. "If you hear anything, I'm to be notified immediately. As far as I'm concerned, you both are accessories if anything is withheld. Anything."

——

Fennimore had family at the plant, and I was certain that my father's management style didn't agree with Fennimore. Likewise, the detective was no fan of the church. His second marriage had been put off ten years earlier for the lack of an annulment of his first marriage, a document he couldn't afford at the time. Instead, he left the church, was married by a justice of the peace, and had his reception at the picnic grove on the edge of the alder stand. Needless to say, the detective was not about to allow either institution to stray too far.

I heard the detective and the pastor leave, their cars rumbling through the gravel like distant summer thunder. I watched the dust from the driveway envelop their vehicles as they vanished from my view. My father's leaden footsteps made their way across the house and out onto the portico to join my mother. From my window, I overheard bits and pieces of their conversation. I didn't quite understand how, but the letter was traced to Caldwell. Worse, there was the impending investigation. If word of this got out, I was certain that Tommy . . . I put that thought out of my head. I couldn't bear to think of him suffering another beating—or worse—as a result of my intrusion. I had to reach out to someone before things went too far before the details were let to wander the streets of Alder Ferry and put Tommy in harm's way.

I was startled from my thoughts by a knock on my bedroom door. This was it, I remember thinking. This is where it all goes down. My father cracked the door before letting himself in.

"Aubrey, have you been seeing that boy from the plant, Genardo's grandson?"

I gulped. I thought we hid our meetings well enough, but maybe we hadn't.

"No, not at all. You and his grandfather kind of made that impossible, remember?" My comment hinted that maybe there could be something between Tommy and me, a teenage yearning struggling to rise above parental authority with no regard for consequence.

"Keep it that way." It was a command. I learned to take him seriously at times, and this was one of those times. I knew from his tone that he wouldn't back off this issue.

"Yeah, sure," was my response, turning my back to him and pulling down the headphones over my ears to drown him out. I'd figure it out somehow, how to clean up this situation, and how to make sure I could keep my meetings with Tommy secret. There was no going back at this point, the ball had been carried forward too far to retreat. Forces were at play that were well out of my control.

CHAPTER 18

CROSSROADS

THERE WAS ONLY one person I could trust with my story: Mrs. K. Certainly she would understand and could offer the consolation for me to ease the justification for my actions. I sent the letter to put Pekennick on the defensive, but to my dismay, it had the opposite effect. He went directly to the police. I was certain at first it was a play on his part, but now I couldn't be certain of that. I simply did not know enough of the situation, and knew nearly as little about the players, to anticipate their moves.

With the police involved, an investigation would undoubtedly reveal what happened to Tommy at the hands of the twisted individual cowering behind the camera. This town wasn't filled with understanding or compassionate people. Far from it, Tommy wouldn't be seen as the victim, he would be seen as a willing participant. Tommy had been all but neglected by his family, church, and community. To believe that the same people would offer to see him through a trial such as this was near difficult to consider.

Tommy was the child that everyone saw roaming the town. They would ask themselves, "I wonder where his parents are?" but would never stop to see if he was all right, or if he needed anything. Instead, they would go about their business and assume his situation would sort itself out rather than saddle themselves with offering him any assistance. Good, Christian people, filling the pews on Sunday, wanted nothing to do with the message of their savior the other six days of the week.

So I took the situation into my own hands. No one else dared to speak up for the vulnerable child left to the elements when his grandparents were away. No one dared speak up to his grandfather for putting that child in harm's way. No one. Not a single person that saw Tommy outside, in the cold of winter or the heat of summer, questioned it. If they did, they kept those feelings to themselves. Except for one person, that individual who saw an easy target, and took clean advantage of the boy.

That person must have been a hero at first. I assumed it was Pekennick but now wasn't sure. Still, I was certain he was involved; he had to at least know. His crucifix hung in that picture. The priest even admitted as much that it was one of a kind. Right there in his office, the deed was done. And he let it happen; how many times I didn't want to know. In some ways that picture destroyed what remained of my innocence.

I was no savior. I just wanted justice for my friend. But I knew that I had reacted in haste, out of anger, looking to inflict pain in a vengeful act. It wasn't my business to avenge Tommy. But it was too late to second guess my actions. It was done, and now I was forced to see a way through the quagmire I created. It was all done with the hope of protecting the only friend I ever knew from becoming hurt any more. That picture summed up his character: his shyness, his shrinking away from people, and his life in the shadows of the alders. He was safe when unnoticed and left alone. At any other time, he was a target: for his abuser, his abrasive grandfather, his vagrant mother, and a town that didn't care.

In my haste, I feared I, too, would end up in that category.

— —

I looked up the worn sidewalk that bled from the front steps to the street. It seemed forever and a year away; but that was only my fear, cementing my feet to the asphalt to avoid the inevitable conversation that had to happen. The house was a squat bungalow, neatly maintained but obvious in its age. Green moss clung to the undersides of the gutters, leaves from the previous fall remained stacked under the hedges, some turning black with mold in the humid summer air. It was apparent to me that a single woman lived here. The maintenance items left unchecked were a sure sign I arrived at the right place.

I made my way up the walk and knocked. The aluminum storm door rattled with a violent percussion each time my fist rapped against it. I decided on three attempts. After that, I would leave and formulate another plan.

"Aubrey?"

I nearly jumped out of my skin; I was expecting an answer from the door, not from the street.

"Mrs. K!"

"You here for me? If so, you have the wrong house," she motioned towards another house two doors down and on the opposite side of the street. This one was properly maintained, with an impeccable yard. Her neighbors must have loathed her. She was the only person on the street that managed to keep her property up to this condition.

I ran over and we embraced. It had been two years since we last spoke, and I always remembered her advice at our eighth-grade graduation: *"If there is ever anything that either one of you needs . . . I am here for you. Always."* My only regret was not seeking her out sooner.

"Let's sit around back." She showed me to the rear of her home. A pitcher of sun tea was brewing on the flagstone porch. She fetched two glasses filled with ice and poured the tea. I puckered slightly, as it was unsweetened, my young palate feeling dried out by its tannins. I looked down through the glass and across the yard, realizing that from her property the Genardo residence could just be seen. The overgrowth of the other properties attempted to block it out, but still, there it was. I shivered as I thought about the place and how close we were to it.

"Are you okay?" Mrs. K saw me shudder. In the warm summer air, it was a definite indication that something was wrong.

"Yeah. Well—no." I ran a finger along the rim of the glass, the vibrations sounding off, a foghorn slicing through the thick air and the thicker tension in my voice.

"Well, what is it, Aubrey?" She placed her glass down and leaned in. "I can't help if you don't let me know what's bugging you."

I knew I looked nervous. We were sitting in the shade, and I was sweating, even though the temperature was still very moderate, comfortable even, the summer air beginning to crisp up as fall approached.

"I've done something and I don't know what to do."

She slid her chair close to mine and took my hands in hers, looked into my eyes, and asked, "What is it?"

"It's Tommy, I . . ." It was challenging to discuss the subject matter, if not awkward. At times I felt guilty for even harboring the picture. It had been a challenge enough to come here and to want to trust her, but the weight of the matter was crushing. I feared that no matter who I divulged this information to, it would never end in the desired result.

"Aubrey, it's okay, you can trust me." It was hard for me to trust anyone. All adults had been anything but trustworthy by my experience. Still, our times together in the past were some of the only pleasant memories of adult interaction that remained with me.

"I found a picture of Tommy. He was, young, very young . . ."

She looked at me, with a quizzing stare, almost as if she were about to finish my sentence. "Go on," she said with a prepossessed look about her. I could tell she was by now being pulled in by my demeanor more than anything else.

". . . and naked." It was a relief to let that last line out. Blurting out that line was a purging of my soul. No longer did I have to keep this to myself. It was out now, no more a burden that I carried alone.

"I don't quite get what you are trying to say, dear."

"I found a picture of Tommy, as a young boy, naked. Not of him as a toddler running through a sprinkler. He was posed. The picture . . ."

"I get it." Her voice raised itself momentarily to cut me off. I was thankful she stopped me, saving me from trying to find the right words to describe what I had seen. There could never be the right words to describe the scene in the picture. If I could ever describe that scene, then I was just as guilty. Guilty for looking at it too closely, like it was some highway accident begging for gawkers. That picture deserved no detail; its very existence spoke of the evil that precipitated its exposure to the light, and the light of a young boy purloined to darkness.

"Let's take this inside."

I followed her in. It was probably the right move. Although the neighboring homes were spaced apart enough to afford us privacy, we couldn't be too careful with the subject matter of this conversation.

"So, this picture, what was in it?"

"It was Tommy, standing in Pekennick's office." Mrs. K cocked her head slightly at the last part of the sentence.

"You're sure it was his office?"

I nodded my affirmation to her question.

"But you see there's a much larger problem now."

"Well, Aubrey, I don't see how things could be much worse than what you've already told me."

"I sent the picture to Pekennick, anonymously."

"Oh . . ." She perked up, "That is a problem."

"And," I continued, "he called the police. They somehow traced it back to Caldwell, I don't know how, but they did."

"Why do you think that could be?"

My mind froze. I used the copier in my father's office to duplicate the picture. The paper in it was recycled letterhead, a memory that returned to me too late to be of any use now. Details. I failed to notice the fine details that stood between anonymity and drawing the ire of the three monumental bureaucracies of this place: the church, the police department, and Caldwell. All three were slow to move, but once started, things would quickly steamroll. Their momentum wouldn't be stopped.

"I don't know how they traced it back to Caldwell," was my response. I just couldn't accept responsibility for my oversight. It was a detail that if left out, just maybe it could keep me in the clear for a little while longer. Still, I felt a sharp stab for my lack of precision, the mistakes of my haste to send off the letter before leaving for camp were continuing to cascade.

"But what I do know is that Detective Fennimore is threatening to interview the employees of Caldwell and St. Germaine's—everyone, including you and the other teachers."

"Shit." Mrs. K's reaction was spot on to my line of thinking. She expounded that thought, stating, "And if they do that, Tommy is sure to suffer the consequences once this story gets out."

I was relieved. Someone finally was on the same wavelength as me. While finding the individual responsible was important, protecting Tommy was my priority.

"I know Fennimore is itching to catch the person and throw them in prison. That much I overheard from my father."

Mrs. K was aware of Fennimore's zeal as a detective. He was the only detective on the police force, and he went over every investigation with a fine comb. He was meticulous, picking up on the subtlest hints, and pulling leads from the most minimal of clues. She knew he would not cease in his efforts until the guilty party was brought to justice. That investigation would destroy Tommy's reputation for sure, and the other men at Caldwell would be the first to take him to task for it. It didn't matter to them that he was a boy and that an adult forced him to pose—or worse. Their homophobia prevented them from seeing the truth: a boy victimized by one of their very own.

"Listen, Aubrey. There's very little we can do here. Maybe I can make a phone call to Father Pekennick, try and sort this thing out."

"But what if it was him? What if he did it?"

"I know Detective Fennimore, Father Pekennick knows him just as well. He's the last person to bluff, trust me."

"But . . ."

"Just because it happened there doesn't mean he was involved. Plenty of people use those offices."

"May I use the bathroom?"

"Sure, down the hall and across from the bedroom."

It was just a matter of steps, the bungalow being a mere postage stamp of a building. The bathroom was smaller than my closet. I felt, again, the advantage of being a Worthington. This is why I would never be liked. I had far more room in a small corner of my bedroom than most of the people in this town had in their primary living spaces. I felt small again, in her bathroom, and wanted to just withdraw from this town and the angst it caused. Still, I wouldn't have traded anything, no degree of sadness or strife, for the opportunity to have become friends with Tommy.

I turned to close the door to the bathroom which faced directly into Mrs. K's bedroom. Her bedroom door was fully ajar, the bed properly turned down, an aged afghan blanket draped along its bottom edge. A mirror on the door caught a reflection, drawing my eyes up the wall. There it was. Against the pasty, white-washed wall was a crucifix. Not just any crucifix, but the same crucifix from the picture, identical to the crucifix that adorned Father Pekennick's office. How many of these things were out there? Maybe Pekennick wasn't guilty after all. There was just no way to know. I was awash again with the ambiguity of purpose I felt earlier. I was thrust back to where I was the previous evening, questioning every action I had taken, and asking myself again, "Who can I trust?"

I stared into the mirror for an amount of time that I knew was out of the ordinary for a trip to the restroom, all the while wondering what step to take next. I washed my hands, rubbing them with vigor, feeling the need to rinse myself of this entire situation. I needed to be cleansed, but no amount of scrubbing made me feel clean. My skin was crawling all over.

"Are you okay, Aubrey?"

"Yeah, be right out." Nothing could remove me from that house fast enough. The crucifix made me nervous—could that be *the crucifix?* I didn't know and didn't want to find out. I splashed water on my face and rubbed my eyes in a vain attempt to remove from them the image of the crucifix. I found it trying to release any doubts that I now felt about Mrs. K, about anyone involved in our lives, anyone that could have played a part in this situation.

"Aubrey, you look like you've seen a ghost!"

"It's this mess that I'm struggling with, I'm sorry. It's got me all messed up inside."

"No need to worry. I'll take things from here and you just try not to worry. I know that doesn't sound easy—"

"No, it's not easy. This is the furthest thing from easy." She looked down at me, and I could see the compassion behind her eyes. There was some truth behind them. I wanted to believe her and thought I should believe her. Women didn't do this; it was always men. The same men who ran our lives were responsible for this. I felt sorry for even thinking she could be involved.

"Mrs. K?"

"Yes, Aubrey?"

"I'm sorry."

"Child, you have nothing to be sorry about."

"Sorry . . . for Tommy, for putting you in this situation."

"It's no bother, I'm glad you came to me. We'll straighten this out together, as best we can for Tommy, all right?"

I nodded and made my way out. There was still a twinge of guilt left in me for even trying to associate her with what happened. I looked back and waved as I made my way from her property and crossed the street. It was refreshing how she watched me, almost making sure I was safely on my way, not leaving her doorway until I was out of sight. She couldn't have had any part in this. I trusted in my instincts so long that it was hard to separate myself from them at times, but this was one occasion where I would need to let it go, to place my faith in someone else and have the courage to believe they would follow through.

— —

Mrs. K watched as Aubrey disappeared down the street and closed her door to the outside world, maintaining the confidences of her home. On instinct she went to her phone, this moment having been rehearsed in her mind for years. She lifted the handset from the receiver, hesitating but a moment, and entered the telephone number that had been committed to memory. Each button sounded out its respectable tone, playing an eerie S.O.S. to her ears as she waited for an answer.

"Hello?"

"I'm fine, thanks." Mrs. K rushed through the pleasantries with her caller, and warned, "Listen—it's serious. They know."

She made perfect on her promise to make a phone call that afternoon.

CHAPTER 19

JUDGMENT DAY

THE CRUCIFIX HAD an angry aura, with its sculpted face resembling more the Jesus who swept the peddlers from the temple than that of savior. The rosewood's contours and knots aided in giving it this disposition by darkening the face, its hue sombering the wood. The dun of the grain imparted an angry, vengeful face on the savior strapped to the cross. The forlorn, forgiving Jesus was forgotten by this caricature looking down with despising eyes on its subject.

He looked up at the crucifix and understood the anger and the lack of pity for him at that moment. All he could do was drop to his knees and prostrate himself before the very God he failed. Tears rolled down his face, switch-backing across the cracks in the weathered skin that impeded their journey, inevitably delaying their falling from the edge of the cheek, only to splash to the floor and lose the memory of the moment for which they were shed.

All the while the only words he could manage, with a whimpering murmur enforced by his reluctant sobs, were, "I'm sorry, I'm sorry." He incited this incantation with monotony. He knew being sorry was the first step in seeking forgiveness, enacting his contrition, and allowing absolution for his sins. But there was no time for that now, and instead, he repeated his contrition to the crucifix, its impassive gaze neglecting his pleas for forgiveness. The figure of Jesus on that cross was indifferent, taking pleasure in the melancholy mood of the degenerate below.

But there are some acts for which forgiveness is impossible in religious dogma. This act was one of them, for contrition would be impossible. He closed his eyes and braced himself with the cold acceptance of what he had done under the eyes of God. Those same eyes in the rosewood crucifix came to life now, looking at him in disgust, refusing his prayers for forgiveness. The red hues of the wood burned into his soul, shackling it to the earth. He moved to let himself go, to set his body into free fall, becoming numb to the fact that there was no escape from this set of circumstances as he submerged into a subconscious netherworld.

—–

Father Pekennick caught his head just before it planted itself against the smooth-grained wood of his desk. His chair had gone out from him, the castors sending it careening into the wall. The near miss with the desk and floor stirred him, rousing him from the semi-sleep state he had been living since the picture's arrival. He knew his back was against a wall. The police would conduct their investigation, the diocese would do their best to minimize damage to the church, and he would be sent away somewhere to be forgotten. He looked about his office. He had invested too much in this parish and in its people. Perhaps he was too cold and distant for them to know just how much he had done to perform Mass seven days a week and to keep the school open while others in the diocesan system shuttered their doors.

His staffing was minimal to keep costs in check. The interviews of St. Germaine's employees wouldn't take long. Even then, they still weren't sure to find the culprit. Numerous seminarians had come and gone over the course of the decade, assisting him with the daily habits of maintaining the parish. Some had gone far away; others remained near. The net cast by Detective Fennimore was wide. It had to be and Father Pekennick knew that. The mere bureaucracy of the church created this problem of developing talent locally and then casting it out to the corners of the globe. In some ways, it ensured that problems like this could be easily swept away.

But he wanted no part of that bureaucracy, none of it. He resented the politics of his beloved church and the archaic traditions that prevented him from performing his most entrusted duties as a priest: tending to his flock. One of those members, a young tender lamb, had been culled from his watchful eye and devoured by the wolf. There had to be an easier way. In his fatigued state, he had been overlooking the obvious.

The crucifix. It was the only clue in the picture, the only link between the scene of the crime and the culprit. He had to stop

Detective Fennimore before his investigation sprouted legs and ran amok over the good name of his parish. Several hours later, he met with Fennimore to discuss the lead.

"Detective, I think we can narrow the investigation quite a bit."

"How so?"

"Let me see the picture if you will."

Fennimore looked at him with a cautious eye. "Not many people ask to see something like this a second time, Father."

Pekennick contained himself at the comment, knowing full well that what he was about to add to the case held the potential to solve the crime.

"Cover that up. I'm only interested in the top quarter of the page."

Fennimore did as instructed, sliding a manila envelope over the page, stopping at Pekennick's finger near the top right border.

All that remained visible, on a barren white wall, was the crucifix.

"Okay, we have your lord and savior Jesus Christ. He didn't come down from that cross before, don't see it happening now."

"He doesn't need to Detective. He's right where he needs to be, as always." Pekennick's remark was truthful to the matter at hand and a jab at Fennimore's lacking faith.

"Enlighten me then, Father."

"This crucifix, you see it?"

"Yes." Fennimore was losing interest, shifting his weight to his rear foot in an attempt to create some distance between them, not certain where the conversation was headed.

"That crucifix is very unique. A friend of mine from the seminary made it. Along with four others like it."

Fennimore perked up immediately. "So then, we find this crucifix, we solve the crime. Or in the least, we find the crime scene."

"Exactly, Detective. Exactly."

Pekennick was different from his church leaders in that he sought justice. It didn't matter that someone close to him committed this insidious crime and violated the sanctity of a young boy's innocence, desecrating the very body that he believed to be the temple of God. He would protect no one, no matter who did this. The perpetrator would not be allowed to be hidden or ensconced away before charges were filed. No, this person would be held accountable and his church, his little kingdom on Earth, would be vindicated, along with his purpose to serve and protect his parishioners. It pained him to no end knowing that he was dreadfully remiss in this single instance. He punished himself without any mercy over the previous twenty-four hours for his failure to the young Tommy.

"One of the crucifixes hangs in my office. Another was gifted to my housekeeper. The third was given to Sister Mary, who has since passed away."

"And the last two, Father?"

"One was given to Ms. Kaliczenkoff for her years of service as a teacher. The last went to Deacon Hatton."

"So then Father, in reality, we have two potential crime scenes, and maybe the perpetrator."

"Great detective work." Pekennick's quip gained a look from Fennimore. His ire was drawn, but he couldn't help but appreciate his attention to that one small detail that could tidy up the situation.

"Not a word of this to anyone, Father. I'll call Worthington and make certain that he doesn't go and start prying around Caldwell. Let's hope we don't need to carry this investigation too far."

"Thanks, Detective."

"No, thank you, Father. This means a lot." Fennimore was genuine in his thanks to the priest, thanks that the man often didn't give out to anyone.

"And Detective," Pekennick paused, looking down, with reflection, "if you and your wife ever desire to renew your vows, I'd be honored."

Fennimore smiled through closed teeth. "I'll keep that in mind, Father." In some ways, the cooperation began to erase the years of discord between them. It was a level of discord not effectuated by either of the men, but the very bureaucracy of the church abhorred by Pekennick and Fennimore alike.

— —

Fennimore approached Hatton's residence on foot, leaving his vehicle at the end of the street to avoid being noticed. He knocked seven times with no answer. There was no motion he could detect within, as he peered through the minuscule gaps that formed occasionally in the heavy curtains stained yellow by years of cigarette smoke. The smell permeated the wooden front door and emanated from it with the same persistence of the incense that smoldered on high holy days. The home seemed empty, Hatton perfecting the role of widower, with the décor frozen in time to his wife's passing.

He made a cursory circuit around the property, checking the doors and windows. All were locked; the windows, in fact, had been painted shut. The cellar doors were rusted in place, also blocking out entrance to the outside world. An old, aluminum shed sat in ruins at the rear of the property, its contents of no obvious value to the property owner. Fennimore was certain Hatton was unaware of being linked to this crime, but still the seasoned detective was concerned about the slight probability that he was forewarned. Even so, nothing at the house seemed off kilter. It was almost too perfect he thought. He left to fetch his dinner at the station.

He returned in the early evening twilight to see if he could capture any sign of life at the residence. The house was completely dark, inside and out. There was no tell-tale flickering of the television, and no shadows cast onto the lawn from figures moving about inside. The house was dead to the world, a lifeless shell with its sole occupant nowhere to be found.

There was nothing quite like the element of surprise to draw information out of a witness. His last stop, he thought to himself, should be at Ms. Kaliczenkoff's residence. His cruiser turned down her street and rolled to a gentle stop where the curb greeted her front walk. The manicured lawn set the property far apart from those adjoining hers. Rows of annuals lined the walk, drawing the eye towards the wreathed front door flanked by perfectly manicured rose bushes. In the cool evening air, the blooms had begun to open again, welcoming him as he made his way up the walk.

She answered his first knock. The shock on her face was apparent. It was the visit she feared, but knew would call for her.

"Good evening, Mr. Fennimore . . . how may I help you?"

"May I come inside? I just have a few routine questions about an incident I'm looking into at St. Germaine Parish." He stepped forward before his request to enter was granted. He would be the one setting the pace of conversation that night.

"This is happening all too quickly," she thought to herself. How he landed at her property so soon was an indication that something had gone awry. To have come to question her this early in the investigation was not a good omen.

"Thank you. Listen, I was looking for the Deacon Hatton. Seems he isn't around." He looked her up and down, probing her every gesture for the slightest clue. She played her hand well. Nothing in her body gave away the fact that she was several steps ahead of the detective.

"I haven't seen him, but he usually is home. How about a cup of coffee?"

Her move to deflect the conversation bought her but a moment, but not nearly enough time to prepare for the flurry of questions that followed.

"I'm just worried, an older gentleman, all alone. I've seen it before. Days go by with no one checking on them."

"I spoke with him yesterday afternoon, just to check in. He seemed fine then, he didn't let on that anything was wrong. His voice seemed strong—"

"So, you know him outside of St. Germaine?"

"Sure, he is my uncle, after all." She gave him an incredulous look, a look that insinuated this was common knowledge he should have known. The truth to the matter was quite the opposite. For years she distanced herself from the man, his reputation as an abusive alcoholic always preceding him in conversation, even years after he quit drinking. The scars of his drinking career ran so deep that they couldn't be healed. By the time he became the deacon, enough of the parish population had turned over or died off so their familial relationship had become an unknown.

"I'm a bit concerned for his safety, the house is so shuttered up . . . did he mention that he was going anywhere?" Fennimore posed the question while feigning an authentic concern for Hatton, leaning in slightly and placing his hand on hers.

"No, he didn't say. If you like, I could call."

"If you don't mind. I'd feel better myself if I could end this night not worrying about his safety."

She picked up her telephone and, again, dialed his telephone number out of pure instinct. She knew he was homebound, his car had not been roadworthy for some time; he had been relying on her for assistance with errands and such.

She waited, and dialed again, then again. She dialed a fourth time, this time watching as her fingers skipped along the keypad to verify she was dialing the correct number. Fennimore watched her with an odd curiosity. She could feel his gaze as it swathed itself about her, keeping her present in that awkward moment. Her nerves were short-circuiting, and her face had grown long with despair as she anguished to make the call. All the while a feeling was beginning to well up from deep within her. It was a feeling of utter dread, assuming only the worst of possibilities for the outcome of this encounter.

"It's busy."

"Give it five minutes and try again."

Five minutes with him. Five long minutes, alone with him, her thoughts now flying through her mind with the unabashed impulses of classical furies. Her mind didn't just race but it contorted itself into an awkward conglomeration of memories, plans, and scenarios. None of which made sense anymore. Instead, they all fell apart, evaporating into an ethereal stew of mental notes broken down into words and misfired cues that no longer added up to a single cognizant thought. All the planning, the what-ifs for this crime being discovered didn't matter. None of that prepared her mentally for dealing with this man, who, with very little effort, had all but broken her.

She dialed again, hoping to some higher power that he would answer. "Still busy," she reported through a thousand-yard stare straight through the detective. She replaced the receiver with clumsy fingers, it having slid off the base twice before she finally secured it in the cradle. She was spent and that was apparent.

"I think we should check on him," was Fennimore's stark remark to the frazzled woman. In his line of work persistence and diligence were always rewarded. This situation was no different. He could have let this interview wait another day; another day where evidence could be lost.

"Okay. I have a key, somewhere around here . . ." She fumbled through her purse, finding the key and raising it for him to see.

Fennimore offered to drive, an offer she accepted. She had been so shaken, so worried by the events, that she didn't know if her hands could be made steady enough to steer her car over to the house.

They pulled up to the house and immediately she sensed something was wrong. Her uncle was a night owl. The television would cast its glow through the small slices of open curtain and onto the front lawn late into the night, every night. But now there was nothing of the sort. Not a trace of light radiated from the interior of the home. Everything was dark as if all light within it had been snuffed out for perpetuity.

"Detective, if you don't mind . . ." She handed him the key to the house. She had a premonition not to enter first. She followed him up the fissured sidewalk, pieces of it separated and drifting off into the neglected lawn like islands, slowly retreating into the earth never to be seen again. She wished for a moment to be one of those small slabs of concrete, as insignificant to the world as they had become, and slide deep into the earth to be long forgotten.

Fennimore opened the door, his right hand groping the wall in search of a light switch. He found one and flicked it to the on position with no second thought. To his surprise and delight, he was greeted with nothing but an ordinary vision of the living room inhabited by an elderly man. Newspapers were stacked along one side of the worn sofa, on the side table by his recliner resided an ashtray with spent cigarette butts cascading over its side. The whole room was filled with the acrid aromas of stale smoke and urine. It was unpleasant, but not out of the ordinary.

He could see straight through to the rear of the house. Directly ahead of him through an arched opening were the kitchen and the rear entry to the home. He passed through the arch, the only architectural feature in this otherwise nondescript abode. He found the light switch and with a firm push of his thumb coerced the old fixture into powering the light. He surveyed the room from the archway. Again, nothing out of the ordinary here; a half-empty pot of coffee, a few dishes in the sink, several over-ripened bananas on the kitchen table swirling with fruit flies. If Hatton left, it wasn't in a hurry.

There were only two rooms left in the small, postage stamp of a bungalow: the bedroom and the bathroom. If there was an accident, it would have happened in one of those two spaces. He leaned against the archway, facing into the living room, and looked directly at Kaliczenkoff. He motioned for her to enter the bedroom, the door of which was only slightly ajar. Nothing but unspoiled darkness spilled from its interior. The room itself was so dark that even the light from the living room failed to permeate its depth.

"Please, after you," was Kaliczenkoff's response to Fennimore's motioning for her to enter the room. She too sensed that he saved these areas of the home for last, the intimacy of those two spaces befitting a tragedy more than any of the remaining square footage.

He pulled himself from the archway and passed through the terse hall that separated the bedroom from the rest of the house. The darkness of the room was quilted over by the heavy silence accompanying it. There was no odor, no movement, and no hint that he would stumble across anything out of the ordinary. There was an ordinariness to the silent darkness that calmed him, quelling any fears as he entered the room and fought through the darkness, his arms making ever widening circles as he sought out a light source and moved about to prevent himself from stumbling over anything that blocked his path.

There was no light switch, and no overhead illumination available to guide his entrance to the room. As his eyes adjusted to the darkness he began to make out the silhouette of a lampshade. Reaching across to the lamp, he fumbled over a piece of furniture that had fallen across the floor. "Damn it!" he yelled. His shin had taken the full force of the collision, rocking him back.

"Are you okay?" Kaliczenkoff called out to him.

"Fine. Thanks for asking." She sat out there, immovable. In the least she could have sought out a flashlight, he thought.

He finally came upon the lamp. Pulling its chain, a cone of light released from its aperture. Upward it shone, illuminating the presence that had connected the dots in his investigation. The rosewood crucifix was there, perfectly illuminated by the cone of dull, yellow light that made its way to the artifact before curving along the ceiling in an oblong oval. The eyes of the crucified Christ looked down on him and the overturned chair at his feet, overburdened with worn clothing that must have sent it toppling over.

Fennimore looked up at the crucifix, thankful for the relic. Without it, his investigation would be stalled in its infancy. He looked into the eyes of the man on the cross who appeared to be exchanging glances with him. But his eyes were not looking at the detective. They were distracted, looking over his shoulder. Fennimore turned, following the statuary's line of sight into the closet.

Deacon Hatton's eyes were frozen into an eternal gaze up at the crucifix, his head cocked slightly by the stiff cord holding his neck in check, his feet barely grazing the floor. His hands, folded in prayer and bound by his scapular, had become stiffened into that position, immotile with the onset of rigor mortis. The image of St. Michael the Archangel, adorning the woolen cloth of the scapular, gazed up at his cold eyes with little empathy. Heaven's vengeful protector held out his sword, stabbing at Hatton from the image, calling him out and urging him on to do it, to sin the final sin and become one of the unforgiven in the eyes of his maker. Hatton succumbed. In passing he finally humbled himself before his God, acknowledging that he was not worthy of forgiveness.

CHAPTER 20

ABSOLUTION

HATTON INSULATED ANYONE from becoming implicated in his abusive relationship with Tommy. At the scene, he scribbled a brief but telling confession: in large block letters, he inscribed "I'm sorry." Beneath the note was a manila envelope containing well over one hundred photographs of Tommy, ranging in all manners of undress to fully nude. In these photos there was no indication of the crime scene; nothing hinted at the place where these acts occurred.

Maybe it was by some act of God that Tommy made off with the one photograph that would lead to Hatton's capture. It was but a small victory, this one abuser of Tommy's tormented past meeting with his just end. Maybe it was God's way of saying, "See, I was always there, watching over you." Still, God allowed this to happen. If anything, it was just another terrible interpretation of divine intervention.

"We know the who and the where," Fennimore explained to Pekennick and Worthington the following day. "Oddly enough, Hatton wrote his farewell on the same Caldwell letterhead that was sent to you, Father."

"He was a former employee, it could be possible that he had some of that old stock on hand," was Worthington's response. "I'm sure the guys took it home all the time for their kids to use, scratch paper, whatever."

"Whatevers don't solve crimes, Worthington." Fennimore's response caused Worthington to curl his bottom lip over his upper, biting down on it to choke back any comments from escaping. "What is troubling is the letter, and why it was sent to you, Father. Clearly, Hatton committed the crime. I can only think of one scenario: someone came across this picture and rushed their judgment."

"It's been the most trying three days of my priesthood, detective. Never had I imagined I would encounter this situation—"

Fennimore cut back into the conversation, "I think someone tipped Hatton off, too. It was too clean, too neat. Only a few people knew of the direction this investigation was going."

Both men looked at the detective, growing more uncomfortable by the minute.

"Detective if you are insinuating—"

"Worthington, I'm not insinuating anything. It's a fact that this investigation was small in scope. How Hatton knew that we were on to him is . . . it's odd. That's all I'm saying. Now unless you have some guilt over this, we don't need to take it further."

They knew Fennimore let them off the hook. He knew that prosecuting the case to the full extent was useless. In the end, it would only harm the victim. Finding the witness who brought this situation to light was about as necessary as thanking the individual that warned Hatton to suicide. As far as Fennimore was concerned, the case was closed. He knew full well, anyway, that the district attorney wouldn't bother to prosecute a case where the perpetrator admitted guilt, leaving all the evidence behind before sentencing himself to death.

"I'll interview Alton Mackay. So long as he implicates no one else, case closed."

There was a brief moment of awkward silence. Pekennick and Worthington knew they escaped the prying eyes of law enforcement by chance alone.

"Hatton did you two a favor. Say a prayer over his grave for saving you both the embarrassment of trial. Good day, gentlemen."

Fennimore was brusque with them. Even though he and Pekennick had mended their relationship to a degree the previous day, he had to end the conversation on this note. Far from advancing favors, he made it perfectly clear that he was halted from going any further by the circumstance, not out of concern for their reputations.

— —

I was unaware of the circumstances that led Detective Fennimore to Hatton. By the next day, the gossip had begun and it was found out that Hatton killed himself to avoid arrest, and unfortunately, the details of his crimes were not kept confidential. Nothing was sacred in Alder Ferry, especially the drama of the events surrounding Hatton and a young boy the town had forgotten. The same young boy, if someone had taken the time, who could have been saved from this circumstance. Instead, he went on to become their gossip column, the continuing object of their ridicule.

I couldn't let myself forget how that happened. It wasn't just Hatton; he had an accomplice. The town's failing of Tommy made them an accomplice to his victimization. They just were not capable of grasping how their indifference to his situation led them as a town to the unraveling crime drama that they all fancied to gossip about over bitter coffee and stale cakes served on dull, cracked china.

The town didn't just fail Tommy. Its institutions failed him, too. All of this drama could have been avoided, and the situation long forgotten, if someone had not hidden this crime. For whatever reason, there was a cover-up, a willing accomplice after the fact that protected the sinister individual who took everything from this boy. A young and innocent boy who was nothing but endearing to anyone he met.

I knew that she knew. Nothing else could have tipped him off about the impending investigation. She would have been in that round of interviews. This was her bid to escape being questioned, and being forced to lie. It was obvious to me that Mrs. K warned Hatton. Twenty-four hours after I ran to her, pouring my trust in her, he was dead. The institutions also failed me that day, shattering any inkling of trust I could place in an adult. She was my last hope in that regard, and her actions stole that small piece of innocence from me.

She may have played the system and managed to evade detection, but she had not crossed paths with an angry teenager. A teen girl with unpredictable emotions, neglected by her parents and left to her own devices and her own wits, to navigate the rocky terrain of her world. The rocky terrain lain down by adults like Mrs. K. She was no different than any other adult who ever held a position of supposed trust in my life. She made herself available to me, and she allowed me to come close, all to protect herself.

I would have none of that. She crossed the wrong girl.

—

Father Pekennick received a second letter the Saturday of that week. This time, more care was used, giving no clues of its origination. From the school flyer sent to each parishioner, I cut out

Mrs. K's photograph and affixed it to a blank piece of white paper. Above the picture, I simply wrote, "SHE KNEW." That was all that would be needed to get the point across. Into the mail the letter went, and within a day the post office had done its duty, sending another anonymous directive across the desk of Father Pekennick.

— —

He eyed the envelope with caution. A tad gun shy, he debated whether or not to open the letter, not prepared to deal with another maelstrom, especially since the first had barely blown completely through. He remembered Tommy and thought of how he failed him. He couldn't delay opening this letter if it could help to make the situation any better. If it didn't, if instead things were made worse, he would accept that challenge, too. It was his duty, a duty he fully and faithfully accepted.

After examining the envelope, certain there were no clues on its exterior, he set about tackling its contents. He brandished his letter opener and with a long, clean slice the sealed edge was perforated with the acumen of a surgeon. It was—no, it could be—evidence he reminded himself, as he withdrew the single sheet of paper from its sheath. Tri-folded, the contents were hidden from view. He placed the lone sheet of paper on his barren desk, where it loomed large as it lay there alone, commanding all attention as if it were the only actor on stage preparing to deliver a soliloquy.

He jabbed at the letter with his opener. Its blade separated the folds, prying them from one another. With his left hand, he pulled the top fold down, his opener pinning the underlying sheet to the desk. He saw her face and the caption. Rage filled him. If she knew, if she used her authority, if she dared . . . as much as he wanted to doubt it, he couldn't. Hatton was her uncle. Hatton had the old letterhead. She, as much as anyone else, could have sent the first letter as a ploy. Somehow, she knew of the investigation and tipped off Hatton. His suicide protected her more than anyone else if the letter was true.

He looked up at the crucifix on his wall for guidance. Its likeness was the only constant in this ordeal. It was the only thing that didn't change and remained passive regardless of what it saw. Yet in it, he saw inspiration. His fears receded knowing that it was there to guide him, and to push him on to do right. He was ordained not only for himself but for the humble, the meek, those who didn't have a voice to protect themselves. He was, no he could be, a savior of sorts, if given the opportunity. This was one of those opportunities, one of those rare chances to right a wrong without placing his charge in any more danger of public humiliation.

He picked up the phone and dialed. He waited, tapping his finger on the desk with each ring. The answering machine. That would do just fine he thought, I'll leave what needs to be said for next week.

"Ms. Kaliczenkoff, it's Father Pekennick. I'll need you in my office first thing Monday morning. Thanks." He hung up the phone and went about preparing for that evening's service.

——

Ms. Kaliczenkoff sat across the room from her answering machine. She recognized the number, but it was too soon to talk to Pekennick. Everything was still too fresh in her mind, and she was too hazed by seeing her dead uncle: his tongue swollen and expelled from his mouth, and the eyes nearly squeezed from their sockets from the surge of blood pressure when the noose cinched up about his meaty neck. She couldn't, not even over the phone. But she knew she had to do this, and it had to be on her terms, not Pekennick's.

——

Pekennick returned to his preparation for the evening. Saturday evenings he offered reconciliation during the hour leading up to mass. In less than two hours his faithful could have the previous week's sins absolved, receive communion, and leave on time to see that their Saturday night would ensure another visit with their pastor in the coming week. It was a perfect agreement he had come to terms with among his faithful. He knew he could never stop the rowdy, working-class community from letting go on a Saturday night after a week of being under the thumb of their bosses and of life in general. There was no stopping them. So he offered this compromise, confession and communion, and the opportunity to stay in God's grace for a short while at least. For Pekennick it stopped the attrition of parishioners. No one wanted to attend mass hungover on a Sunday; it was easier to roll over than roll out. Eventually, they would stop coming altogether if the Saturday option were removed from the table.

This Saturday was no different. At four in the afternoon, he opened the church doors and settled himself in the confessional and waited. It began as a trickle, ramping up and then tapering off at forty-five minutes past the hour. Mass was scheduled to begin at five o'clock, a start time he was strict in maintaining. Grateful that his parishioners came on Saturday rather than skipping Sunday or leaving the parish altogether, he saw to it that their evening plans would not be altered by his failure to keep time.

He looked down at his watch. Ten minutes until the top of the hour. It had been slow that afternoon, with many families away on vacation before the new school year began. He was about to leave when the door to the booth opened to a ray of light filtering in and then becoming extinguished by the shadow of the penitent.

"Forgive me, father, for I have sinned. It has been six months since my last confession."

He recognized that voice. It was her. The bitch, she dared to come at him this way to preserve herself and protect her position. She was mocking the system, the same system she used and duped to protect the identity of a man who had done the unspeakable.

"Welcome my child. For what sins do you seek absolution this afternoon?"

There was a pause, not an awkward pause, but a pause reserved for reflection. He could feel that in the air. As angry as he was for what he perceived she had done, he still felt a small amount of compassion for her as the sinner. It was his duty. He wasn't quite certain if she was involved at all, it was only a calculated hypothesis on his part. A hypothesis that, given the circumstance, he was confident would hold weight. This would be the moment to put that hypothesis to the test.

"Father . . ."

"It's all right my child. Your sins are private here."

"Father, I lied . . . I held something back."

She was aware of what happened and she had taken the right of surprise from him by entering the confessional. But now she was forced to play according to his rules.

"Go on."

"My uncle . . ."

"Yes?"

"He . . . he took some pictures of a little boy. A boy that would eventually be my student here at the school."

"Continue."

"I was visiting him one afternoon, almost ten years ago. I walked in on him and . . ."

"And what?"

"I saw them, together, in the bedroom. They were . . ."

"They were what?" This question was less probing than it was demanding. The confession, for a moment, evolved to interrogation.

"The boy was naked. My uncle was photographing him."

"And when you saw this, my child, what did you do?"

"I left, Father. I was scared, I . . . I didn't know what to do."

"You were scared. Maybe the child was scared too?"

"I confronted my uncle the next day. I told him . . . I told him that boy was never to be in his house again. Not under any circumstance."

"And you saw that reaction as a fit response for what you witnessed?" He was pressing her with challenging questions. Through the screen dividing them, she sobbed. Still, he pushed on. If she wanted absolution, her confession would need to be near perfect. Her heart would need to bleed regret, sorrow, and true contrition.

"Looking back on it, no, Father. It was the furthest thing from what I should have done. I was scared, scared to see my uncle off to jail, his reputation—"

"Or your reputation? Instead, you sentenced your uncle to death. A sin for which he may never be absolved, his soul be damned."

"But, Father, I watched over the boy from that point on, made sure it never happened again."

"Child, can you be certain it never happened again?"

"No, Father."

"Finally an honest answer. Please, continue, and remember, the Lord above—he knows."

She didn't know how to take this. Was it a bluff? Did he know more? How? She couldn't risk holding back, for fear if she did, that he would report this confession, even though it was frowned upon by church law.

"Father, I did my best to protect the boy."

"Child, you may have protected him from future assault. But you also shielded him from the help he so obviously needed."

"Father, I'm sorry . . ."

"I do not need your apology. Please reserve that for our Heavenly Father."

"Yes, Father."

"Is there anything further, my child?"

"No, nothing else."

"Are you ready to receive your penance, so that you may be absolved of these sins?"

"Yes, Father, I am."

There was a pause. Anticipation began to fill her, sensing an end to this chapter. She turned the tables on him, she thought, seeking shelter through her faith. Knowing the priest, she was confident he would follow the strict rule of canon law. She would escape this quandary and finally be able to move on from what she had been hiding for the past decade.

"For your penance, turn in your resignation to me by nine o'clock Monday morning. Along with your resignation, you are to surrender your pension and health care package to the church."

"But Father!" She was dumbfounded. Everything she had worked for, it was now gone.

"Once your penance is complete, I will absolve you of your sins, my child."

"But Father, how do I—"

"Not all sins are equal. But all penances equal the weight of their offense to our Lord."

Her sobs grew louder, bordering on wailing. He looked at his watch, it was nearly the top of the hour, and his parishioners were waiting on him. He was angered by her selfishness, as she knew full well that the clock would dictate their session before he took to the pulpit. He was through with her and her conniving ways that nearly destroyed the very institution he worked so hard to protect and maintain.

"Now get out of my church."

CHAPTER 21

LET ME IN

I T WAS A SOMBER beginning to sophomore year of high school. While for some it marked the beginning of a high point to their life story, for me it marked the beginning of just another year until I would be able to break free of my parents. I never viewed high school as my peak. Far from it, I wouldn't have dared waste my energies peaking at a moment in time when I was still quite far from realizing my potential. The world around me reveled in its youth while I gazed into the future.

The few weeks leading up to that year of high school were anything but uneventful for me and Tommy. In a span of a few days, the town was rife with the gossip of Hatton's suicide. Those who remembered his violent past nodded in accordance to the others telling the story of him and Tommy, "I told you so," constantly rolling off their lips as if they knew what he had been up to all along. The late summer's barbecues and picnics were swallowed up by the story, enjoyed alongside charred hot dogs and hamburgers singed over charcoal swimming in lighter fluid, all offering up an aftertaste reminiscent of the town's industrial past.

Still, no one could have seen that story breaking. If I hadn't intervened, it may never have broken. In many ways, I blamed myself for the fallout, placing blame on the wrong man, assuming with incorrect fervor that another priest had violated another young boy. It wasn't a total stretch of the imagination, but it lacked foresight. In my thirst to gain retribution for Tommy's suffering, I only opened him up to more of the same. Constantly the object of hazing from peers and adults alike, those recent events made him an even greater target.

Eventually, this too would come to pass, I thought. But people in Alder Ferry didn't have short memories when it came to these things. There was little drama to distract from the performances of their own lives, their own miseries playing out day after day. This was the distraction they needed and it struck to the core of their town: the church. It was the one institution they refrained from questioning. They accepted its place in their lives out of a traditional reliance upon the religious dogma it encouraged them to practice.

The church would survive, the institution itself immortal to the acts of its followers. Without knowing the total backstory of the investigation, Alder Ferry's long-standing religious institution escaped public scrutiny. As did Caldwell. No one knew that the entire situation was precipitated by an anonymous letter sent on its letterhead from the photocopier sitting in the office of its president. Instead, people were made to pay at the expense of the reputations of the institutions. In the wake of the aftermath, Hatton was dead. His demise was not mourned by anyone. His final act, however, did preserve the integrity of the two institutions that, with irony, failed in their duties to protect Tommy.

For her part, Mrs. K was now relegated to that same legacy as her cohorts in Alder Ferry. Before the beginning of the new school year, a small luncheon was held in her honor to celebrate her years with the parish. Left out of that celebration was the fact that a third of her career was spent hiding the knowledge of a horrific crime against one of her students. Her details for retiring at what appeared to be a young age in comparison to her peers were sketchy. She hinted at traveling and seeing parts of the world about which she instructed her pupils but had not experienced herself.

How she would do that would be uncertain. She knew it was now close to impossible. She barely escaped prosecution, but at a cost that confined her to her home. Gone were her income, her pension, and her health insurance. All that remained of her worldly worth was the equity in her modest residence. She locked herself in the home that became her de facto prison. Her youthful dreams of someday escaping Alder Ferry were vanquished, and she morphed into the reclusive, aged woman we all knew from our childhood: wrinkled, gray and alone, her house in disrepair. The next generation of Alder Ferry would come to know her as the witch in the haunted house, taunting one another to stand atop her front step, tempting fate. On occasion she would humor them, appearing from behind the drawn curtains with broom in hand, her wild and unkempt hair sweeping across her face, and hiding it from view.

Those were the unintended consequences of my actions that concerned me the least. Hatton's self-destruction was a gift to humankind. As an adult, I wondered what hell was like for him, and if it compared to the hell he would have faced in the state penitentiary. Even I shuddered at that thought, not wanting to take it a step further, fearing those images becoming burned into my brief but monumental memory of that animal of a man.

The truth of the matter to be told, I did feel a bit of remorse for Mrs. K's inglorious fade from the public eye. In some ways, death would have been far easier for her. She was a vibrant, outgoing woman with a pleasant career. Instead, she suffered all alone with the regret of her past. She did prevent Hatton from harming Tommy any further. But she also kept Tommy from the support he needed to recover from the trauma of those events. Had I known her role, my actions may have been different, but I couldn't look back on what I did. All was sorted in the end, and the parties that destroyed my best friend's youth paid a hefty toll for their actions. What grief I felt for her circumstance was readily consumed by the anger-stoked fire burning inside of me to see that those traitorous adults were made to suffer.

But there were other unintended consequences of my actions, consequences that would affect me. My father eyed Tommy now with even deeper suspicion. Tommy was not just Genardo's grandson. Now he was the troubled youth, chased by demons that could also drag down his daughter. My parents had their reputations to uphold. Their daughter couldn't be seen with someone like Tommy, someone scarred so deeply that his life no longer mattered to him. Someone who they thought would be prone to lash out against all authority as a response to his troubled past.

Time was short in those few weeks to address my concerns with Tommy. He was the greatest unintended consequence of my actions, the last person I wanted to see centered in the unwitting drama I composed. He was left alone on the stage, the other players removed through the tragedy that became him. The object of contention between Hatton and Mrs. K at one time, he now was their undoing. All the while he was left alone to recover from the pain of his past as the audience looked on to see what would come next.

Fortunately, Tommy could look past these things. Maybe it was a lesson he learned from the trauma of his troubled life: better not to be seen or heard. Tommy mastered the art of disappearance; with little ease, he could melt away and go unnoticed. The very same qualities that made him a victim also served to protect him as he aged. It didn't always work, but it would allow him the time to formulate a plan to deal with the issues facing him. Regretfully this wouldn't always be the case.

I tried my best to reach Tommy before summer ended. I even offered to assist with the filing at my father's office to catch a glimpse of him. A request summarily dismissed, my father still aware of the wiles of his youth, those same wiles that led to my conception. A mistake in one blind moment of his life and my mother's life that led to the situation we all were made to deal with in our own way. Our family was a tenuous creation of circumstance. We were now a family beset with outside circumstances standing to threaten the financial successes we all enjoyed, as well as the uncanny ability to go about our lives separately while cohabitating under a solitary roof.

Any attempt to contact Tommy at Caldwell would have been for naught. My father took it upon himself to terminate his employment after the scandal with Hatton broke. Tommy was spared the humiliation of facing his co-workers and their taunts. However, he was left to deal with his grandfather, all alone, when the past events came to light. There was no refuge for the boy. At the plant, he would have at least been visible. Instead, he was forced again to disappear.

I made my way to the alders every day, hoping I would catch Tommy there. When Labor Day weekend arrived, I surrendered myself to the thought that he had already been sent to his aunt's house in the city, since school was set to begin in three days. My parents left for the weekend, rejoicing in the fact that they could leave me behind and live a life without me in tow. Coupled with the fact I had no social life, they doubled their pleasure knowing that there would be nearly no chance of teenage revelry during their absence.

— —

The Saturday morning of that weekend began like any other for me: brew the coffee, smoke a cigarette, and spend an hour on the portico gazing into the alders.

I passed the majority of that day with a book, the only companion I could always count on being there when I needed company. Reading wasn't always my favored pastime. It was an act I acquired from Tommy, seeing how it had left him the means to cope with the angst of life that always embroiled him. In many ways, I turned to reading not to escape my own problems, but to be connected with Tommy, knowing that somewhere out there he was probably doing the same. It was an act of mindfulness, an act that allowed me to take my eyes from myself for some time, and understand life through the characters living on the pages before me. It was therapeutic.

Mid-afternoon I found myself antsy and needing a distraction. I peered down the expanse of the lawn, the river sparkling, gulls dropping from the sky, dive-bombing their prey. Their calls cut through the late summer air, peeling it apart like sharp claps of thunder, the bright white flash of their underwings reflecting the sunlight back to me. Everywhere about me, life went on, except there on the portico. I rested my book on the table and pulled my knees up together under my chin. I had to move, just to feel alive again.

I struck out for the alders to stretch my legs and gain a break from the confines of the Grand Old Lady. While some people would revel in her grandeur, it often grew tiresome. It was a place definitive of lonesome, and it removed any societal aspect of living. I found our secluded hideaway with ease and slid down into its cool chamber. There was a slight chill in the air compared to the subtropical heat that grabbed hold of the weather with the might of a vice grip. I settled in to enjoy the damp, cool air, the insulation afforded by the mellow earth and massive rocks that embanked the cavern. In the distance was a growing din of activity, growing louder as the afternoon aged. At times I concerned myself with the thought that the stand itself was about to be overrun with swarms of humanity.

The picnic grove at the alder stand was chock full of locals barbecuing, drinking and otherwise laying waste to what remained of their summer. It was one of the few instances where I could remember hearing any outside sounds interfering with the quiet that defined the alders. It was unnerving. In some ways, I felt violated. The purpose of the alders, to me, was to block out life. I was angered by the distraction caused by the swarm of locals who invaded my personal space.

I had to see the train wreck of humanity that was giving rise to the commotion. Frustrated by the intrusion on my day, I made my way to the trail along the river that connected with the picnic grove to avoid being seen wandering from within the alder stand. On the expanse of lawn, children ran about, arms waving, their squeals piercing the air with obnoxious rapidity. Their parents sat in their chairs and watched, drinks in hand, not letting their refreshments stray too far. The younger crowd kept to themselves, downing beer after beer before the warm air could steal away its chill. They weren't going anywhere. No one would be in any condition to drive.

Any chance at peace that day was shot.

But it wasn't. In the corner of the parking lot, the Genardo family established itself. They sprawled out over into the lawn, claiming far more real estate than any other family. Empties littered the grass around their lawn chairs, the charcoal glowed red even in the sunshine, and they basked there indifferent to everyone else. Huddled, alone, with a beach towel over his head protecting his near ivory skin, sat Tommy with a book in hand. Distracting him from the chaos would be a chore.

I waited it out as long as I could bear.

He eventually rose up from his chair and sauntered towards the restrooms at the opposite side of the parking area. I made my way over and intercepted him, certain we were out of his family's view.

"Psst!"

His head turned, looking for the sound of the noise.

"In here."

I had locked myself in the men's restroom.

"What are you doing in there?"

"Trying to get your attention."

"Well, it worked. You'll get us both killed if we get caught."

"Better to die together than to die alone."

"Now's not the time for that." He couldn't help but chuckle under his breath, appreciating my sublime gesture given the atmosphere surrounding us.

"When they all pass out, meet me back at my place. No parents this weekend, we can talk."

"You got it. May be a little late . . ."

"I won't be going anywhere, now cover for me."

Tommy used his body to shield me from the crowd as I dashed back into the alders. We exchanged quick smiles and I parted with a happiness that showered over me and carried me home. Tommy made his way into the restroom, a pair of catkins draped over the half-spent roll of toilet paper, a memento of our chance encounter.

———

Tommy came through as usual on our agreement to meet that night. It was a bit peculiar, being that it was the first time either one of us would be invited into the other's home.

"Wow," Tommy's eyes nearly exploded from their sockets as he entered the house.

"So this is how the other half lives," was his comment to me, jesting as he poked at my side.

"Funny," was the most sarcasm I could muster in response. Even though I knew his comment was meant in fun, still I re- treated backward from him, so he could sense my discomfort.

"Sorry."

"It's all right. Let's go back to the kitchen."

We made our way through the living room, and I knew all the while Tommy's eyes were infatuated by the sights offered to him by the Grand Old Lady.

"Don't go Gatsby on me," I pulled his hand to tug him out of his moment, both of us laughing as we carried ourselves into the kitchen.

Moments like these were never easy. By design, they just couldn't be. But Tommy had a way to ease the tension, and re- lease any fears of engaging in conversation that for most people would signal doom.

"So . . . crazy times recently, huh?" It was an icebreaker about as appropriate as possible from Tommy. I could tell this would be awkward for him.

"Yeah, very crazy. Listen . . ." I reached for his hand, wanting to make contact with him to ease the weight of the conversation.

"Hey, if you think any less of me, I get it." He looked down, appearing ashamed more than anything.

"I'd never . . . you did nothing wrong. But before we get to that—" I squeezed his hands, tightening mine around his. I feared he would bolt and wanted to keep him captive to hear me through. "About the whole situation, it's my fault."

"How so?" He looked up at me, quizzing my face with his eyes.

"I found the picture in the alders. I—I sent an anonymous let- ter to Pekennick. Tommy, I am so sorry. I never meant for all this to happen . . . I just wanted to help." I started to cry, and instead of showing anger, Tommy pulled me in, hugging me close.

"Hey, look at me." He placed his hand under my chin, lifting my head to eye level, engaging me with the warm smile from the corner of his mouth that could melt glaciers.

"I appreciate your trying to help, I really do . . . no one has ever gone out on a limb for me that way. You're the only one."

"But, everyone knows, everyone—"

"It's all right, I'll get by, always do." He was right, he weathered many storms, always alone. "Bree the only difference now is that I don't have to do it alone. As long as you'll still be my friend through all this."

"Of course I will, why would you even ask?"

"Well, people think I let him do it. That I enjoyed it. But really, he was the only man in my life that ever showed me any attention. He was the only person that ever took me in when it was cold or raining . . ."

"Tommy, he took advantage of you." I was shocked by his demeanor, by the remorse he seemed to feel for Hatton, instead of anger.

"He also cared for me," his eyes wandered, the confusion of his past, how his relationships were defined early on, were now all coming to a head.

"That's fucked up and you know it. He didn't care about you. You were an easy target for that man."

"It's easy for you to say, Bree. Look at my life, my home. I had nowhere to go, nowhere."

It was true. I still couldn't understand his victim mentality, the only comparison in my mind was that he traded one abuser for another, an abuser that had a perverted penchant for worshipping his under-age body.

"It was only pictures, nothing else. Then one day, it stopped, all of a sudden. I would knock, and there would be no answer, nothing. At church, he would even avoid me after Mass when I served as an altar boy." He reflected further, his sweaty palms sliding out from mine and burrowing deep into his wavy blonde hair. "I would have never turned him in, I was more afraid of being judged by everyone around me more than anything else."

And that anything else just happened, on my watch.

"Tommy, it gets worse."

"Really? How can this get any worse?"

"Mrs. K, she knew. She knew all along, and never reported it." But looking back, on this one detail from Tommy, maybe she did help all along. Still, I could never forgive her. In the end, she prevented him from getting the help he needed. Because of her, his plight continued unnoticed.

"But she . . ." Tommy's voiced trailed off. His favorite teacher, the one adult who had never sought anything from him in return for her services, she had betrayed him. He looked defeated. Like me, he had lost all hope in the adults that portended to have our best interests in mind.

"So that's why she was let go . . ."

"That's my guess, Tommy."

We were both crying by now. The kitchen counter was the only surface that propped us up, keeping us from swimming in our tears pooling onto the floor.

"Can you do me a favor?"

"Anything, you name it."

"Next time you want to help, can you ask?"

"Sure." The mood lightened, and I knew that we were safe, that we would weather this event together, just like the others in our brief history.

"I knew my relationship with Hatton was odd, trust me. He really was the only person up until that time that . . . that took any interest in me." He was sad, and still, I could see he was struggling with the entire situation. Years of repressing the events had taken their toll. Their immediate release without warning certainly didn't help his state of mind.

"Yeah, Tommy. Like I said before, it was fucked up. I need a smoke."

"I'll take one, too."

Moving outside we left the difficult portion of our discussion behind us. Nothing more needed to be said on that topic. When it was time, he would share, or maybe write about his experiences. I would be there when he was ready if that day ever came.

"You know what's really confusing about this whole mess?"

"I'm sure plenty, but what's your angle?"

"It's, you see, pretty personal."

"Uh-huh."

"All my life, I've liked things that aren't well, manly."

"So what?"

"Well, let's see. At home, I open a book. Immediately I'm asked about the title, and told how it sounds like a 'queer' story."

I didn't quite see where he was going but followed along.

"Everyone was drinking beer and getting smashed at the park earlier. I drank my iced tea instead, not because I'm against drinking—"

"Yeah, so what?"

"They throw another bottle of iced tea at me, saying 'Here's your fag tea,' it's always 'fag this' or 'faggot that,' everything I do is about being a fag, you know?"

"I never associated reading a book or drinking tea with being a fag, Tommy."

"Neither did I. It's just . . ."

"What is it?" I was tired of him running around in circles, I just needed him to get to the point of his story.

"I don't know if I'm gay or not."

Crickets. Nothing but awkward, loud, and obnoxious crickets filled the portico. The entire evening had just been washed away by his statement. It wasn't what he said, not the revelation of his true inner self. It was the fact that he had repressed for so long his feelings about himself and questioned them, not in a matter of personal discovery, but out of fear. I was more than saddened by this. His whole identity, everything he thought about himself, he questioned. He held back from being his total self to escape persecution.

"If they knew about Hatton, I would be 'gay' to them, even though that has nothing to do with being gay." I felt for him. He couldn't express himself at all anywhere, except there with me on the portico that night.

"I didn't want them to know. I didn't want them to have that twisted justification in their minds. All I heard the past few days from my grandfather in passing was 'hey faggot,' or 'where's the fag?' Overnight my name changed to faggot."

"Fuck them, either you're gay or you're not."

"I think I am."

"Good. Otherwise, this whole situation would never have worked out." I put my hands up in the air and twirled them about us as if we were the center of a whirlwind, which in many ways we both were. He looked at me in a funny way, a bit confused but more challenged by the statement.

"Come on, you know boys and girls could never be just friends," I declared. We both tried as hard as we could, but it was no use. We broke out in uncontrollable, deep laughter that freed the soul; laughter that liberated the mind from the body.

"So, feel any different?"

"Not really . . . well . . . maybe. It feels good to finally tell someone." His face lit up again. A weight was removed from both of us. His past was no longer a dark place off limits, and our future, our friendship, was cemented. It wasn't an easy road, but we somehow managed to get to that point of mutual agreement and understanding, a place so many relationships struggle to find.

"Then we have a deal."

"Deal?" Tommy furrowed his eyebrows, wondering what terms were about to bind him.

"Yeah, you don't keep secrets from me. And I won't help unless asked." More laughter ensued, and we both knew that going forward there would be no more acting alone. We would always, when possible, strike out at life together.

CHAPTER 22

LEAP OF FAITH

I T WAS A RARE event to meet Tommy without looking over my shoulder. It was the first time we could relax and remain worriless in our time together. That evening proved to hold the warmest conversation we ever had, a conversation that completed our understanding of one another. After that night, we were no longer children. All the events we had either suffered through or witnessed had come together to create the moment of that evening. The virginity of our youth, as tainted as it was, had been sacrificed that night.

Afterward, everything would be different. The past had forced us into the situation we faced, being two young adults still living the lives of precocious teenagers, forced to combat the effects that years of abuse and neglect had upon us. It wouldn't get easier as we would come to find out, but the years had already hardened us to veteran status in the conflicts of life.

I let part of Tommy go that night. The young, innocent boy I had known and fallen in love with was gone. In his place, a more mature Tommy, free to explore who he was, appeared on the portico and vaporized into the alders, the quest for himself well underway. He stopped momentarily, turned back, and with a wave he was gone. How I loved him was without any definition. It simply was love. That night my love for him increased by bounds, and it was sickening to see him leave all alone.

I would never forget that night, the memories of our friendship becoming rooted in symbiotic fashion, like the roots of the alders. Under the earth, they intertwined, each sustaining the other. The two of us had become rooted together in much the same way. No matter what the trauma, one of us was always there to catch the other. Sometimes we missed, but we never quit on each other.

Our friendship had its cornerstone in trust, laid upon a foundation of common suffering, pointed with love.

Love. Like no other emotion I had ever known. I had thought of love, imagined how it would feel, but my love for Tommy—our love—it was nothing of the kind. It couldn't be put into words and folded into a greeting card. It lived because we allowed it to flourish and bloom. We farmed our love, cared for it, harvesting it for our well-being. At any time, we could have walked away from the pain we endured and the traumatic events we suffered through together. But we didn't, because this was love.

As he departed it occurred to me that, day or night, it made no difference: Tommy always made his way home through the alders. He could always manage to move through the trees without impediment. He was and would always be their sprite.

The next morning came with a vengeance. After Tommy left, I broke out my mother's wine to cap off the evening. It wasn't as much fun celebrating alone, but I made it work.

A pounding on the front door roused me from my sleep that morning. It wasn't an authoritative banging, but an agitated rapping that increased its intensity with each passing minute. We never had visitors, and this was a Sunday morning, on a long holiday weekend. With a begrudged attitude, I slid out of my bed and squinted through grainy eyes to see who interrupted my sleep.

I rubbed my eyes to make sure they weren't lying. The grainy sands that crusted over my eyes only forced their way in deeper, irritating the already bloodshot and light shy organs. I kept rubbing, but she was still there, now aware of my presence. She continued to bang on the door without concern, now calling out my name, "Aubrey!" with increasing amplitude.

It was Mrs. K. This was the last person I had hoped would ever come knocking on my door. I watched her through the glass windows that ran alongside the door frame. The glass distorted her figure, giving her an even more bizarre look, her appearance similar to the hybridization of a shriveled hag moving about with the energy of a chimpanzee fed a steady diet of caffeine and nicotine. She looked mad, her eyes were red and swollen. My only thought was that she had a mental break. Now here we were, all alone, in what equated to the middle of nowhere in this suburban nightmare.

"Aubrey, please, please open the door."

"Why should I?"

"It's about Tommy—"

"No apologies Mrs. K. Not today. Go away."

She stopped, frozen in her tracks. A morbid look came across her face, with a seriousness about it that caught my attention.

"I'm not here to apologize."

I considered walking away and locking her out of my mind. But I couldn't. For some reason, I felt the curious suspicion that I should trust her on this one occasion. I unlocked everything but the chain and the door creaked open several inches. For the first time since everything had gone down, we were eye to eye.

"Aubrey, I need you to come with me . . . it's Tommy . . . he's in the hospital."

"What do you mean? He was fine last night. What happened?"

"I'll explain in the car if you can trust me just this once."

My instincts were rarely wrong, and this time they told me to go. I obliged her, welcoming her into the house as I threw on some clothes. She looked like she hadn't slept in a week. Her hair was still flattened from her pillow, her make-up slung upon her face in haste, and her tears caused it to run in streaks that she just hadn't taken the time to blend back into the rest of her face. With reluctance, I threw myself into her car, and she careened down the gravel road well on our way to Mercy Medical Center in the city.

"There was an incident late last night," Mrs. K struggled to tell the story as she drove. She lacked the wherewithal to perform either task at that moment. Her driving was so erratic that I was torn between watching the road and looking at her. I feared that if I looked at her, we would also end up being carted off to the hospital. I chose to look ahead in stoic fashion, feigning indifference given our recent history.

"A jogger early this morning was heading past the picnic grove and stopped to use the water fountain. He saw something piled up by the restrooms. It was Tommy." I couldn't tell if her speech was rehearsed or not. Her delivery was devoid of emotion. She was in shock, and it gave her the bit of clarity she needed to deliver the message.

"Is he . . ." I asked and stopped. I didn't want to know the answer because it was too much to bear. Everything at that moment disappeared: my hangover, my horrible breath, and my distrust for the woman driving me to the hospital. Everything was gone because none of it mattered. Nothing mattered if I didn't have him to share these experiences with. My eyes became flooded with tears, tears that flowed uncontrolled and alone, with no sobs to announce their arrival to the world. My psyche poured out of me with those tears. No sound I could make would account for the incredible hole that had just been punched through my chest.

"He's in critical condition," she too had trouble talking in anything more than a few words at a time. "They had to induce him into a coma . . . he was beaten. Beaten bad, Aubrey,"

"I—I don't know . . . this can't be happening. I should have gone with him."

She reached down and across the console, taking my hand in hers. At that juncture, we had no past, only the present. A present that was moving in slow motion and fast forward all at once. Everything seemed slow: the car, my reaction, her words. But all the while everything was happening too fast to comprehend. I should have walked him home, or at least to the halfway point.

"No need to blame yourself for what happened," she looked over while craning her neck, giving the impression to the other drivers that she was eyeing the road rolling out before us. "If both of you had been there, there's no telling how bad it would have been."

———

We arrived at the hospital after a twenty-minute drive that seemed to take hours. The entire ordeal had already begun to age me; in that interval, I began to feel old. I braced myself for what I was about to see, not knowing what to expect. Just inside the room was my dearest friend, my true companion through life's journey, comatose.

We entered the room, shocked to find it empty. Maybe I shouldn't have been shocked, but still, I was. Tommy's bed was curtained off, preventing any view of him from the doorway. I made my way into the room and grasped the curtain by a fistful. I closed my eyes, not wanting to see what was behind that curtain, not wanting to remember him in this condition. I breathed a deep breath, exhaling slowly, the odors of disinfectants filling my nasal cavity. Like those cleaning solutions, I too was becoming barren to anything that touched me. A cold rush ran along my arm and down to my hand, causing it to jerk the curtain immediately to my right.

I still harbor guilt for the relief I felt after I opened the curtain. There he was, quiet, sleeping, at peace for once. His face bore the marks of several bruises, and his left eye was swollen shut. He seemed in good shape to me. Outwardly he was fine. But weren't we all? On the outside we shone, hardened to the world. But inside, we all hurt—Tommy even more so than the rest of us.

Mrs. K was directly behind me, her hands on my shoulders. Even though I knew she betrayed us both, her intentions were a sincere act of graceful kindness. As the tears made their way down my face, I took some comfort in her presence. I didn't know what to expect, and I was in no condition to face the unexpected alone that day. Her actions that morning healed part of the hurt she caused. Truly contrite, she sought nothing in return for her genuine act of goodwill that day.

I approached Tommy's bed with nimble steps, navigating through the tangled vines of wires and tubing emanating from nearly every part of his visible body. A breathing tube was in place, the ventilator pacing his mechanical breaths, and inflating his chest to capacity with each cycle. His chest rose and fell in time with the heart monitor that bleated out its call with a tedious duty, everyone in its presence tuning out its monotonous call. I watched as he lay there, and moved in closer.

I swept the backs of my fingers delicately across his cheek, taking care to avoid the tubes running from his nose and terminating somewhere behind his motionless head. He felt cool to the touch. I wondered if it was the room or if it was his life slowly exiting his body. My hand gently traced along his cheekbone, finding its way to his thick, blonde hair. I allowed my fingers to pull through his hair with a dainty touch, taking care not to disturb him, pulling the hair back and over his ear. I leaned in close and whispered, "Tommy, it's Bree, I'm here." As much as I hoped he would respond, there was no response. I eased away, my hand finding its way back to his cheek, which I continued to stroke, more so to console my own grief. My tears processed down my face, free-falling into the void between Tommy and me, absorbed by the hospital bedding and lost to the world forever. Every time something traumatic occurred I swore I wouldn't cry. And every time I failed in that resolve. My emotions were too raw to be tamed. To lose touch with them, I knew, would make me no different than the persons that did this to Tommy.

"Who let these two bitches in?"

I knew that voice, and I hesitated to turn and face it, the moment now flush with fear. I looked again at Tommy, and fear was no longer an option. I turned to face the man filling the doorway to the room like an ogre. Genardo. Behind him, made diminutive by his figure, was Tommy's grandmother. It was clear she had been crying. Up to that time, I didn't think it was possible for any one of them to shed a tear for the boy.

"I did, Mike. Let them be." Father Pekennick's booming voice took control of the situation. "Ladies, please come with me."

We followed the priest out into the hall, and down into a family waiting room. He poured us both a cup of stale coffee from the urn that was percolating through the previous night.

"Ms. Kaliczenkoff, I think it is best that you go. I'm certain we are both in agreement that your presence here . . . well, it complicates things, let's just say."

"Yes, Father." She hung her head, hoping for some commendation for her efforts that morning.

"I appreciate what you've done today—truly. It's just, your relationship to Hatton . . ." The priest trailed off. But it was the best he could do. No one else knew her role in Hatton's abuse of Tommy. And no one needed to know. But her relationship to Hatton, which was well known to Genardo, was a fact that could set the man off.

"Father, I agree. He's suffered enough." She slipped out the door quietly. I watched as she faded from view, her form slowly vanishing down the length of the hallway. It would be my last memory of her, our last interaction. For all that she had done, I appreciated her bowing out with grace, her concern for Tommy evident as she exited without pomp.

"Aubrey," the priest then turned his attention to me, "I know this is difficult, but I'll do my best to see that you and Alton, that your friendship . . . that it survives this awful set of circumstances."

"Father?" I questioned not to ask anything of him, but to seek his attention, almost to challenge what he had just said.

"I know what you know about Ms. Kaliczenkoff." I gulped, wondering where the conversation would take us. "She told me how close the two of you had grown, a true friendship. Tommy is going to need that to get through this more than anything else, more than modern medicine can provide, more than I can even provide. He is going to need you—he has no one else in his corner." He nodded his head in the direction of Tommy's room. I knew what he was saying. Still, I was cut down to almost nothing hearing it from this man. He was the last person I thought could understand the bond we developed. And it was all Mrs. K's doing. Her final act made possible an open expression of the relationship between Tommy and me.

"Tommy almost didn't make it, Aubrey. If you think you can handle—"

"It doesn't matter what I think I can handle, Father. I need to know—for his sake."

His eyes examined my face for any sign of panic. He took a long sip from his coffee and turned his head towards the window. "I know, seeing him in the bed, he doesn't look too bad off." He turned back towards me, motioning to the chair in the corner of the room. I sat, watching his every move, tuned into his body's language, hoping for a clue as to what was to come.

"But it was bad, really bad. I don't want to be blunt, but I can't find any way to make this come out any softer."

By now he had paced across the floor several times. I sat there quiet, attentive to him only. Nothing else interfered to distract my attention from him.

"He was raped, Aubrey."

I almost threw up when I heard those words. My hangover had just caught the best of me, and those words wrenched my stomach with such force that I could taste the bile making its way up my esophagus. The acrid taste smoldered in my mouth, leaving a flavor of burning tires that seared every taste bud, making them as numb to feeling anything as the rest of my body had become.

"They used a broken, plastic baseball bat. His insides were torn apart. He nearly died from the blood loss."

Pekennick finally stopped pacing and looked down at me. He kept his distance, not wanting to get too close. But I needed him to continue; I needed to know what was next, what Tommy needed to survive.

"Are you okay?"

"I don't know how I am." I was numb.

"He had surgery a few hours ago. He's expected to make a full recovery. It's just going to take time."

"Father, who did this?"

"We don't know. Truth is we'll probably never know."

"Father, can I . . . I need to say something."

"Yeah, whatever you need to get out."

"It was me. I sent the letter."

He looked at me. Then he broached a small smile to evade the awkwardness developing between us.

"I rushed to judgment, I am so sorry, so sorry that you had to—"

"It's all right, Aubrey. Everyone failed him, every person that could have helped him, including me. We'll let it go at that. If he were my friend, well, I'm sure I would have reacted just as you had."

He dropped down to one knee. He looked at me, and for the first time, I saw a sparkle of life behind his eyes that I failed to notice before.

"Going forward, we make everything right by him. The diocese has a fund, so the medical bills won't be an issue. He'll just need our support." He put his hands out, palms facing upward, and I placed my hands in his. "Mainly your support Aubrey . . . I'm sure there are very few adults left that he can trust."

Which was true. We were left with very little to trust, especially the institutions and people that should have had our welfare at the top of their list. I still wasn't sold on religion, but Father Pekennick at least refreshed my hope that somewhere out there, an open mind and understanding heart waited to be found.

"It's not going to be easy," he took on a bit of a more serious tone, "and remember that you didn't hear this from me: I want you to always remember to have faith, to believe in something."

I looked back at him, appreciating his perceived understanding of the challenges we faced. He rose to leave, offering one final bit of advice before we moved to say our farewells to Tommy:

"Always believe in something."

CHAPTER 23

AN OPEN WOUND

I BID FAREWELL TO Tommy at the hospital before a peculiar audience. Behind me was Father Pekennick, and along the far wall of the room were Tommy's grandparents and a smattering of their family's friends. Between those two worlds were Tommy and me. This moment reflected our lives: we stood together, alone in our separate sphere. But when I shut out the rest of the world, like I did that day, it didn't matter. What mattered most was that young man, his ravaged body near lifeless, and my role in seeing him back to health.

My farewell to Tommy that day was made easier when I tuned out everyone else. There was no reticence, no downturn in the volume of my voice. Without cue, I took Tommy's hand, taking care not to disturb the lines that surfaced from under his skin, and lowered myself to his level. I looked at his swollen eyelids, my stare penetrating the tombs they erected above his eyes, and said aloud, "I love you, Tommy." The words came on their own, no pretense paving their way. Off my tongue they rolled, with the gentle projection that I hoped would penetrate the fog enshrouding his senses.

The Genardo family was as sterile as the hospital room. My goodbye to Tommy caught them off guard, flooring them all. How often had they heard those words? By the looks of their perplexed faces, I knew it was seldom. I could see they were struggling to translate those three little words, spoken in a tongue foreign to them, struggling to place them into a syntax they could comprehend.

I took one long, last look at Tommy before leaving. As my head rose, the blank faces of the Genardo contingency caught my attention. I just rocked their world, usurping what power they may have had over their very own flesh and blood. I vowed not to let

Tommy down, not to allow them the opportunity to jeopardize his recovery. I looked each one of them in the eye, fearless at that juncture, made so by my concern for Tommy. It was one of those rare nothing to lose moments that strikes at the heart of the opponent, your need to win stronger than their desire to fight. It was a cavalier display of fearless resolve.

Father Pekennick was at the door, and the priest put his arm around my shoulder as he escorted me from the hospital. I could tell the past two weeks aged him, his face worn from a lack of sleep, coupled now with the guilt he felt for Tommy. Of all the people in that town, he alone rose to the occasion. To my surprise, he became the one person that could understand our friendship and its rarity in comparison to any other relationship he had ever understood. It wasn't the ostensible avant-garde teacher that became our champion. Instead, it was this stoic Catholic priest. A man who challenged my questioning of authority and my understanding of religion, through his understanding of Tommy and me. He was the man who taught me that faith and religion need not coexist to be viable. To the contrary, he proved to me that only faith could exist independently. Everything else was dependent upon it.

I was grounded by the entire experience at the hospital. It caused me to become numb to my surroundings. At the same time, my eyes were opened to this man beside me, the priest who had gone far out of his way to help Tommy, and to support our friendship. It was a challenging day on so many levels. But each layer only became complementary to the next, each experience building upon my understanding of not just this situation, but preparing my journey into the world outside of Alder Ferry.

I came to as we pulled into my driveway, releasing the seat belt while the car decelerated and coasted to the front entrance, cloaked by a small cloud of dust. Not many words needed to be spoken. The events of that day had done all the speaking, clarifying all the characters cast in this drama where I now assumed the lead role. Instead of even attempting to engage in conversation before I departed his car, Father Pekennick left me with these parting words: "I don't care what you believe in, but whatever it is, don't ever lose faith in it."

--

Alone again. Less than twenty-four hours after our experience on the portico, we were separated once more. For the foreseeable future, it would be that way. Tommy was incommunicado and I was left with no support system, no one to whom I could express myself. It was tiring, always ending up there alone. I looked around and thought maybe I wasn't so alone. There was something that would listen, that could hear and understand me. The alders. They always listened.

Regret was my only companion that lonely afternoon. Regret for the letters to Father Pekennick and for allowing Tommy to go home the previous night unescorted. My actions caused the sequence of circumstances leading up to Tommy's rape. Hatton's actions didn't matter. It was the knowledge of his actions that mattered. It was inconsequential as to how altruistic my intentions were. It could have been argued that Mrs. K's intentions were altruistic. But their net result spoke of the true impact they had. My intentions didn't matter; they didn't cause this situation. My actions bore all the blame for the continued suffering poured upon Tommy.

Regret was a pitiful companion. I struck out to the alders, to be there with the essence of Tommy, to not be alone in the only strange way I knew. I hoped the trees would listen to me as they always did, for they were just as alive and feeling as I was. The catkins danced about the branches, reflecting my mood, absorbing the chills that careened along the length of my spine each time I thought of what happened to Tommy. And each time I thought of it, I grew only angrier, sadder, the two emotions feeding off each other, fueling the acceleration of their combustion.

I was at our home in the alders, our respite from the world where we had always met. The night before I watched Tommy disappear into the embrace of these very trees. Safe. In here he would have been safe. But the alders, they let him leave, allowing him to cross the threshold into the human realm, where he was vulnerable. In my fragile mood, I blamed the trees for letting Tommy down as much as I had. They shared in the blame for his suffering the previous night.

Outside the alders, he was an easy target for the predators that took it upon themselves to brutally violate his body. The manner of their assault on him defined the madness of the human condition; by their actions, we were all made less human. We were no better than any other creature walking the earth. No different except that we were quite content in the willingness to use our intellect to inflict unmentionable physical agony upon another human being for the sheer pleasure of it. As much as I considered myself above the wretches that did this to Tommy, I would certainly take as much pleasure in exacting an equally cruel torment against them if given the opportunity.

My head spun, or so I thought. Maybe the world was spinning, and I was locked into this position, stilled by the anger and depression fueling my gathering rage. Everything was quiet, yet the beating of my heart was deafening. Outside of me, all was still and calm. But within was a torrent that drowned out all restraint, stifling my own conscience.

I entered the cavern and ransacked the entire chamber in my rage. Nothing settled me, there was nothing that I could throw or break that would take away the pain and anger consuming me. Those emotions owned me, and I lost control over them as I ripped the hammock from its anchors in the stone. I sent Tommy's precious library to the ground and watched as his notebook flew, fluttering through the air like a wounded bird, its pages torn by the current of wind caught up in it like a sail.

The notebook came to rest in a dark corner opposite the entrance. Its marbled cardboard cover had become creased, causing it to expose the delicate pages within to the rage I threw about with reckless inconsideration. Tommy's handwriting showed itself to me. I fell to my knees wailing, having taken a very secret and intimate part of him and violated it. The open notebook bared his soul to me, and in my rage, I tore into his soul like those animals who had torn into his body. His precious, well-crafted words lay there in the dirt, their pages tattered and unkempt. I broke down into uncontrollable tears, pounding my fists into the ground, my head bowed over and now kissing the earth. My tears and snot congealed in the dirt, caking upon my face, and crusting over my eyes and lips. I choked on it. It was taken in with each whimpering, uncontrolled sob, passing into the back of my throat where it caused a gag reflex so severe that I choked on my own saliva.

I picked up the notebook and cradled it. I cradled it like I would have cradled Tommy if they would have let me earlier that day. I caressed the cover of the notebook, smoothing it over, ironing out the crease with my palm and setting it back in place. The tattered pages were another story, they were ruffled and torn, intermingled, each requiring individual attention to separate it from the masses and allow it to settle back naturally into its comb. Just like Tommy, the notebook would never be the same.

No matter how hard I tried I would never be able to fix either one of them.

I would never be able to fix him. Never. What was done to him, past and present, could never be repaired. They broke him, and by extension, broke me. I held the notebook tightly to my chest, now its protector, and rose to my feet. The tears receded, my brows furrowed, and my fists clenched. Sadness again was overwhelmed by anger. The anger came over me in waves, each one cresting higher, the surge of the storm increasing with rapid accession, building upon the height of each preceding wave. I looked about and found the hatchet used by Tommy to cut down limbs for the occasional fire we would build. It glinted in the lowering sun, calling to me. Its edge seemed to catch the rays of sunlight with special attention, multiplying them, the beams captivating me, calling me towards the source of their gathering power.

I reached down to the hatchet, its wood handle worn and splintered. I could feel the heft of its steel, and the weight of it tugging at my arm. I squeezed the handle and could feel the wood lose part of itself to me, small shards of it working their way under my skin. Like everything and everyone else, they were under my skin, driving me to near madness, the pain at times becoming pleasurable. I relaxed my grip and opened my palm to my eyes. It had become reddened with the blood of numerous, minuscule wounds caused by the old tool's weathered facade. I tightened my grip and stormed outside.

I let out a shriek that I never considered myself capable of producing. A shriek so primal, so shrill, that it would send hounds running for cover. I looked skyward screaming out, "Why?" repeatedly, waiting for an answer. None would come. I gazed up only to see the retreating sunlight filtering through the canopy of trees in shimmering waves that captured each piece of dust in the atmosphere, freezing them in time. I hollered out over and over, at the top of my lungs, asking for answers. Still, none came.

I raised my arms high above my head, the steel of the hatchet now glinting in the rays of sunlight. It refracted the light like a mirror, sending rays to the trunks of the trees and to the forest floor. I was enraged. Nothing made sense then and there, and nothing mattered that was worth mattering. I raised the hatchet high above me in my right hand, my left pulling at my hair, tilting my head back, as my crazed eyes streamed with a wild glower to the heavens. The rays of light caught the steel again, the mirrored polish of its edge casting multiple refracted shards of light across the forest. I chased each, swinging at them with reckless abandon. With each swing I missed. They seemed to anticipate my every move to evade the blade's fury. I let out a cry, pouring all my energy into my arms, feeling the adrenaline course into them, giving them a strength that was god-like. This time I did not miss. I caught the sprite of sunlight dead on. With a dulled thump, the hatchet buried itself deep in its prey.

So good. That was how it felt. It felt so good to sink that hatchet into the flesh of something else that could feel pain. I hoped it hurt as awful as I did. I looked down at the hatchet buried into the hide of an alder. I pulled, angling my arms upward to release the blade from the hold of the fleshy interior of the tree. I swung again, and again. With each swing I burrowed deeper, exacting a gash along the tree that would have surely been mortal. As the pulpy interior became exposed to the air, its flesh-hued to a rich shade of red. The alder was bleeding. I caused this mystic being to bleed.

In my rage, I struck out at the one thing that mattered in a world where nothing seemed to matter. The alder was there that day to absorb my rage, my sorrow, and my pain. It sacrificed itself so I could heal. Still, I was aghast at what I had done. The wound I inflicted grew an even deeper, crimson red, a shade matching my anger. My screams subsided, my arms dropped to my sides, exhausted and spoiled. The hatchet worked itself loose from my weakening grip and fell to the forest floor. The splinters of the alder crusted upon its edge had also grown red, staining it with evidence of the brutality I was guilty of inflicting upon the harmless tree. A tree as harmless as Tommy, but nevertheless an easy target, an easy way to let out my frustrations without any fear of retribution.

I ran my fingers along the gash in the trunk. Its woody interior was soft and malleable, fleshy almost. I could feel the electricity of the earth passing through its trunk, like nerve impulses, trying to call my attention to something greater than me. My hand on the trunk, I looked around. Quiet. Not a leaf stirred in the forest. There was a reverence in that moment of understanding, in the realization that the tree took it upon itself to release me from my angst.

Still, I was saddened by what I had done. This wouldn't bring Tommy back. It wouldn't erase all that happened. Instead, a gaping wound was left, bearing the heart of this magnificent deni-zen of the stand to the elements. For years this majestic tree had withstood the very same elements that now had an entry point to its lifeblood that flowed openly and glowed red as the setting sun.

I pulled my fingers from the wound and wrapped my arms around the rugged trunk. "I'm sorry," the words rolled off my tongue in a velvet whisper. Over and over, I muttered those words, as delicate and true tears of sorrow made the long walk down my face to nourish the ground below me. It was a true apology to the tree and a true form of sincere appreciation for what it had done. It had taken the raw emotion from me and turned it into this, a good cry that cleansed my soul and prepared me to go back out into the world. Back out there, to see Tommy back to health.

My arms closed around the tree and I faded off to sleep, worn from the emotion of that day.

CHAPTER 24

EASIER SAID THAN DONE

"THE BEAUTY OF it is, I get to read *The Catcher in the Rye.*"

Tommy always saw the positive, but the negatives always haunted him. They drove him to become the young man lying there before me in the hospital bed. Still the ever-Aquarian, he was optimistic in his chances. He was a survivor. Even this tribulation he would not only survive but take from it whatever he could to improve his condition. These were the moments I always reflected upon. No matter what life threw at me, it would never be as difficult as the circumstances Tommy weathered. He suffered them with a dignity that was nothing short of in-spirational. When my circumstances seemed daunting, I would always think of Tommy, and how he would push through the pain with passion, hoping to further a greater good in his life.

"What?" I shouldn't have questioned him, thinking he was just delirious. But I couldn't see what the reference to the book had to do with his stay at the hospital.

"The book, it's still banned in Catholic high schools. At least it is in mine. The principal removed it from the reading list. But my tutor isn't aware of that." Tommy smiled his wry grin, knowing he bucked the system, a small victory in comparison to what he had just been through.

I looked at him and responded, teasing him, "I read it last year in English class. I never knew the book was still so . . . provocative."

"To the Catholics, it must be. Nineteen hundred and fucking ninety-one and they still think we all live under rocks."

We both shared a laugh. If anything, it was a great segue into the conversation we needed to have.

"Tommy . . ."

He looked up at me, knowing the conversation would take a turn away from the lighthearted.

"Yeah?"

"About that night. I need to know—do you remember what happened?"

"Well, all I remember is leaving your house. I'm glad I don't remember it at all. I shudder when I think of it, I wonder why I'm here, why they left me alive. I should've been dead."

A tear welled up behind his right eye, then his left. They were followed by another, and then another, the next in line succeeding its predecessor with rapidity. Soon the tears flowed freely down his face and mine. There were no sobs from him. The tears were flushed with pain, the shock of survival still overpowering his grief. They flowed unabashed, each one carrying a part of him with it. One by one each of those tears, over the course of that year, would slowly erode the pain of that incident. It would never totally be gone but would decay into a more manageable hill to climb.

"But you're not dead. You're still here, and so am I." He slid his hand into mine, and I wiped away his tears with the gritty hospital tissues, which were more a close relative to cardboard than tissue paper.

"Bree it's just that, I don't know anymore. I don't know if I should go on."

"What are you talking about?"

"Every time I seem to make a little progress, something happens."

"Well, I hope you can see this more of the aberration than the norm."

"Really? Why did they do this to me? No one knows what you know about me." It was true. No one knew at all. I had my suspicions about his sexuality all along, but he didn't bare that fact to me until an hour or so before the attack.

"Why did they rape you? I can't answer that. They're sick. If you're thinking that they should have finished you off, I get it. But they didn't and—"

"And now I have to deal with it. Deal with the bloody shits, the three inches of colon that were removed. Sitting on this goddamned balloon because my ass can't handle the pressure of sitting."

"At least you don't have to shit in a bag. At least you'll recover fully. Rising like the Phoenix from the ashes, that's what you are doing. So, fuck them. Don't quit on me now."

He looked defeated. He didn't have to feel that way. If he only could accept that his survival and success would be the greatest blow to them, he would win. It was an easy thought for me in retrospect, standing there above his hospital bed.

"They never caught them, did they?"

"No, Tommy. And you don't remember the attack, so, unless they feel guilty about what they did . . ."

"Yeah right. But then what? Eventually, I have to leave this place. I'll be back out there with them. Everyone is out there, waiting to pounce. I don't feel safe out there."

"We just have to weather it a couple more years until college. You're not alone. I've been here the entire time you've been in the hospital, and I'm not leaving your side. Not now, not ever. Don't you forget that."

He squeezed my hand. I knew we had an understanding.

"I never will, Bree."

I leaned in close to him, and whispered: "Just remember Tommy, I love you." I drew out the word love, allowing it to linger in the air as it rolled off my tongue and melted into the "you" that closed the sentence.

"I love you, too. I should've said it before, but just accepted it. I accepted that you loved me. No one else ever said that to me before . . ."

"Well, now it's done." The tears were now happy, almost celebratory, the awkwardness of the simple "I love you" having passed. It wasn't awkward because either one of us were afraid to say it—we weren't romantically involved. This was far deeper than that. We were two young adults never told that they were loved. Never told someone felt about them the way they felt about each other. But somehow, we figured it out. It was an innate human need to be accepted and to be loved, and we never had that until we found each other. Simply put, it was awkward expressing a feeling, an emotion, that was never demonstrated to us. We reconciled that failing of our families. We would not be like them. We had lived to learn how to love.

"Now back to the book. Let me remind you: you are no Holden Caulfield!"

And so it went, through our daily meetings at the hospital, nurturing our friendship and love. All the while, our families grew to despise us even more. Our relationship did not fit into the struggle between the two opposing worlds from which we hailed. The struggle between those two worlds defined them, and without it they were nothing. It was a negative synergy that enabled the continuous looping of a social cycle regardless of the players cast to its stage. We threatened that existence.

CHAPTER 25

MEMORIES

A S MUCH AS I loved Tommy and cherished our time together, the first half of sophomore year killed a part of me. For those four months, the hospital stood in place for the alder stand. That year began with me, every day after school, completing my homework beside Tommy's bed. When Tommy was brought out of the coma, we were right where we left off that fateful night on the portico. Thankfully his memory went blank after leaving my house that evening. For Tommy to remember the rape would be unimaginable. For this reason, I felt an odd and calming sense of gratitude that he had been induced into the coma.

At the urging of Father Pekennick, the diocese hired a tutor while Tommy was in the hospital. It was the same tutor that unwittingly included *The Catcher in the Rye* as part of the lesson plan. I sensed that Tommy had something to do with this, but the boy earned a little something for what he had been through. The kindness of the old priest served Tommy in many ways, allowing him to continue his studies and graduate on time. By graduating on time, Tommy would be spared any more time in that town than would be necessary.

Tommy's body amazed me. He rebounded with far greater resilience than I could have imagined was possible given his injuries. His body was a willing participant to the scalpel, and with each surgery, he became physically stronger. It was a struggle for him, and painful for me to witness, the pain always evident on his face, but seldom did a complaint cross his lips. As those months wore on his repaired colon adjusted to digesting solid foods and the bloody, strained stools subsided, fading from memory with the elapse of time.

The hospital became his sanctuary. For once he was at ease during all hours. This was what I cherished most of his recovery:

the peace he experienced there in his hospital room. His stay there guaranteed that he was free from harassment by his grandfather and the scrutinizing, ogling eyes of society. There he was finally free to breathe and live without fear. His creativity and intellect flourished in that environment: he was free to write unfettered, to draw upon his past experiences and reflect on them without looking over his shoulder.

After his discharge, Father Pekennick saw to it that he was kept safe when he returned to school. But this was only part of each day. It wasn't enough, there would always be the fear that it could, that it would happen, again. Tommy could never feel safe again, knowing his attackers remained free, always lurking in the shadows of his fear to finish the deed they began. Even though I swore to stand by his side when I first saw him in the hospital, I could never take this fear from him. His feelings were justified, and as I assumed the role of his protector it pained me to see him carry on through life crippled by the fear haunting him after the attack.

Which is why for me, senior year could not arrive soon enough. I had grown weary of the drama that accompanied living in Alder Ferry. I dreamed to escape the place, to relocate under the guise of higher education, and to allow my relationship with Tommy—with anyone for that matter—to grow and be enjoyed without fearing reprisal. Staying put was not an option for me, or for Tommy. To survive we would need to escape, and education appeared the most likely route.

All that time spent with Tommy did more than build upon the foundation of our relationship. Through him, I acquired an appreciation for literature I never imagined possible. From the boy in the trees I was introduced, one by one, to a whole new world that manifested itself on the pages before me, and was brought to vivid life only by imagination. No one could take that away from me. Only I could deny myself that pleasure. The escape afforded through the stories I immersed myself in over the years, at Tommy's urging, ensured I always had a companion in even my loneliest hours. I have only Tommy to thank for that, for setting me on the journey that led me to my present set of grateful circumstances.

— —

It was December of senior year. Christmas break was closing in on a week, and we met again in the alders. The holidays were hard for both of us. Tommy's excuse for a family would spend the day drunk, arguments brewing to brawls that spilled out onto the street. More liquor flowed to lick the wounds, and eventually, a black-out ensued for the revelers. At an early age, holidays for Tommy meant stepping over their slumped bodies, taking care not to disturb them, lest he become the target of their rage.

For me, the holidays were plain cold. The chill of my parents grew icier with each year. As I aged they drifted further from each other, and from me. Not to say that they took an interest in me as a child, but during the holiday seasons of my early youth they at least feigned to care. When I had caught on to the ruse of Santa Claus at an earlier than expected age, they became ecstatic. No more pomp and circumstance. Gifts were simply left to be opened, and each of my parents retreated to celebrate in their own way. My mother would become drunk and bitter in the kitchen as my father gnawed a cigar over a tumbler of bourbon in his study. Dinner was always late, what part of it survived their feud.

It was a cold December afternoon. The sky had that omnipotent gray color indicative of the time of year. It was bitter cold. The air so frozen that it had heft and was weighty. In some ways, the cold air that day embodied the dank moods of Christmas's past we had both suffered through. The burden of enduring the holiday was not much different than the burden of finding the perfect gift, as we were expected to fall in line with the tone of the holiday set by our families. This was meant to ensure that we would take no pleasure in what was touted to be the happiest time of year.

I sat under that cold, gray December sky, cigarette in hand, pulling deep draws on it to ward off the chill. Each breath only amplified the sharpness of the air, the smoke streaming up in a stiff column from the stick of tobacco, prisoner to the wintry grip, as its particles became trapped in its icy vice. Nothing escaped the cold. It was everywhere and always found your weakness. It was unrelenting and unforgiving in its advances. Maybe that's why I came to love it so.

A rustle through the fallen leaves stirred me back to attention. I dropped the cigarette, crushing it into the earth as I turned. It wasn't Tommy, but instead a snowy, white owl. I had never seen anything so white, and so magnificent. All I could do was stare back. The air had frozen my joints and the righteous bird locked me into place with its eyes focused on me like lasers. Just as soon as it landed, it took to the air again. Up into the alders, it soared, its white coat vanquished by the gray December sky.

"Hey."

I jumped out of my skin, turning to face Tommy.

"Don't do that!" I swatted at him, giving his shoulder a playful push that threw him off balance.

"Wow, sorry to interfere with your moment." He laughed it off and took a knee in the leaves beside me. "So, what's up?"

"It's cold in here. Let's head out to get some coffee or something." After my encounter with the owl, I was keen on moving our conversation elsewhere. I didn't feel threatened but wanted to distance myself from the alders. Holding a conversation anywhere else always proved difficult, but then and there I knew we had to move on, at least on that morning. Tommy looked at me with an air of confusion, but nodded his head and shrugged his shoulders in agreement. We wandered our way through the alders to the parking lot, the scene of incredible trauma in our lives only two years prior.

"Tommy, I have some news."

He looked at me. I looked up at him. At that moment I knew why I moved us out of the alders. That place was special and healing, and the news I was about to drop would break Tommy's heart. I looked up towards the sky and nodded thanks to the owl for moving the conversation away from a location that had only hosted beautiful memories for us.

"What is it?" He looked away from me, not wanting to make eye contact.

"I've been accepted to the state university. I leave next August, after graduation." It was spoken, out there to be chewed, digested, and spit out. Tommy's bottom lip burrowed under his upper lip, biting his tongue and fighting back the emotion he felt.

"Well, congratulations are in order!" He held out his arms and took me in them, squeezing the life from me. I could feel his joy for me fighting against the pain of my departure. It was a battle that he didn't want to fight, but one that had to be fought. It wasn't his place to let me go. But it was his place to let go of that piece of himself that wanted me there all the time, by his side, so that the other piece of him, that piece that ached to see me succeed in leaving Alder Ferry, could shine through.

"Tommy, I couldn't have done this without you—you need to know that. Everything here, going off to study literature—I learned all these things from you. You instilled this passion in me." I caught him looking down, his head turned away, then turned back to me, his saddened eyes gazing into mine. His eyes were glassing over, the cold air crystallizing his sorrow before it could race down the length of his angular face.

"Bree, I am so happy for you. I hope you know that. I'm just going to miss you, miss this." He waved towards the alders, and towards me. Placing his hands on my shoulders, he continued, "But I know that you need to leave, we both eventually need to break free from here. Maybe it's just that, I don't see it happening for me. But I don't want that to take away from this moment for you at all."

"Tommy, you deserve this too. More than me." I took his chin in my hand and lifted it up so his eyes squared off against my face. "Everything that I will be studying, I have to work at. But for you . . . for you it comes so natural, there's no effort in putting a pen to paper, in reading a book in one sitting."

"Yeah, well, I just don't see that break happening for me."

"Promise me that you won't quit trying."

His eyes squinted. "I don't have the resources you do."

"You got me there. Touché."

It wasn't fair. He had an extraordinary gift that remained unrecognized. His family, his teachers, the entire system of his life failed to recognize his talent. His was an amazing potential that he rightfully feared would go unrecognized.

"I'm still going to need you to edit my papers until you get in somewhere. So, don't think you're getting off too easy." We both swallowed deep, cold breaths of air that chilled our bodies and stirred our minds. There was nothing wrong with my leaving, but there was sadness in Tommy's staying on until he could manage to find his way out. We finally relaxed our bodies, smiling at each other and swinging our arms as we walked hand-in-hand, two people obviously in love with each other. A love incomprehensible to most people we encountered.

"I have one other request." Tommy's eyebrows lifted upward as his eyes rolled back in contemplation of my next proposition.

"Careful now, you've been asking a bit much from me." I caught his smile forming in the corner of his mouth.

"You still owe me for playing nurse." I teased him with my eyes and turned my head with a slight inclination away from him, nodding with a playful smile that would have sent any other boy running. "Keep prom season open, you're all mine."

We both burst out into a deep laugh. It was a laugh that shook the ground and would make other people uncomfortable in its genuine show of emotion. It was a laugh reserved for the privacy of the home, not the public's scrutiny. Standing there in the gravel parking lot we had forgotten our surroundings. We weren't alone, the morning dog walkers and joggers still strode by, glimpsing at us as they passed, pretending not to see us standing there. It was like life: people were always around, but always blocked each other out for fear of engagement.

"Excuse me, folks?"

The couple stopped in their tracks, stiffened by my plea to them. It was almost rude, I thought. No, it wasn't rude. Just out of the ordinary. It was sad to note that approaching another human being had become out of the ordinary.

I fumbled through my pocket for the camera that was my companion for the previous three months, co-conspirator to my senior year photography elective. The camera proved that my eye was lacking any artistic vision. Any hope for me would rest upon placing words, one after another with deliberate thought, onto paper.

"Excuse me, can you take our picture?" I waved furiously at the couple. I must have seemed mad to them, but I didn't care. There were no pictures at all of me and Tommy. The middle-aged man looked at his wife and shrugged, handing off the leashed collie to her. I clapped my hands and skipped forward in small steps with glee as he broke off their walk and made his way toward us.

"Thank you so much!" I pushed the weathered thirty-five-millimeter camera forward to him, almost throwing it in my excitement. He reached outward just in time to keep the camera from being sent to the ground in the happy commotion I was causing.

"Not a problem, young lady. Now if you two could, yeah that's it. I want to have the trees in the frame behind you." We slid in close to each other. I had never been held that close by anyone. Even in our darkest moments, we had never been so close. Maybe it was because we knew that there was an end in sight, with our troubled teen years finally on the wane. Maybe it was because we never had the opportunity to be photographed. Whatever the reasons, they all coincided that day, at that moment, in a harmonious union between our bodies, huddled together to stay warm, to remember the past, and to forever frame our love for one another in that photograph. I leaned in close to Tommy, my right cheek tight to the lapel of his pea coat as he turned toward me. I was elevated to the tips of my toes, my arms wrapped around him as we focused our bodies on each other and our eyes on the camera. For a moment, all was right in our world.

"Henry!"

Shattered. That moment was ended by the impatient wife on the other end of this marquis event. It didn't last as long as I hoped. Moments like that never did. That day I learned to always be in the moment and appreciate it for what it was, for the simple reason that moments like those are meant to go the way of the wind and be remembered fondly for the brief bridge to perfection they bring. Memories, they can be like the wind; they are fleeting, captured but for a moment in the sails of life's memories.

"Coming! I'm so sorry, I only snapped one shot, hope it turns out for you."

I peeled myself from Tommy with reluctance, reached out, and accepted my camera back from him. I thanked him, dejected, fearing the shot was ruined.

Tommy took my hand and spun me around back to him. "It's all right. We'll always have the memory."

CHAPTER 26

LAST DANCE

B Y THE TIME PROM season sprung we had tired of hiding our relationship from the outside world. If anything, hiding it only weakened us, allowing the world to divide and conquer the small piece of the universe we claimed for ourselves. We didn't flaunt our time together, and the alders remained our place to meet without any outside interference. I always feared for Tommy's safety after his attack. If anything, being out in the open for all to see quelled my fears somewhat, reasoning that being together in full public view made it more difficult to target either one of us.

Prom night was the second night Tommy was invited onto my parents' property, although it was only the first instance of which they were aware. He never made it across the front porch, where we stopped for the obligatory photographs that my mother had developed a peculiar interest in taking. I sensed a sadness in her, not knowing if it was for me, or her own situation. I wasn't the daughter she wanted or dreamed of, but then and there a bit of clarity struck her as I stood in my dress, gazing into the depths of Tommy's deep blue eyes as he pinned the corsage above my left breast.

Just inside the door sat my father, bourbon in hand, clenched fist strangling his cigar. He sat in the shadow cast down the hall by the porch roof, his silhouette haunting the moment, the scent of his cigar lingering in the air like a ghost yet to be exorcised from this plane of existence. His threat was real, and with each drink his inhibitions released, his anger overwhelming his senses. My mother knew how to deal with his temperament, but Tommy and I were no match for the man in that condition. With no hesitation, we made our exit via Tommy's battered Dodge sedan. I looked back through the dust cloud churned up by the four wheels and saw my mother watching, one hand up, sending us off. I blinked, then shook it off. If she felt guilt, it was all hers to feel. I wasn't about to allow it to hamper our evening.

Tommy's car waited patiently behind the rented limousines escorting the scores of couples to Alder Ferry High School's gymnasium. It set us apart from the others, being in a vehicle underscoring the indulgence of the evening. But it was also refreshing, knowing that most of my classmates would remain here after graduation, their next and last limousine ride to be on their wedding days. I was more than glad to bank my ride for a later date, and for a moment of magnitude in my life.

Why we decided to do this I couldn't say. We were the last to adhere to tradition, the first to steer from its tentacles. Still there we were, waiting with anxious patience to partake in the classic American coming of age tradition we were made to believe was a rite of passage not to be eschewed. We sat there in the car, watching the limousines make their rounds, dropping off couple by couple who strolled along the plastic red runner ushering them into the gymnasium turned dance hall.

"You ready for this?"

Tommy nodded and reached under his seat. "Yeah, just need a little encouragement first."

It would be his first night in a crowd since the attack. The bottle swallowed his nervousness. Not a drop of sweat appeared on his brow, his hands were warm and dry, and he was calm.

"How much have you had?" I pulled the bottle of Irish whiskey from him, swirling it in front of him.

"Just enough."

"I don't drink this stuff."

"There's a cooler behind your seat with a few beers."

"Bottles, Tommy you shouldn't have!"

"It's a special occasion, canned beer wouldn't do." He leaned in close to me, our foreheads touching, our eyes spaced just far enough to catch one another smiling out of pure happiness. That night was more than a prom. It was a statement, our coming out in public as a couple, even though we were far from a couple in the traditional meaning of the word.

Tommy strolled around to my side of the car, opened the door, took me by the hand, and asked, "Shall we?"

I giggled through my response, "Let's get this over with." He saw the humor in my voice, and we pointed ourselves to the gymnasium entrance. Eyes were on us the moment I stepped out of the car. To call us an odd couple was a complete misunderstanding. Tragedy would have been a more proper description. Everything in our lives: family, school, and society, they all aligned against us. We simply were not meant to be. We carried on our rebellious march across the parking lot to everyone's disbelief.

"I haven't been in here since I was a kid," Tommy remarked. "It hasn't changed a bit. My dad would probably recognize the place if he were alive."

"Let's go, this way." I pointed to an empty table to the right of the oversized speakers flanking the band platform in the front of the room. Everything was off, like any low-budget high school production. No matter where one sat, conversation consisted of yelling at the person next to you. The gym teacher was playing the part of disc jockey, the musical selections coming from his personal library. Everything that blared through the speakers was as dated as he.

Halfway through our plates of tepid roast beef and pasty mash, it happened.

"Come on. Dance with me, Tommy."

He had no choice. I stole his hand and he trailed behind me as his napkin fell from his lap and floated to the floor. The speakers no longer blared with impudence. There was now a softness to them, a reverence to the gentle flow of music emanating from them. The Beatles' "Something" filled the room. I fell into Tommy's arms, swaying to the gentle riffs that kept us in perfect tune to one another.

"I guess this is our song," Tommy whispered into my ear. I squeezed him closer to me, laying my head on his chest. I looked up at him in approval, and with a gentle crescent of my lips smiled to him. The words of the song were sublime, catching every emotion I felt for that boy turned man. I prayed the song not to end, then cursed it for its brevity. But it was perfect for us and that occasion. We lingered on the corner of the dance floor after the song concluded, basking in joyful ignorance to everything going on about us.

"Let's get out of here." Tommy nodded his agreement to my order. Not even halfway into the evening, we were set to leave. That moment on the dance floor was a special moment that could not be matched if we stayed. Rather than spoil its memory, we left.

"Where to?"

I looked at him. "The alders, of course."

"Right on." He steered the car from the lot as I hopped into the back seat to change.

"No peeking, mister."

"You have no worries there, we've had this conversation, remember?" I caught him smiling in the rearview mirror before he turned his eyes away. The car crept along the gravel road, groping in the dark to the parking lot at the alder stand. We hopped out, beer and whiskey in tow, and stumbled away to cap off the evening.

"Beats going to the diner," Tommy commented.

"For sure. I deal with those fools all week. Last thing I need is to waste a Saturday night on them. Tommy?" I had his attention. "Tonight really was special. The dance, everything. Thank you for being my date." I lowered my chin and raised my eyes to him in flirtatious gratitude.

"I would do anything in the world for you, Bree. Anything." He accented that last word and smiled back to me. We lit our cigarettes and broke out the beverages. It would prove to be a long night in the alders.

"So, any news on what you'll be doing after graduation?"

Tommy stirred his toe through the dust on the floor, buying time before he answered.

"No, not yet. There's always community college, I guess."

"But that doesn't get you away from here," I responded to him.

"Right. I just don't know how to go about going off to school, it's expensive, you know."

"I know it is. And I know our situations are different, as fucked up as they both are." At times I felt like I was pushing him too hard. I knew he understood the urgency of the situation, it was either leave or fall prey to the tragedy of living out his life in Alder Ferry.

"Trust me, Bree, I know that." He looked down, nodding his head, his lips puckered inward as he pried his mind for the right words to convey his situation. "You see, there are only two places where I ever found refuge—in nature and in a book. That's why I always retreated here, to the alders."

I turned my head to the side and my eyes widened to circles under an understanding brow. I felt for him. I knew that for a large part of his life this very spot was the only place on earth where he could find peace. But that was as a child. Moving into adulthood it was inevitable that things would change. There was nothing I could do to add to his statement; it neatly summed up his life's experience. The alders were his security blanket, but could also be his purgatory, holding him hostage somewhere between his past and his future.

The conversation led on well into the early morning hours. I was slightly buzzed but not drunk, as was Tommy. We spent the night alone, filling it with heartfelt conversation, and soothing cheer as we turned our eyes towards graduation that was a mere two weeks away. It was to be another milestone for us. We were on the cusp of surviving the final leg of our primary education before heading off in different directions. My path was set, but Tommy's still uncertain.

The sun was beginning to filter in over the trees that graced the bank of the Lowanachen when I stepped onto the portico.

"Where the fuck have you been?"

It was my father, still drunk.

"Out. Now I'm going to bed."

"Like hell you are!" He grabbed my arm and turned it. I allowed my body to submit to his grip, fearing he would shatter my arm if I resisted. "Where have you been?" The smell of bourbon on his breath was so strong I was drinking them in, nauseated by the taste.

"Since when do you care?" I was hurting now, my arm had pain shooting along its entire length, and the muscles were burning from lack of oxygen.

"Leave her alone." Tommy stepped out from the alders.

"Tommy, no—" I wanted to plead with him, to get him to turn away before the situation took a greater turn for the worse.

My father's grip loosened and I pulled myself away from him, now distracted by Tommy's challenge.

"And what are you going to do about it you little faggot?"

"Come down here and I'll show you."

Tommy, even with youth on his side, was far from equipped in going up against the ex-Marine. My father's drunken state slowed him somewhat as he stumbled down the stairs toward Tommy.

"Dad, leave him be!"

He didn't listen. He charged at Tommy, drilling him into the ground and knocking the wind out of him. His right fist landed squarely underneath Tommy's left eye socket. A deep bruise formed immediately as the shattered blood vessels erupted under the skin and sent streaks of red that fissured the white of his eye.

Darkness fell. My father was left in darkness as the baseball bat he kept by the backdoor made perfect contact against the base of his skull. It was Tommy's only chance, and I wasn't about to watch him sacrifice his body for my sake. Tommy looked up at me in disbelief. He seemed almost more scared of me holding the bat as I stood over the two of them. I rolled the lifeless body of my father off him, yelling, "Get outta here! Run! We'll talk later."

We exchanged a hurried parting hug before Tommy made his way into the alders. I checked my father, who was still breathing. I propped his head up and left him there to sleep off the alcohol by the sleep I induced. I was sure there would be hell to pay, knowing that some little faggot kicked his ass. I'd be certain to remind him of that. As wrong as it was to characterize Tommy in that way, I took an immeasurable amount of joy knowing the blow it struck my father's ego.

CHAPTER 27

WATER FALLS

THE MORNING AFTER prom solidified for me and Tommy the need to forever distance ourselves from our families and from Alder Ferry. While my classmates slept off hangovers or came to in a bed of regret, I was left to figure out how to cope with the set of circumstances set to rule my immediate future. We had done nothing wrong that evening: we had rightly celebrated our friendship and our survival through the previous four years of high school. It was ironic to a degree how, after leaving the alders, we were greeted by prompt and furious resistance from my father, the event capping off what had been a wonderful evening.

The beauty of our friendship would always remain as a misunderstood application of love and devotion between us. We weren't the star-crossed lovers that the other kids exchanged gossip about, but our early departure from the prom spoke otherwise to them. That dance we shared remained untarnished forever in my memory. I told myself again and again that the events which welcomed me home that morning would have played out eventually in some fashion. Regardless, it was not the fashion I imagined. I did take pride in the fact that, for once, Tommy and I stood our ground together. We would remain undivided in our willingness to be rid of the circumstances that brought opposition to us.

I knew my best course of action would be to maintain a low profile going forward. No amount of time would heal the wound to my father's ego. That Sunday I boarded myself up in my bedroom, and through the window I looked back in time, seeing again the Lowanachen at the end of the expansive lawn. This time the reflections of its waves weren't diamonds. Now they were shards of glass, my shattered childhood being transmitted back to me for reflection. Like my will, the waves of the river were constantly building and falling back onto themselves. The cycle repeated with a mesmerizing and monotonous evolution, a monotony that at times could be said imitated life: drudgery repeated, and interspersed with brief moments of excitement to keep one believing in the myth that living was all there was to existing. The waves negated this fallacy. Living and existing were two separate identities; they were two distinct paths. Consistently most of the waves died, collapsing back into the greater whole of their race. They were like most people I knew, ebbing and flowing with the tides, honoring the tedium of a cycle that gave them the most minimal of support to survive.

In due time, certain individual rogue waves would gather enough momentum to break free from the tide and force their will upon the shore. Over the past four years, through all the setbacks, Tommy and I had done the same: we maintained our momentum. We were always pushing forward, never turning back, even when it looked that we here headed in the wrong direction. We were those rogue waves challenging the tide, choosing life over an existence, at a cost that came close to bankrupting our wills. But it didn't, and when it didn't we came crashing upon the shore, our abhorrence to just existing rippling through the other waves, stalling them for a moment before they carried on with their predestined tides. This building momentum gave us the strength to weather the force levied by the tide and saw us through our final year in Alder Ferry.

I would need to survive another three months until leaving for the state university. I didn't know how I would do it. I just knew that somehow I had to conjure up the strength to withstand whatever the forces that opposed me could muster in that amount of time. History as my testament, I knew it could be the most challenging three months of my life.

Monday morning should have been as mundane as any other. But it wasn't. My father was nowhere to be found, and likewise, my mother had vanished. All that remained in the driveway was the second-hand car purchased for me to shuttle myself to and from school. On a typical morning, my father would be leaving the house as I awoke. My mother, on the other hand, was never one to rise from bed at such an early hour. It didn't fit the lifestyle of an alcoholic unbound by the striking of the clock.

As I departed the house I was met with a clue that led me to take faith in my suspicion that something was amiss. It was the morning paper—the same paper my father stole away with him every morning. But that day there it was, calling to me, begging to be released from the rubber band holding it captive. I obliged the wishes of this simple messenger cast down a couple hours sooner and unfurled its smudged glory. In oversized bold typeface the headline read:

"LARGEST ROUND OF LAYOFFS EVER TO HIT CALDWELL ANNOUNCED."

My cowardly parents fled. They would avoid the media frenzy that was certain to consume Alder Ferry. There again I was, all alone, to wade through the wreckage left in their wake. All alone to walk the gauntlet at school, to be stared down by my peers, teachers, and staff turning their eyes away with indifference.

I read down through the accompanying article to confirm what my mind suggested to be the ultimate goal of this act. Among those let go were Mike Genardo and the remaining old guard at Caldwell who continued in his staunch support. My father had executed an act of revenge that was calculated to cause the deepest amount of strife in Tommy's life. Fortunately, he was in the city when the news broke. Whether he would return to Alder Ferry now seemed indeterminable. What was a toxic situation for him had become downright dangerous.

Not again. I had my keys, my car, and my freedom. I drove to the city and waited outside Tommy's school. Before Tommy would return to his aunt's house after class, I had to find him.

—-—

"Get in."

"What are you doing here?"

"Haven't you heard, the layoffs, at Caldwell?"

"No . . . he didn't."

"He did. Your grandfather, all his friends. Gone."

"Holy shit."

"Yeah, holy shit, Tommy. If you go home . . ."

"I don't think I'll be going home. The old man is probably pissed as hell and drunk by now. I'll camp out in the alders, just bring me some food tonight."

"You got it."

"And Bree . . . thank you."

I placed my hand in his and smiled over to him as the light before us faded from red to green. "Anytime, anytime."

There was an urgency in our conversation that kept it succinct. While we finally had the means to evade these circumstances, it wasn't going to be easy. Tommy would for all purposes be homeless until we could figure out a detailed plan of action.

I returned to an empty house at dinner time. The sun was still high, but preparing for its long descent over the western horizon. I threw together a care package for Tommy and set out into the alders.

"Knock, knock."

"Who's there?"

"Dinner."

"Well come on down!"

"Any word on what's been happening?" Tommy was as uninformed as could be, a modern cast away to the alders.

"Not much more than we already know. Except now the police are over at Caldwell, bomb threat or something. Could be a long night." I sighed as I reported the latest bit of news to him. Tommy hung on every word, and hastily bit into his sandwich, half of it nearly gone with one swallow.

"Slow down, you're not going anywhere."

He let out a forced laugh to hide his embarrassment. He was a slow eater, always enjoying what he ate. His apprehension was apparent, choking it back with the sandwich in hand.

"I think you're safe in here. Going to school tomorrow?"

"Yeah," Tommy responded with indecision and hesitance in his voice.

"Tommy, I doubt he'll go to your school."

"Doesn't mean he won't be waiting for me outside." It was a valid point. Genardo was a wild card that could never be dismissed.

"Then lay low a day or two. Just try and call the school, let them know you don't feel safe."

"There's no phone here, Bree."

"Never mind," I rolled my eyes. "I'll call."

"Tomorrow, be here at the same time?"

"Definitely, you keep safe. Come to the house if it gets too weird in here."

"Spent plenty of nights here, it's like home." I pulled him to me and held him, wanting to linger. Expecting my parents to be home, and waiting with questions if I returned too late, prevented my staying. I wasn't about to undergo an inquest that evening.

——

With little regard for the day's events, I turned back to the Grand Old Lady. I glided through the alders with carefree ease, navigating the gnarled root stumps and damp depressions as I witnessed Tommy doing four years earlier. I remembered that first chase through the stand, how amazed I was with the grace that he moved through the trees. His movements were ethereal, his feet caroming from the forest floor with minimal contact. Now I moved through the stand with the same quality. I had an intimate understanding of its every twist and turn, like the knowledge a lover gains of their companion's body after their fingers have traced its every square inch.

I flung myself up to the portico, startled by the reflection of headlights mirrored off the screen door. I made it home in near perfect time. My parents could question me all about my day, and now there would be no need to explain my whereabouts. It should have been me asking them where they had been, leaving me alone to navigate the minefield they had strewn. Confident and cocky in my situation, I found the switch for the small, stained glass light fixture above the kitchen island. I settled in and waited for their entrance, riding the river of excuses that would provide a convenient cover explaining away their actions. Cowards.

Minutes passed. I was sure they were rehearsing their story. Then I heard it, the solid thud of a car door. Followed by another. In quick succession, it was followed by two more doors closing, then what sounded to be a trunk sent to its home position. Four doors, and maybe a trunk. My parents never brought company home. I didn't see why tonight would be any different. If anything, they would be more likely to stay away than to invite guests under the circumstances.

I snuffed out the kitchen light, darkening the entire house. From the front window, I could see the figures of four men standing about an old, battered, dinosaur of a sedan. The cherries of their cigarettes gave away their position, their muffled voices and laughs sending lightning bolts of alarm through me. But I had nowhere to run. I was now prisoner to them inside this house that was far removed from town, far enough away that no one would see or hear anything taking place.

"Worthington, get your chicken-shit ass out here. Now!"

Peering through the curtains, parted but a sliver to avoid giving away my position, I saw Genardo. The baseball bat moved up and down with a pendulum-like motion, striking his meaty palm. From inside I could hear the slap of the bat against his flesh, each strike growing louder as the bat gained momentum, its arcs shortening, and its potential ready to be released. All it needed was a victim.

I shuddered at the thought. The old house was barren when hiding spaces were concerned. The closets held barely enough space for the clothing stuffed inside them. The basement was an open cavern, empty save for the antiquated boiler that glowed red with anger, its appetite for fuel oil insatiable. There was only one place, one place out of sight that the men could possibly overlook. The kitchen crawlspace. It was an addition, many years the junior of the remainder of the home, and not part of the original footprint. A small crawlspace beneath the kitchen served as a conduit for the plumbing and heating service to the room.

Inside the pantry was a false wall that served as the crawlspace entry. The narrow opening was shielded in part by the shelving above, and the wall-piece fit firmly in place, with no identifiable seams to surrender knowledge of its location to the unknowing eye. In fact, I only became aware of its location a year earlier during the kitchen renovation.

Angry knocks sounded at the front door. The back door was still unlocked and it was too late to negate their entry through the rear. I pulled the false wall away and slid inside the crawlspace, fighting against thick, cottony spider webs to make my way inside. The false wall snapped in place to the sound of breaking glass coming from the front porch.

I snaked my body deep into the crawl space, my nasal cavities becoming engulfed with cobwebs and dust. It took every ounce of strength to remain still, as I felt numerous other living things fleeing my advance, while others crawled over and around me to see what had just taken up residence in their space. I feared to open my mouth, the cobwebs and dust slung to my nostrils with each breath. My heart raced and I felt suffocated from the lack of oxygen my stunted breathing supplied to my lungs.

The men entered the house and moved methodically from room to room. With each pass, furniture was thrown over, hideous laughter following their deeds, and profanities filled the interims.

As they entered the kitchen dust from the floor joists above me rained down, forming small mounds of mud in the beads of sweat that covered every exposed piece of skin on my body. Dishes crashed to the floor, food was thrown from the refrigerator, and in final form the faucet was snapped from its base, sending water showering into the kitchen. Within minutes the water began to trickle into the crawl space, its dirt floor now muddied by their work.

Then I smelled it. Cigar smoke. They settled in my father's office and uncovered his trove of cigars smuggled from Cuba. Would they ever leave? I was drowning in the crawl space, the water cascading over the circuit of wires and plumbing that made their way along the floor joists just inches from my head. My body sank halfway into the mud, frozen in place by its grip. I was shot through with fear and couldn't move if I tried.

After what seemed to be hours, all was quiet. The soft gurgle of running water offered a peaceful interlude following the preceding melee. I heard their car make its way down the driveway. But I didn't hear the doors close—I was too far from the driveway to know just how many of them left. The water continued to run and I remained paralyzed by fear, not knowing if one or more of the men stayed behind to wait for my father. There I remained, a prisoner to my fear, throughout the night.

At daybreak the first rays of sun to reach the house filtered into the crawlspace through a minuscule gap between the foundation and the subfloor. Now I knew why that room was always so cold, but that no longer mattered. My best hope was to leave for college and never spend another winter, not another moment at all, in that house. Genardo and his men were reckless, but they weren't foolish enough to be seen at the property in the light of day.

Not having heard any movement above me for hours, I slithered backward out of the crawlspace, turning off the water at the shutoff valve just inside the false wall. My entire front was caked in mud, my back saturated from the water that dripped over me with torturous design throughout the night. Before me was a sight of horror. The entire first floor, fully renovated under my mother's watchful eye, was under a shallow layer of water. Every piece of furniture had been toppled, the contents spilled out, items with any buoyancy bobbing along, enjoying the brief freedom of their ruin. The stained-glass slats flanking the front door were shattered, giving prying hands ease of access to the deadbolt made useless by its proximity to the glass.

I was in horror by the scene and chilled by the cool morning air of late spring. I didn't care about the house or its belongings. I didn't care about my appearance. I didn't care about the food floating about, islands for swarms of houseflies colonizing their shores. All I remember was feeling small and insecure. I ran from the house and to the alders, looking for Tommy, looking for security in his company.

He was gone when I arrived. How long he had been gone I didn't know. I couldn't even tell the time of day. Exhausted, I fell into the hammock to wait for his return.

"Bree, Bree, wake up, it's me. Tommy."

Scared, I jumped from the hammock. When I saw Tommy I collapsed into his arms, shivering with fear and the chill offered by my still damp clothes.

"Where have you been? I've been here all day waiting for you," my words echoing to him through tears and chattering teeth.

"Never mind me. What happened?"

"I thought you were going to lay low?"

"I'll explain that, but what happened to you?"

"Tommy your grandfather and his buddies busted up the house last night. I hid and waited it out." I felt myself melting deeper into his arms, finally able to let my guard down. Tommy held me, running his hands through my hair, dislodging lumps of dried mud with each pass. I watched as they crumbled to mere dust, and then burst into small clouds that slowly faded away, never to return.

"Where were you?"

"Bree, I figured a way out of here."

I looked at him with a stare of perplexity, not knowing what he was hinting at, not sure I was ready for what he was about to say.

"I was with the recruiter, Coast Guard. I leave a week after graduation."

PART IV

CHAPBOOK END

CHAPTER 28

THE LONG SUNSET

T HE AGED BRASS bell was all that sliced through the heavy weft of fog shrouding the parade field. The salt air clung to everything, leaving behind an exfoliating layer on the skin, coarse but barely noticeable to the eye. But its presence could be felt tightening the skin, stretching it taut to the body's frame.

The August sun paced its rise to the occasion and burned a growing hole into the fog. Opposite my position was the old, weathered bell, its polished brass reflecting the scant sunlight in my direction, casting out long golden rays that sliced through the salt-laden mist. With each ray a bit of the mist fell casualty to its warmth, its essence returning to the sea and sky, partners in its conception.

The same long, golden rays refracted off the brass insignia scattered below me. In the thinning veil of fog, the ranks began to assume the semblance of military bearing. At first, they were a sea of blue. The fog's evaporation brought the mass into focus, revealing the individual members construing each column. From the retreating mist, the formations rose to assume their rightful places of prominence before the gallery of onlookers.

On cue, the entire assemblage snapped to their feet and stiffened to a position of rigid attention. The notes of the national anthem carried themselves across the field, slashing through what remained of the early morning haze, and settling within my eardrums to resonate. For the first time in my young American life, those musical notes took on meaning to me. They were no longer the prologue to a meaningless sporting event or played to stroke the ego of a politician. Those notes now gave witness to a group of young men and women answering the call to serve their country, the reserved few who could truly claim to hail from the land of the brave. Everyone else that assumed those verses of the anthem and wrapped themselves in it were nothing better than imposters.

It had been nearly three months since the layoffs at Caldwell. Three long months I spent almost entirely alone, except for the small bouts of time I found to spend with Tommy before he embarked on his passage from Alder Ferry. I waited out the rest of the summer for my time, witnessing the restoration of my parents' home from the invasion by Genardo and his goons, an event scored by my father as a cost of doing business. In the end, the cost to him was minimal. Genardo exacted his revenge, and at the same time, my father rid Caldwell of the men who challenged his position.

It was my first trip to Cape May, New Jersey. Tommy had all but vanished from his grandparents' house in the weeks leading up to his departure for boot camp. I was the only invitee to his graduation, and I wasn't even sure if what passed for his family even realized he enlisted. The second generation of his paternal line in the United States now gave its second son to the service of their adopted homeland.

"Seaman Alton Mackay."

I jumped and cheered at his name, shocking even myself with the volume and projection of my voice. I was unaware of the modicum of decorum for these situations but didn't care. He never had anyone cheer him on, and I was resolute in my willingness to break that tradition. I exchanged glances with the families around me who looked me up and down, dismissing me as the crazy girlfriend. I acknowledged their looks, whispered the obligatory "I'm sorry" and returned to my seat, content with my display of affection.

Finally, the only thing that remained between me and Tommy, his graduation ceremony, concluded. I ran down from the stand and flung my body at him, catching my arms about his shoulders. This day was the high school graduation we never enjoyed. There were no parties or barbecues in our honor back then, we both retreated from those ceremonies to weather the tempests of our personal lives. But this day was different. Finally, we could celebrate an achievement without looking back.

I lowered myself down from Tommy and pressed the creases back into his shirt, brushing away the smudges of makeup that stowed away across his collar. My hands slid down his shirt, stopping and taking his hands in mine. He smiled his coy smile, but this time there was a light behind it, a sense of accomplishment no one could ever take from him. I was more than proud of him. I was overwhelmed with relief and joy. Joy in knowing that this beautiful specimen of humanity escaped a life that was nothing but a dead end for him, a true suicide note for the talents he possessed. Relief knowing that he was safe. Each night he would place his head on a pillow and sleep without fear.

"Hello there, sailor!"

"Stop it Bree," was his response, but try as hard as he could, he couldn't stop laughing.

"I am so proud . . . so happy for you." A tear strolled down my face, taking the time to absorb the joy of the moment before it blended in with my makeup. Another fleeting memory, but one that would always be etched into the foundation of my mind.

"Thank you." What else could he say? It was the simplest, heartfelt thank you I ever heard, and have yet to hear. It was monumental, to climb above the wreckage of his youth, and for once have an unobstructed view along the horizon of his future.

"Bree, I know this all happened fast, I should have let you know before I signed up . . ."

"Nonsense." I was too happy for him to consider questioning his actions. "You don't need my permission to live your life. Best friends, remember?"

"I could never forget." He put his arm around my shoulder as we made our way off the parade field and to my car.

"Let's head over to the beach after I get out of this uniform."

"I kind of like the uniform . . ."

"Government regulations, can't wear it off duty." Again, that smile carved its way out of the corner of his mouth, and I watched as he strutted with confidence to the barracks, a walk he never exhibited before. His uniform fit him perfectly. It was the first set of clothing tailored for him. Everything about the experience transformed him—in all the right ways. He was still my Tommy, but now had confidence in his abilities and a foresight into his future.

"So, feel any different?"

"Maybe a little, it all hasn't sunk in yet. The past eight weeks were a blur."

"Well, nothing's changed really at Alder Ferry. Caldwell is still running, your grandfather is drinking away his early retirement, life there goes on."

"Except for one thing," Tommy paused and looked upward, seeking some sort of direction before resuming, "except that we are gone, that place will never have to know us again unless we let it."

"Truthfully Tommy, I am grateful for one thing—you. You are the best thing to come out of that town." He pulled me in close as we sauntered along the beach, the waves kissing our feet as they rolled through the wet sand.

"Have you been to the alders at all?"

"Not since the night before you left for boot camp. It's kind of odd without you, like being home alone."

"That's the beauty of it, it is home, to me, it was anyway."

I knew those trees were more of a home to him than any other structure in his formative years ever proved to be. I listened to every word he spoke that afternoon, each one sinking in deeper, affirming what I knew about him. It also gave me a bit of clarity to hear the stories of his childhood resonate from an adult's perspective. I winced at the thought, but indeed we were adults. Not only legally, but life had cast us into adulthood at an early age. We were experienced in life's ways much further along than our peers, much further along than anyone our age need travel.

"Here it is." Tommy pulled an envelope from his cargo shorts. "My duty station."

"Where is it?" My thoughts immediately turned to Miami, somewhere warm.

"Would you do the honors?"

I swiped it from him, the envelope tearing under the pressure of my thumb and forefinger. I slid my finger beneath the seal, walking it along its edge, and removed the contents. I waved the single piece of paper in the air, feigning to lose it in the ocean breeze.

"All right, ready?" I looked down at the bold letters centered on the page, trying out of desperation not to show my disappointment. "You got Portland."

"West Coast. Pretty good."

"Portland, Maine."

"Oh."

It wasn't the sexiest destination, I remember telling him, but he could always put in for a transfer after a couple of years. No one stayed in one duty station.

"So, five days from now I'll be reporting to Portland, Maine."

"All you can eat lobster, Tommy." He laughed it off. I knew it wasn't his first choice, either. It was far enough that visiting would be more than difficult. The logistics of traveling between Portland and my campus reduced the likelihood of seeing one another to almost zero. No matter where he ended up, it would have been difficult. Even Miami, although getting there would have been worth the effort during Northeast winters.

"We'll make do, don't worry. Anyway, I like getting letters. I expect lots of them." Until now, I didn't realize just how hard it would be to say goodbye.

"Me too, Bree. Me too."

We sat on the beach and watched the sun explode into a radiant, blood-red fireball. It struck me as peculiar, the sun that night. It was the same color as the alder wood I hacked into after Tommy's attack. The same deep, crimson color that my wound to the tree generated now splayed across the western sky. It oozed from the sun's orb like the broken yolk of an undercooked egg, its contents running their course in contradiction to the frolicking waves upon which it rode. We stayed there long into the night, at times in absolute silence, and at peace in each other's company. There we sat, finally free to just be, right there in the wide expanse of sky and sea unfurling before us.

CHAPTER 29

FOLLOWING SEAS

B Y SOPHOMORE YEAR of college, I had become quite bored with my schoolwork. It felt almost to be an extension of high school, apart from my English classes fueling my desire to continue. Another year and I would begin the search to identify potential graduate schools. Until then, I would need to hunker down and tackle the few remaining general education credits that stood between me and focusing solely on my major.

It wasn't much different than sophomore year of high school. It was that in-between time, waiting to break free of the stigma associated with ninth and tenth grade, waiting for someone to finally take you seriously. College was the same way. You could declare a major freshman year. No one held you to it, and no one in the English department at my university considered you one of their own until you entered your junior year. Less than a year and I would be there, finally a college junior, finally allowed to enjoy the opportunity to discuss literature and writing with the professors on the level I needed not only to maintain my attention but to give me the foundation necessary to find success in the world of writers and the written word. Writing was never a natural talent for me. I seized at every availability to squeeze any tidbit of knowledge and experience from my professors in the hopes that just something would take hold and make a lasting impression.

––

It was a cold day about a week before Thanksgiving. I woke to the delivery of a note from the dean of my college, requesting my presence in his office at eleven that morning. My grades were fine, and I was puzzled as to why I was being summoned. I was made nervous by the request, wondering if I had done something wrong, even though I was about as stoic as the elm at the center of campus. I kept to my studies above anything else.

Arriving at the dean's office was overwhelming. The official airs given off by the dark woodwork, attaching the present day to a bygone era, were judicial in their tone. Already I felt judged, although nothing had been said or done. It was intimidating. I became ostensibly smaller as I entered the waiting area, not knowing what to expect.

When I was shown to the room I choked back my worries and stepped in, allowing the heavy door to seal me inside. The room was an odd "L" shape, a cornered office whose layout was given very little thought. Behind his desk was Dean Fenning, who stood to greet me, his voice offering a somber affect, vacillating between concern and compassion.

"Ms. Worthington, please." He motioned me deeper into his office. His voice wavered, almost adolescent, cracking back to the boy that still lived somewhere deep inside his consciousness.

We waded across the parquet flooring to the ninety-degree bend that led us to the lengthy portion of the office's "L" shaped design. The light filtered through the heavy, aged drapes, dust particles frozen in the sunbeams that fell across the floor and crawled up the opposite wall. I was caught off guard—ambushed—as I turned the corner. My face froze in fright, my eyes widened while the irises shrunk to a mere sliver to lock out the scene. A man in a Coast Guard officer's uniform stood there, hat in hand, looking down but also looking at me, deferring his eyes away from the emotion brewing on my face. Behind him were a woman and another university staff member, the identification card draped around her neck simply stated "chaplain" across its face with her name in minuscule letters beneath it.

"What happened to Tommy?" The words were automatic even though I knew the answer. Before they could speak, before I even spoke, I went into shock.

"I mean, Alton, Alton Mackay." He would always be Tommy to me, but at that point in time, he was only known to the rest of the world as Alton Mackay.

"Ms. Worthington . . ." The officer stepped forward but was stopped by the woman behind him, her hand making light contact with his right shoulder, causing him to part from her path.

"Excuse me, Commander. Ms. Worthington, you need to sit. With me." She took my hand and we moved to the small sofa

204 \ H. A. CALLUM

that spanned the wall, flanked by bookshelves whose volumes hadn't been disturbed in years. She was petite, close in age to my mother, and dressed very well but not to extravagance. The warm blue color of her jacket was comforting, taking me in without a second thought.

"I'm Linda Reisler, Coast Guard Ombudsman, and this is Lieutenant Commander Warren." She motioned toward the uniformed man, whose hat kept his fingers busy. While his face was devoid of emotion, his fingers belied the impassive stance he was attempting to display.

"We're here to talk to you about Seaman Mackay, or is it Tommy?"

"I called him Tommy, it was a term of endearment." My responses were programmed, by now I was just tossing out information on demand. I understood what they were trying to do, but it wasn't working. I was moving further away from them each second, no matter how physically close to me they came.

"I know why you're here. Please, please, just get to it." I never understood why people delayed relaying news like this, especially when the distressing look about them made it so obvious what they were about to deliver.

Warren chimed in, "All right. Three days ago, Seaman Mackay's cutter was sent to aid a small fishing vessel caught in a large offshore storm." The officer paused, catching his breath, and crouched down before me, holding me captive in his eyes.

"A wave came across the side of the cutter and swept him overboard." The officer's eyes were now far from emotionless. Behind them I could see the sea in all its rage, the waves crashing down on the cutter, stealing away Tommy before they retreated from the decks.

"Ms. Worthington . . . your fiancé sacrificed his life in the line of duty."

Fiancé? The word stopped me but before I could ask, Warren continued.

"I saw it from the bridge. Seaman Mackay was one of my crew. I am so sorry . . ." I could see the sorrow in his face, the responsibility he felt for what happened. Oddly, this man's candor was all that kept me from breaking down right there before everyone. He gave me the strength to carry on a bit longer and retreat to a private space to have my breakdown.

"Thank you, Commander Warren." They were the only words I could muster for the man who traveled many hours to deliver this tragic piece of news to me. It did help though, coming from someone that knew Tommy, someone that through his delivery of the message made it obvious that he had a deep-felt respect for Tommy.

"We realize that Tommy," Reisler spoke and dropped her head towards me for approval to use that name, to which I nodded my agreement, "he had no next of kin, is that right, do you know?"

"His dad died long ago and his mother abandoned him. So, to answer your question, yes." I didn't know how else to answer, and I knew Tommy would have agreed with it, leaving the Genardo family out of the picture. "I'm all the family he had."

"There are just a few arrangements to make, but we can discuss the details later. We would like to have a ceremony honoring him at the command, back in Portland . . . that is if you're up for it." She paused while shuffling through her paperwork. "And, Tommy named you as beneficiary to his group life insurance policy."

I was dumbfounded. Tommy had just died, they thought I was his fiancé, and now I was a widow of sorts—widowed by the sea from my best friend.

"Ms. Reisler, this is just too much right now. I can't go to Portland, it's too . . . too soon. And the insurance, I can't talk about money. Not now." As far as I was concerned I would never go to Portland. That place took him away from me forever.

"We know this is a lot. Here's my number, call me anytime." Reisler left a small packet of papers with me to go through. "When you're ready, I'll come back and we'll go through everything. Except for the life insurance, we'll submit the paperwork for that."

It seemed like I had no choice but to take the money.

"Ms. Reisler, I don't think I ever want to come to Portland. Let's just call off any ceremony."

She nodded her agreement.

———

The ordinary became extraordinary under the circumstance of that meeting. As I walked back to my dorm, nothing seemed ordinary and nothing had permanence. Anything could change, and instantly. Routines now maintained sanity in the face of loss. The routine, mundane chores of daily living were the only constants I could depend upon, and without them, I would go crazy.

Like checking my mail. Every day after class I would check my post office box in the dormitory foyer. I would insert the stubby key, twist it, and jiggle it up and sharply to the left to disengage the lock. It was almost always empty, except for the letters from Tommy. I told him to write, it was something to hold onto, like having him in the room with me.

Insert, twist, and jiggle. Every day, my fingers partnered in this dance with the postal box. Most days, it was a dance that ended up with me going home alone. The postal box was just stingy in giving itself up to me.

We danced the same that day, only I didn't go home alone. Inside was a battered envelope, its crisp, white exterior worn to a feathery edge, its color faded to a pasty yellow. It was from Tommy, postmarked the day before he was lost at sea. His crisp addressing of the envelope was the only outward aspect of the mail piece to survive intact.

I hurried back to my room to hide with the letter from the rest of the world. It was all mine, the last palpable vestige of Tommy's short and turbid existence on this planet. I sat the letter on my desk and stared at it as I looked out the window. Across the sky, the barren branches of the trees scratched and clawed, but to no avail. They remained firmly planted in the ground, unable to climb no matter how hard they tried. Like them, I was rooted, there at that moment, as my hands feared to reveal the contents of the letter. It was not a fear of knowing, but a fear of never knowing again, never anticipating what Tommy would say. Opening this letter would be the last time I would experience the anticipation of welcoming his words to me.

I paused and considered allowing the letter to remain un-opened. There was magic in the letter, given the timing and circumstances of its arrival.

In the end, my heart's longing to hear Tommy one last time won out:

> Hey Bree,
> Remember on the beach in Cape May, and we opened
> the letter with the orders? Our reactions were priceless!
> Nothing cool or fun like Miami or Key West. Nope. Portland,
> Maine. Cold, rocky, and, did I mention—cold?

But you know what? This place has turned out to be amazing. The people have been great, and Portland is becoming a happening spot, especially the old downtown. You should see it—artists, writers, all concentrated and just making things happen. Pretty cool.

On top of that, I have some amazing news. Next spring, I am finally enrolled in a couple courses at the local community college! It's not much but it's a start. I feel like I'm finally making my way. The Coast Guard has been great to me; I would never have this opportunity if I hadn't tried. And my skipper, Lt. Cmdr. Warren, the guy is pretty open as an officer, you know. Not stiff or anything. Sometimes I think he looks after me like I'm his own son. It's so odd to see people taking care of each other as we do on the cutter—I've never really known that outside of our relationship. It gives me faith that maybe it's not all bad out there, maybe we were just cast to a bad spot.

Thanks for always believing in me and pushing me on. When you said you were leaving for college, I admit to being jealous. But here I am, about to start school on my own. Wouldn't have done it if you hadn't believed in me all along.

I know this last bit may seem odd, but for the first time, I think I have found me a home. I can see myself staying here in Portland a long time. I can't wait for you to come up and visit—there's so much I want to show you.

Love Always,
Tommy

P.S.—I remember telling you that I never wanted to share my poetry. It's very personal, you know? But I've decided to take the leap and get something published, eventually. What do you think?

Taped to the bottom of the letter was a pair of catkins.

There would be no way to describe how I felt after reading that letter. But there was one thing for which I was certain: I was glad to have read it. To have left it unopened would have kept me in the dark to Tommy finding his true happiness. It may not have lasted long, but he succeeded in finding happiness before leaving this world behind.

Everything he did was an act of kindness. He always had the interests of others in mind before his own. In some ways, his passing was fitting. In the line of duty, it was his care for his fellow man that sent him out onto that deck. It was not an order. He willingly walked into the storm and faced his fears so that another soul would live another day, to tell the story of the blonde stranger that saddled up on the deck of the rolling cutter and cast a line before vanishing beneath a wall of sea foam.

In some ways, his exit from this world was part of his mystique. Tommy simply vanished, like he would when he entered the alders. There was a spiritual bit to him that defied comprehension and denied rational explanation. He was part of the natural world, and after finding peace in the human realm, that is to where he returned.

I put the letter down and let the tears roll down my face. They were gentle tears. I cried for Tommy that afternoon instead of grieving. In his letter, I saw the peace he found, and that same peace overcame me, knowing that when he passed there was, at last, a lightness to his heart that gave him a freedom few of us will ever know. It was a freedom that no man, no government, no piece of paper could ever delineate or dictate.

I allowed myself to regain some of my composure. I lifted the phone from the receiver and dialed Linda Reisler.

"It's Aubrey. When can we have that ceremony for Tommy? In Portland, of course."

CHAPTER 30

THE LONG GOODBYE

THE WAVES LAPPED at the wreath, their minuscule crests failing to take hold of its tattered edges. They grasped to no avail, their watery fingers splashing against the wreath's side with each attempt. The waves were like a ghost, trying in desperation to make contact with this world, but physically unable to break through. They did give the illusion of pushing the wreath closer to shore, each wave lifting it gently and tilting it towards me, the donut-hole center filled with the algae green color of the sea upon which it rode. In fact, the tide was doing quite the opposite. With each passing wave, the wreath was pulled out farther with methodical repetition, underway to its own burial at sea.

It mirrored in some way the reticence I felt in letting Tommy go. I always found myself during that time grabbing for him, grabbing for our past, attempting to pull it back to shore with me. But those memories were ghosts. Like the waves upon the wreath, they simply melted at the touch of my fingers. Cherished is all they were meant to be, only moving further away every time I reached for them

"Whenever you're ready, Aubrey."

I turned back one last time and watched the wreath ride the waves. It was now much farther from shore. The ship's bell across the harbor clanged out through the cold, clear air, carrying its chime far out to sea, sounding out the impending arrival of the wreath. Far from shore, where we stood, across those emerald waves that stretched thousands of miles to the Irish coast, across those same waves that brought Tommy's grandparents here in the not so distant past, somewhere in between was Tommy. I imagined the bell's solitary chime piercing the depths of the sea and reaching him, carrying along with it a final "I love you," accompanying him to the afterlife.

The waves continued to wash about the wreath, giving the appearance of smiling back at me, their perfectly rounded crests curling under themselves just as Tommy's lip curled under the corner of his mouth. The waves, like Tommy, were a bit secretive, not willing to offer much unless you stopped to listen. I was fortunate to have been the one to stop and listen to Tommy. I became the woman I am proud to be for having known him, learning from him the true meaning of love, its hardships, and the perseverance required to keep it strong. I lingered on and listened to the waves, the barely audible whispers each one made as their crests fluxed back into the sea. I wrapped my arms around myself, squeezing my overcoat gently to chase away the chill of the damp sea air. In the waves, in their whispered eulogies, I felt Tommy's presence. I turned my back to the ocean, this part of our farewell complete.

"I'm ready."

I followed Linda Reisler from the pier to the command center, where the remainder of the crew gathered following our farewell to their shipmate. The farewell was a small and intimate affair in the shadow of the cutter moored to the pier where we stood. Looking up at the cutter, I was impressed with its height. My stomach dropped as I imagined Tommy's fall from the deck, how his eyes must have watched in horror as he viewed the churning seas approach him with no deterrence, there being no ability on his part to avoid the impact that ensured his fate. I wiped that image from my mind, replacing it instead with the sight of Tommy moving along the deck in stalwart fashion, squaring off against the waves buffering his cutter. He always looked back with his guarded smile, acknowledging what was to come, before vanishing into the wall of green sea foam that greeted him.

For once I was the guest of honor, a privilege earned at great cost. I wished over and over that day to have been able to avoid the situation. But I couldn't avoid it. This was the reality I had to make terms with if I were to continue living.

"I can't thank you two enough for putting this together . . . it's helping to make peace with Tommy's passing. You made me feel like he didn't . . . like he didn't die in vain." Reisler put her arm around me and gave a hug radiating warmth and concern.

"It was our pleasure, Aubrey. Our pleasure."

"Commander Warren?" I rustled through my purse as I asked for his attention, rifling through make-up vials and crumpled gum wrappers. I pulled out Tommy's last letter and caught his eye attempting to read the hand-writing that was fortunate to survive the morass of my purse, a mirror to my life at the time.

"You have my full attention." I looked back up at them both, embarrassed by my lack of preparation. He was fighting hard to keep the smile from spreading across his lips as he watched my clumsy display. I caught Linda Reisler gently nudging him. She, too, was also struggling to keep a straight face.

"Listen, if you don't mind, I want to read you something." My change in tone solemned the conversation.

Warren looked towards me with understanding eyes, ordering, "Please, go on."

I swallowed hard and ran my fingers across the letter to get to the lines I needed. Tears began to well up, Reisler put her hand to her mouth, sensing the sincerity of the moment, herself trying to hold back tears as I read from the letter:

"...my skipper, Lt. Cmdr. Warren, the guy is pretty open as an officer, you know. Not stiff or anything. Sometimes I think he looks after me like I'm his own son. It's so odd to see people taking care of each other as we do on the cutter—I've never really known that outside of our relationship. It gives me faith that maybe it's not all bad out there . . ."

"You don't know how much this means . . ." I was on the verge of a complete breakdown, tears falling without trepidation, "... thank you for finally giving him the experience of knowing what it's like to have a father."

Warren pulled in Reisler and she collapsed into his arms, crying.

"Aubrey, we should be thanking you. You don't know what those words mean to us. The crew, everyone here, they're our family." Reisler wiped away her tears as she spoke. "We were never able to have kids, so we made the Guard our family."

I looked at them, and began to ask, "You mean, you two are . . ."

"Married. Don't let the different names fool you." Warren answered my question before I could finish. His smile chased away the grief and ushered in a touch of happiness. Only knowing Tommy could change such a situation. It was a reminder of how he touched us all.

"Now Aubrey, don't ever think twice about coming to visit." Reisler and Warren were in a sideward embrace as they saw me off at my car, Warren holding her close to his side.

"I'll see what the future holds." I was never one to commit and wasn't sure if I would ever be able to return to Portland. Too many memories of Tommy were there. But, those were great memories, and Tommy was right: the warmth of the people here chased away the cold. That entire day I felt a sense of belonging to a place that I had never before seen.

I hoisted Tommy's belongings into the trunk with Warren's assistance. He commented, "Tommy was never one to pack heavy."

"No, he wasn't," was my response to Warren. "Tommy never acquired much . . . or had a place calm enough to call home to store his things."

Warren turned to me, placing his hand on my shoulder, to keep me from leaving. "Bree, there are a couple more things." He handed me a packet wrapped in brown paper and bound together with a piece of old rigging cinched up by a square knot. "Tommy always had his books with him, I didn't want them to be tossed into his sea bag and forgotten."

I was delicate with the packet, running my fingers along its edges and tracing the outline of the square knot that lay flat upon its top. I commented to them, "I always remember Tommy with either a book or a notebook. He was never far from one or the other. Books were his first friend, his first means of escape from a rough childhood."

"Take care, Bree. And don't be a stranger." Reisler's words grounded me there a bit longer, and I hugged both of them. Our trio became one in a simple moment that solidified our friendship, the small but close circle created only because Tommy lived.

"Thank you." The emotions in me prevented any other words from escaping. I fought back more tears and collapsed into my car, with the packet of books riding shotgun in place of Tommy. As I pulled away I watched the couple holding each other, their love apparent as they shrunk into the distance and faded from sight. It was a familial love I had never known. I took solace knowing that Tommy's last days were spent in that warmth.

I turned to the highway to make the long drive back to Alder Ferry. I didn't want to go there, but like Portland, I had to go. It was part of my farewell to Tommy and to the past as I sped off into a future made possible by Tommy's last gift to me. After tomorrow I would never again have to return to Alder Ferry. Tommy's group life insurance policy would see me through the remainder of my education. I was free of the financial burden chaining me to my parents, making me return to them after every semester and be reminded of just how fortunate I was for their generosity.

———

I didn't go to my parents' house. I would save that for last. Instead, I pulled into the parking lot by the alders one last time. It was late and cold, and I hesitated to leave the warmth of the car for the cold darkness surrounding me. But the alders called me to them, and I brushed back the scrubby cedars at their edge and made my entrance. The pale moonlight pierced the sky above, casting its silver rays to the forest floor where they rippled like the ocean waves. Each step took me closer to our hideaway, our retreat and respite from life. I was visiting an old friend for the last time.

I reached the entrance to the cavern and removed each book from the shelf. Time and the elements had taken their toll on the volumes, but they were priceless to me. I packed them out to the car without any ceremony, each trip guided by the light of the moon. Each sliver of light penetrated to the floor, lighting my path one footstep at a time. It was eerie in that this could be the last visit to this place, the last instance I would sit here undisturbed, left alone to my thoughts, no one around to interrupt the emotions welling up inside of me.

I collapsed into the hammock, surprised that it still held my weight, the ropes fastening it to the stone shrunk tight by time. The place was empty now, except for the few remnants of our time there: a scattering of empty beer cans, the sweater I kept balled up on the ledge that served as a bookend, and the few scraps of paper stirring in the breeze. The books made it what it was, and they were gone, safe for my posterity, however long that would last. Without them the space seemed cold, the wind casting its chill down the back of my collar, causing me to shudder. With the wind, I felt a part of us leaving. The stand had done its part in seeing us through our troubled teen years, protecting us when it could from the outside world that always opposed us. Now it was over. We were both free of Alder Ferry. The alder stand seemed to sense that, and with one final gust of wind I sprung from the hammock and gathered what remained into a pyre on the floor.

I lit a cigarette and touched off those sacred remnants with my lighter. In seconds the parched papers and textiles were engulfed in raging orange and yellow flames that licked the stone ceiling and walls. I watched as it all burned down to embers, glowing bright red, until finally, one by one, each extinguished itself to the memories that only remained. I ran my hands along the stone walls for the last time and whispered "Thank you" to them, the echoes of my words etching themselves into the stone.

As I rose from the cavern the sun was peaking above the Lowanachen. In its golden morning rays, I could feel their warmth strip away the cold of the night, empowering me to camouflage the entrance to be forever hidden. I buried a piece of our past in that chamber. A past filled with drama interspersed with peaceful interludes where we would catch our breath, recharge our souls, and turn ourselves back out to the world for more of the same treatment. This ground was hallowed, a place made sacred by both our suffering and our delight, taking us in for respite when no one else would.

I turned my back to the wind sweeping through the alders from the Lowanachen. With it, I flowed, an airiness to my step. I glided along the forest floor, much like I had witnessed Tommy that first day I saw him here now seven years in our storied past. It only seemed like yesterday, two kids finding each other here, and cementing a common bond in each other that society could not allow. But we found it and held on to it with all our strength. We were lifelines in the storm, cast to each other, preventing one another from drowning in the mire of life.

I gazed through the limbs of the alders as I left the stand. The light, I will always remember the light. Those trees applied a filter to the light that made it clear and made everything else a bit less opaque. I stopped before exiting and looked up, turning in a circle with my arms wide open, taking in deep breaths of air, enjoying the earthy must of the dirt splashing around my feet. The rays of the sun sparkled gold among the previous year's catkins, sending glittering flashes of intense light my way. I plucked one pair from the tree to hang from the rearview mirror of my car.

I took tight hold of the steering wheel to make what I hoped to be my last trip to the Grand Old Lady. It was a shame because I really liked her, but her inhabitants were a bit much. Like Alder Ferry, it was the people who were to blame. It was the people there who took a quaint setting and made it inhospitable for any-one that disagreed with them.

— —

I coasted along the gravel driveway. It was still early and I hoped to be in and out without waking anyone. I snuck in through the kitchen door off the portico as I always did, the aged screen door somehow the lone survivor to incessant rounds of renovations subjected to the house by my mother. I arrived in my room unnoticed and piled what clothes remained in my dressers into an old gym bag and I took one last glance around the room to make sure I didn't miss anything. There, on the inside of the closet door, something caught my eye. How could I have forgotten? It was the dreamcatcher fashioned from catkins, Tommy's first gift to me that August day. It now seemed to be forever ago.

I removed it with apprehension, the catkins having dried out, losing small bits and pieces with each touch. I laid the memento atop a handkerchief and wrapped it loosely before placing it inside the open gym bag. My fingers lingered on it, and I flashed back to that day. It was the catalyst that sent me off into the alders for the first time.

"You know, he was a troubled child. Maybe he was better off—"

It was my mother. Offering her wisdom where it wasn't warranted.

"Fuck you."

"Aubrey that's no way—"

"It could have been me just the same. You're no better mother than what he had, so get over yourself."

There was a rustling in the hall. My father's figure blotted out what light filtered in through the doorway.

"What's the yelling about?" He was indignant in his posture, blocking my escape, and itching for a confrontation.

"The two of you are like everyone else. None of you gave a shit about that boy. You all chased him away. He had nowhere to go and not a single welcoming soul in this fucking town to help him out."

My father stood taller, stepping up behind my mother, excusing himself for all that had happened, "He wasn't our responsibility."

There was a moment of silence. A brief, awkward moment of silence that on the battlefield would have been killed with the report of a rifle shot.

"I'm leaving for good. You can both go to hell."

"Pay your own way through school then, you little bitch." My father walked away, hurried down the stairs and slammed the door on his way out.

"Aubrey, you can't do this—"

"I can and I am. Goodbye, mother." Her face was blanched of all emotion. I had taken the only thing from her that she exhibited control over—me—and threw it right back at her.

I tossed the gym bag into the back seat of my car and thundered down the gravel drive. Dust clouds billowed out from under the tires and rose high in anger, blocking out any view of the Grand Old Lady and my mother. Her head was buried in her hands on the porch, crying. It was just the two of them now, left alone to turn their anger towards each other.

"Farewell," it was the last word I yelled out the window before I let my tires spit gravel across their lawn manicured to a perfection that belied the reality of the spent lives in that house.

CHAPTER 31

FINAL DRAFT

I SAT ALONE THAT night in my dormitory room after leaving Alder Ferry behind in a whirlwind of dust. Perhaps it was fitting that I left as I did since we were always at the eye of the storm. With my exit, I turned its torrents back toward my parents and the town that threw their best at us. In the end, they only succeeded in pushing us away, our will stronger than their ability to wrestle us into submission. Still, I never felt like I won. I would always be at a loss after Tommy's descent into the dark abyss of the North Atlantic.

I sacrificed the chilled incandescence of the overhead lamps for the warmth of candlelight, more fitting for the mood I was feeling. It was an odd concoction of sadness, loneliness, and peace. None of it made sense, and I wasn't sure if it ever would. It was a tidal wave of emotion enhanced by my surroundings that encircled me. Tommy's belongings formed an enclave around me, aglow in the flickering light of the candles, their light waves falling upon his articles like the sun's rays filtering through the canopy of the alders. All that evidenced his time on Earth was there on the floor: his uniforms, the books from the alder stand, the dream catcher, and his notebooks. One by one I touched them, closing my eyes, and seeing Tommy each time, memories of him flashing through my mind in vivid clarity, the visions induced by the objects themselves.

I lingered on each, holding on to the thought that I would be able to communicate with him through those things. While they reminded me of him, and in a way made me feel close to him, they just weren't enough to bridge the gap spanning our two worlds. Someday we would be together again. Until then, the memories would tide me over while time washed away the pain of his passing.

I took great care in folding his uniforms, maintaining the crisp military creases, placing them with gentle hands back into the sea bag for safekeeping. The books found their way to the deep windowsill, looking over the campus green, waiting to catch the sunrise the next morning. They would serve as my inspiration, a reminder of Tommy's kindness, his final gift to me making all this possible. They would be the stalwart guardians of my writing desk, keeping me in line and at task. This would be my honorarium to Tommy: fulfilling my education with hard-earned success, not skimming the surface of higher education but immersing myself in it.

That would be the easy part. I had no distractions, no financial concerns, nothing of dramatic tone to take me away from my studies. All those things were removed from my life, allowing me to be a student first and foremost. Still, I knew there had to be more, something else I could do to honor my dearest friend, the greatest love I had known. It was a story that deserved to be shared, a story that defined the romance that is true friendship. We were lovers of a different sort, true soulmates thrown together to quell the deafening roar of life. In that, we succeeded. Through all that I survived, because of his kindness and endless concern for me.

It was too much to think about. I would never be able to do anything to match Tommy's kindness. I looked over with eyes blackened by the stress of recent days to the notebooks that still remained there, out in the open. I saved them for last. They were my first insight into what made Tommy who he was, and now they were my last remembrance of who he had become through the years. His poetry journaled his experiences. Verse after verse reflected his moods, the turbulence of his life, and the brief points of light that poked through the weft of his heavy heart with blinding brilliance. It was all there.

Writing was his treatment. The words he scribed were palliative, taking away the pain he felt in the moment. Writing could never cure his soul of the scars that adorned it, but what it did was lend him a means to cope with his circumstances, to try and make sense of what life had given him. No child, no matter what age, should have been made to cope with the circumstances he did. For Tommy, it was writing that carried him through a little longer, giving him the means to temporarily endure in a world that bordered on being too daunting to brave.

I breathed deeply and pulled one of the notebooks in close to me. I held on to it, my fingers gliding along its edge, tempting fate to a paper cut. It was all I could do to draw blood, but my dried skin had grown callous to the fine edge of the paper, repelling its attempt to draw life from me. I held the notebook to my face, taking in its perfume of salt air. The ocean's essence kissed me when I lifted the cover from its pages. I rifled the edges, watching as the papers crested and troughed like the waves that called Tommy home to them.

I allowed the wave of the pages to ride to their own denouement. They stopped of their own accord, picking a page that naturally allowed for the notebook to remain in the open position without exerting any effort. There was a peace to it, in the pages slowing themselves without interruption, and the notebook took comfort in the position it assumed with careless intention.

I looked down to the white page, its pale blue lines guiding the writer's hand into tidy spaced verse centered on the page by design:

> There is an eternal Spring;
> A season always at hand.
> No flowers, no thaw;
> No pause in the clocks.
> This Spring is not buffered;
> There are no other extremes.
> No winter ushers its entrance;
> No summer marks its decline.
> Spring is the human season;
> We always look to it.
> But only a few abide its tome;
> Revolutionaries, poets, dreamers.
> Spring is a condition;
> Only a season if we allow.
> To let it wane with barely an adieu;
> Ceases Spring if dreaming ends.

I found myself running my fingers along the circumference of the catkin dreamcatcher in rhythm to the lines I read aloud. Dreams. We always lived for the dream of a better life, of escape. We never gave up hope. If we had, I for certain wouldn't have been sitting there at that moment, my face reflected in the candlelight, tears splashing onto the page below. I would be somewhere else, hopeless, no spring of the mind to lead me. I was living my spring.

The tears smudged the ink on the page as I wiped them away. My instinct turned instead to blot at the tears, absorbing their moisture rather than grinding them into the page and washing away the real sentiment looking up at me from the notebook. Maybe there was something else I could do. It was a long shot and would be a few years into the future, but it made perfect sense at that moment. I would bide my time for the opportunity to make it happen.

—

Three years passed and I was well into completing my Master of Fine Arts in Creative Writing. I had been admitted to a highly respected program only by the many late nights, hard work, and dedication to my chosen craft. Writing still didn't come easily to me, it was a craft that required nearly every ounce of my mental capital. I was still apprehensive in presenting my writings to my peers; it was a challenge to even consider myself their peer, the level of their writings was immeasurable in comparison to mine. I managed to choke back my timidity and bare my soul, learning there in that program what it meant to be a writer: placing a most personal piece of yourself out there to be disseminated and critiqued.

My writings were like the buffalo that fell from the herd, the others watching as it became dismembered by the wolves who brought it down bite by painful bite. In time my writing had been culled, removed from indecision, refined to a point where it was becoming respectable on its own. I had no choice but to humble myself, and in doing so, I earned the respect of my professors and peers. It still didn't make what I was about to do any easier.

Every time I walked the halls of academia I felt judged. Despite all my hard work, there was always a bit of self-doubt burned into me, the scathing remarks of my parents lingered on, causing me to question anything I achieved. It didn't matter how hard I had to work to get here. I still made it on my own. Maybe it was rejection that I feared.

I stood before the heavy oak door marred by years of knuckles taken to its façade. Mine rose and stopped halfway through their arc. Back over the shoulder they went, halfway through their wind-up, only to stop again. I clenched my left fist and brought my right hand up again to announce my intention to gain entry when the door fell open, my fist nearly landing squarely between my advisor's eyes.

"Miss Worthington?"

"Professor Donella, I am sorry. I know I don't have an appointment—"

"It's all right, Aubrey, please." She ushered me in, her office lined with floor to ceiling bookcases packed tight with numerous volumes. Still more laid in neat piles across the floor. How anyone had the time to read all that was beyond me.

"How can I help?" She had a smile that was disarming, a smile that welcomed you in, and she allowed it to work its magic on me that fall morning.

"It's about my thesis—I have an idea, but not sure if it will work," I explained the proposition to her, laying out my plans to have Tommy's works published posthumously.

"Aubrey, it's not something we would normally allow."

"Professor, what would Robert Browning have been without Elizabeth?" I fumbled my fingers across the latch of my satchel, wondering if I would even be given the opportunity to show her the notebooks waiting inside.

"A man without inspiration, that's what he would have been." She eyed me up, now with curiosity.

"Tommy was to me what Elizabeth was to Robert. Without him, I would be a writer without inspiration. He should have had the chance I have today."

Professor Donella tapped her fingers on the desk in a light cadence and fell back into her swivel chair whose cushioning had fled to its edges years ago. "Since you were so eloquent in placing it in those literary terms, then maybe it is something to consider." She smiled and waved me towards her desk. "You do know, others in the program would not consider giving up the publication credit from this institution." She looked deep into my eyes, testing me to feel out my resolve.

"I know professor, but he instilled the love of books and writing in me. I more than owe this to him. His writing is a journey into his soul, into the experiences that shaped the verses he wrote."

She looked back at me with a bit of approval. "Do you have anything I can take back to the department?"

Before she could finish her sentence, I had the four notebooks front and center on her desk, at attention and awaiting inspection.

She opened one, then the next, making a cursory review of all four. All the while, she only murmured the occasional "Hmm, hmm" all professors are known to utter, giving no indication of her true feelings. I was on the edge of my seat and just knew that she had to be falling in love with the words in those books.

"Let me read a little more, talk to the department, and I'll get back to you." She spun her chair to the side to rise between two columns of books on the floor. "Don't worry, I'll keep these notebooks off the floor." She smiled and we both shared a laugh, mine a bit nervous, hers delighted in nature. Still, I left feeling that my request would be dismissed.

Attending Professor Donella's lectures were awkward after that meeting. I felt that I was a bit too forward in my request, but I rebuffed my doubts, knowing I owed it to Tommy to have his works made known to the outside world as he intended. I considered this my best opportunity. It would still be a few years before the world of self-publishing exploded, and even if it had been an option at the time, there was something to publication by a university press that offered a weight of approval unlike anything else.

The agony of those four weeks was crippling. Then came the day of reckoning, summoned to a meeting with Professor Donella immediately after a morning workshop. I was totally unprepared for the meeting and caught blindsided by the immediacy of her request.

"Okay, Aubrey?"

I shook my head up and down, harried, just wanting that moment to end.

"After some consideration, we've decided to let you go forward."

I was mentally on my way out the door as soon as I saw her lips begin to move. But her words, they were like magic, freezing me in my seat.

"We have a few conditions, but I have confidence in you. The story is what sold us. Not that the poetry is bad—it's not, far from it." She looked down at the notebooks and slid them to me with the gentleness they deserved. "I would keep these closer to me than anything else I owned if I were you." Her smile again. I hoped someday to have a smile like that, like her and Tommy, a smile that could bring peace to any situation.

I placed my hands on the notebooks and cradled them on my lap. "You don't know what this means, you'll never know." I was at a loss for what to say.

"I'll know when I have a final draft sitting on my desk." She reached over to me and placed her hands around mine. "This is why we write, Aubrey. This is the essence of it all. His memory is *here*." She drove that last point into my soul with all the accuracy of a marksman. Then she patted her hands on the notebooks and firmed my grip on them, stating, "*This is why we write.*"

True enough to my word, I had my final copy on her desk two weeks before the deadline. I would receive only an editorial credit and would author the foreword and a biography on Tommy. Every sentence, every word in every sentence, I liked to say was written with purpose. Hours of writing were surpassed by even more hours of editing and rewriting until I could bleed no more. It was painful, but nothing in comparison to the pain that boy long suffered. This was an act of love, and there was no pain that could prevent its happening. Nothing surpassed the need and the purpose that required this act to be executed with the degree of detail that I saw to it. Not since the crucifix that forfeited the identity of his abuser had such a sacrifice been made in Tommy's name. But this time the sacrifice was different. Instead of fear, it would bring adoration for those remnants of him committed to paper by his own hand.

It was an enchanting moment when the final, published work made it to my hands. The cover bore a black and white lithograph of a pair of catkins, hanging in simple grace from a bare branch and illuminated by a silver moon. Below that was the title:

Whispers in the Alders
A Poetry Collection by A. Thomas Mackay
Edited and Foreword by Aubrey Worthington

Published. I looked down at the cover with joy knowing that his life would live on through the one medium that always saw him through his most trying times. The sky became ashed over with dull gray clouds that blocked all but a few rays of the sun hewing through them in solitary beams, illuminating a large copse of trees on the horizon. Everything else remained dark.

I looked at the rays of light, and whispered, "Tommy, you've finally earned your middle name."

PART V

CLOSING THE HOUSE

CHAPTER 32

LAST RESPECTS

THE MEMORIES OF Tommy, of our time together, of my life after Alder Ferry—they all complemented one another. They couldn't prevail independently; each gave fruition to the other. Those memories were the building blocks of the life I now enjoy and was how Portland came to be home. This city never would have made the shortlist were it not for the memories that led me here. Its welcome to me was unlike any other I'd received before, and for that reason alone I owed it a bit of my allegiance.

I watched as the snow quietly continued to form strata upon strata over the landscape below my loft's window. Portland never looked better. Until next year, when the scene below would repeat itself and I would cherish it the same, never for once taking the gift of this life for granted.

I could see the masts of the ships in the harbor peeking out over the rooftops. Up and down they bobbed, paying homage to the sea, rising and falling in adoration to its power, and riding upon the reason for my return to Portland—out there somewhere, Tommy lingered. He would always be there, saddling the waves, washing about the harbor of the city he had come to cherish. It was here that he found peace and experienced for once the feeling of family through his Coast Guard unit. It was here that, for a moment of his human sojourn, he found unhindered happiness in life. Knowing what strain life placed on Tommy, I cherished the thought that he finally came to know peace and happiness here. I allowed Portland the opportunity to prove itself to me, and just as it did for Tommy, it captured my heart.

Those years in Alder Ferry were impetuous. Most people would have simply walked away from the drama that ensconced my friend. But I didn't. Looking back to that time of my life I knew it was worth all the pain and worry, even the despair that defined our passage to adulthood. It was love in its purest sense. In the company of each other, we discovered the romance of living, and how our passion to break free became a common bond forging our friendship. Ours was timeless, and the passion that we applied to our relationship was proof that true love is a romantic embrace with another person in its rawest form.

I continued to watch through the falling snow as the masts rocked to and fro, scratching their arcs across the gray sky. Their paths were only affected by the height of the waves, but their designs on the sky remained constant. The masts licked at the sky like flames, reaching up fully outstretched but falling back on themselves. Like fire, they mesmerized me, the syncopation of their movement placing me under their trance. They were now my catkins, dancing in the ocean wind, riding out storms past and present. Like the alders, the sea became Tommy's retreat— his final retreat. He would always be there in essence, the spray across the bows of the ships dancing and draining through the gunwales, his spirit in them, invigorating the ships and their crews, and keeping them on point. He would touch all who rode the seas from this harbor, all those who sought freedom beyond the horizon to purchase their passage from life's circumstances, even if only temporary.

I tracked my line of sight away from the harbor and pulled it back inside. The thin panes of glass rattled in the wind. They allowed for a chill to permeate the air before them, alerting my senses to the supernatural realm that seemed to have followed Tommy from the alders to the sea. He was their sprite, and I was their muse to be played. The chill in the air kept me in the moment, the cold, at times, nudging me from that uncharted territory between dreams and reality. As I stared out across the horizon into the expanse of emptiness that washed away from me, the cold would rattle my senses, stirring me back to myself.

I was shocked out of this placid interlude by the ringing of my phone. I saw the number and sighed, almost resigning myself not to answer. But I answered as I did every time—with silence.

"Aubrey?"

More silence.

"Aubrey, it's Mom."

I played her along a little longer; I could hear her finger in the background nervously tapping against the phone. After what must have seemed like forever to her, I answered with a solitary, "I'm here."

I put the phone down and waited for her to begin another tirade. I had not been to Alder Ferry in years and made it certain that I would not be making any plans to return.

"Aubrey . . . it's . . ." I sensed hesitation in her voice, which differed from her typical soliloquy. "Aubrey, it's your father. He's dead. It was his heart."

I was speechless. Silence buttressed both ends of the conversation.

"I'll call back later," were my mother's closing words before she ended the call. I was surprised by the succinctness of her delivery, and how cold the message came across.

My fingers snaked their way around the oversized coffee cup I'd poured a few minutes prior, trading the chill of the morning air for the convected heat it offered. I pulled my blanket around my naked shoulders and adjusted my gaze outside, tucking back my unkempt bangs from my eyes. My hair bore the frost of a premature gray; I refused to dye it like other women bearing down on thirty and clawing back at their twenties. Those few streaks were hard-earned, the scars of the past, and represented a wisdom accelerated beyond my years.

I shuddered with the wind as my eyes landed on the picture. There we were, Tommy and I, outside the alder stand that defined our relationship. The wind had been speaking to me. I swore never to go back, and now I began to question that vow. I looked up at the picture, speaking softly to it with a sense of disbelief, "Looks like I'll be going back to Alder Ferry after all."

My hands tightened their grip on the coffee mug, squeezing it, almost caving it in on itself. It's the very same wrath I always wished upon that place. I didn't like what that place did to me or how it made me feel.

Just then I was brought back down by the stream of steaming coffee cresting the lip of the cup and crashing upon the ridges of my trembling hands. Even after all this time I was still overcome with the power that place could have over me, evoking emotions that were as cruel and unrelenting as the sea. I brought the cup to my lips and sipped gently to push back the tears now welling up. The emotional scars were always the last to heal. Spent, I collapsed into the chair by my desk.

I turned my eyes to the left. There, Tommy's collection of books adorned the top shelf of the bookcase, asserting their rightful prominence in the literary dominion I created. The books, all of them, were fortunate to have landed there. I viewed them as pets—their fates rested in the hands of their owner. Some books were simply strewn across the floor, dog-eared into submission, or left to rot in a damp basement, spilled food for pilfering insects and bedding for squatting mice. But not mine. All had been given a loving home, especially those from the alder stand—they paid a much higher price for their adoption. Those books survived more than the elements. They weathered the extreme lows of a young boy who they took under their wing, stealing him away whenever they could from the harsh world he knew.

A small shadowbox that housed the catkin dreamcatcher Tommy fashioned was at the end of the bookshelf, serving as a makeshift bookend. It was my invitation into his world, and the first ticket punched in the long journey that led me here. Everything sprang forth from the dreamcatcher, setting into motion the events that allowed our love and friendship to flourish.

I rose from my chair and padded across the worn hardwood floor to the dreamcatcher, the frosted nail heads securing the floorboards stinging the bottoms of my feet. The shadowbox preserved it for my enjoyment, an omniscient reminder of the true cost of my success. The catkins had dried and become brittle, but their shape, the never-ending circle they formed, remained unbroken, as did my dreams. I traced my finger with an airy touch across the glass encasing this memento, taking care not to disturb its coffin for fear of it shedding even more of its fragile physicality. All that the dreamcatcher promised was surrounding me, its promises becoming fulfilled. As my fingers drew circles across the cool glass I couldn't help but become overwhelmed with gratitude, thinking aloud, "Thank you . . . thank you," for everything made possible by that first act of kindness it represented.

I let my hand drop away from the shadowbox in a graceful arc to my side. I took hold of the blanket draped around me and turned, again, to face the picture. I exchanged glances between the picture and the wintry scene playing out on the opposite side of the window. I was enchanted, turning my head in differing angles to see if it was just the lighting, or if I was really seeing what my eyes were relaying to my mind. I removed the picture from the frame and placed it upon the central pane of the window.

My eyes were not deceived. The gray sky outside blended perfectly with the color of the sky in the photograph. Held up together, they bled into each other, the picture melting into the scene outside. Like the alders, the emotions I had when that picture took hold of me were deeply intertwined and difficult to penetrate.

The picture was alluring—the alders were bare against a battleship-gray December sky, their catkins solely adorning the branches. If I stared long enough, I would see the catkins dancing in the cold wind that brought us close to one another, a moment captured just before the age of cell phones and social media. I smiled knowing that the picture remained private to me, the magic of that moment never to be spoiled by likes and comments from mere acquaintances who would never understand the magnificence caught in that hair of a second when the shutter clicked.

The picture's arrival was more than coincidence. For years it was hidden in the boxes that followed me from my undergrad dorm to my grad school apartment, and the numerous towns in between. It was a stowaway until my arrival in Portland. As I pushed my writing desk up against the window, a thirty-five-millimeter film canister rolled out of the desk drawer. On a whim I had the film developed, not expecting much. I thumbed through the nine prints, mostly overexposed film, until the picture surfaced. Somehow the film had survived all those years, waiting until we arrived here to make itself known again. Once I saw the picture I knew I was home. The picture made this place a home.

I remembered that day clearly. It was the only time I remembered not being separate from everything—the cold air pulled Tommy and me in so close that from a short distance we appeared to be one. It was the only instance where I let go of my individual identity to be one with another person. Fleeting as it was, that moment's perfection was forever hallowed in the picture.

There we were, together. In my closet was the same second-hand pea coat Tommy wore in the picture. I shed the blanket from my shoulders, allowing it to crumple to the floor. In its place I donned Tommy's pea coat, lifting the collar high to prevent the chill from retreating down the back of my neck. I pulled my shoulders in close and grabbed both lapels, taking them in to cover my face. In the warmth of my breath, I could smell his essence.

I plodded without care across the floor back to my writing desk and took up the picture again in my left hand, holding it out at arm's length against the winter sky beyond. I stared at it, stolen back to another time as my eyes sank deep into the photograph. As I looked, the catkins came to life, dancing in the breeze, lulled by the ethereal notes echoed out by Harrison's guitar, his tones from "Something" melodizing the scene. The song would always move me, and its aria would always be awash in the splendor of that photograph, becoming the soundtrack of our time together. I stared for what seemed hours, the catkins catching each note of the song, a symphony going on about us. It was the closest moment to perfection I ever experienced with another person.

Like so many moments with Tommy, I didn't want that interlude, alone with the picture, to ever end.

Again, my serenity was shattered, hijacked from a place of great introspect, a place where much more time would be spent in coming years to make peace with the past and to enjoy the present, all without succumbing to the uncertainty of the future. With an obnoxious sense of delight my phone erupted a second time, the vibration setting it free as it hurried across the table and collided against my coffee cup with an empty clink that pierced the cold air that penetrated the window. It echoed through the room with clarity, chiming in tune to the ship bells across the harbor.

I looked at the number flashing at me in distress and calling to me, pleading then and there to be all that mattered. The phone at times was all too human, never hesitating to cry out above the crowd and make its presence known. With the indignant gesturing of a spoiled child, it would interject its will, seeking to subordinate all other matters to its call.

I turned back to the window, attempting to ignore the phone's plea, knowing that I didn't have to acquiesce. I owed it nothing. There was no written rule where I was bound to please either it or anyone else at my expense. Those days had passed with great pain, a revelation that I needn't experience again.

The light, effervescent snowflakes were replaced by an immeasurable army of minuscule warriors that penetrated every crevice and every defense offered up by the outside world. The snows left nothing untouched. The winds swirled the snow about, causing it to rise in great funnels that touched the heavens, where it receded into the gray sky above, only to collapse down upon the earth again like waves buffeting the shores.

The snow was an apt but unnecessary excuse. There was no need to go back. The alders set us free and cast us out to the world to make our own way. To go back wouldn't be a dance with memories past. It would be a courtship with disaster, beckoning antagonists to take my hand and pull me back into the cycle of misery that would reverse the promise bound up in the dream-catcher looking down at me. The past was gone, but the memories would always remain. I would always have them, and they were all I needed.

I spun the phone about on the desk, playing roulette with its keypad. I hesitated, then began to dial. I snapped the phone shut and spun it again. The phone's rotation came to a gentle stop, its antenna pointing at me with all the potential of a loaded gun. I unlocked the phone and looked out the window as my fingers danced across the keypad.

Instead, I ordered flowers.

— THE END —

ABOUT THE AUTHOR

H. A. CALLUM is a poet and writer hailing from Bucks County, Pennsylvania. His poetry and short fiction have appeared in local and national literary magazines.

His hometown is nestled among the rolling hills, weathered stone walls, and meandering woodland streams interspersed with quaint farm-lots that inspire his writing and guide his eye as a naturalist and wildlife advocate.

Having crossed the United States many times over, and after calling the American West home for several years, Mr. Callum's understanding of America serves as his eyepiece to a culture that is constantly changing, much like the landscape shaping the continent. His writing reflects the ever-evolving definition of what it means to be American.

Mr. Callum holds a bachelor of arts in English from the Pennsylvania State University (summa cum laude) and is an active and visible member of his local writing and literary communities. When not writing, Mr. Callum treasures the time spent with his wife and daughters—his greatest sources of inspiration.

Made in the USA
Middletown, DE
08 November 2018